# CAPWAR EXPERIENCE

## CAPSTONE CONSPIRACY BOOK TWO

# CAPWAR EXPERIENCE

BRANDT LEGG

CapWar EXPERIENCE (CapStone Conspiracy Book Two)

Published in the United States of America by Laughing Rain

Cataloging-in-Publication data for this book is available from the Library of Congress.

ISBN-13: 978-1-935070-34-4

ISBN-10: 1-935070-34-7

PUBLISHER'S NOTE

This book is a work of fiction. Names, characters, places and incidents are products of the author's imagination or are used fictitiously. Any resemblance to actual persons, living or dead, businesses, events or locales is entirely coincidental.

BrandtLegg.com

*As always, this book is dedicated to Teakki and Ro*

*And to Blair Legg 1957-2017*

# CHAPTER ONE

J anuary 20th. The West Front of the US Capitol building was draped in American flags and packed with well-dressed dignitaries, including past presidents, members of Congress, governors, and wealthy business leaders—anybody with enough clout to get there was there. The typically rigid security for an inauguration had been ratcheted up to address the NorthBridge threat. NorthBridge, the domestic terror group which had promised a second American revolution, had already attacked establishment institutions and assassinated a number of political leaders.

The entire nation was on edge.

The country's law enforcement apparatus had saturated nearly a three-square-mile grid around the event with more than 30,000 personnel, including Secret Service, FBI, Capitol Police, and a dozen other federal, state, and local agencies. The US Military, expecting commando-like raids from the terror group, had added another 15,000 National Guard. The US Army was utilizing all protocols and alert levels for combat defense of the National Capital Region.

Arlin Vonner, the billionaire responsible for Hudson Pound's election to the highest office in the land, did not attend the inauguration. However, he was well represented by hundreds of his own Vonner Security agents aggressively scouring the town for NorthBridge assassins. Vonner had learned long ago that the bureaucrats were generally good at only two things—wasting time and money—and were certainly not good at preventing disasters. And that's exactly what it would be if Hudson Pound died before taking office.

Tarka Seebantz, one of Vonner's VS agents, led a team of four, but she'd rather work alone. The six-foot tall former CIA operative had been handling Vonner's problems for six years, but had only recently risen to the rank of team leader at the insistence of Vonner's chief lieutenant, Rex Lestat. He'd been impressed by her file and her skill sets; martial arts, weapons mastery, explosives, and, most important to Rex, computer tech and foreign languages. Rex, who normally didn't directly involve himself with operations such as these, had spent weeks tracking a specific and credible threat to the president-elect. As he continued to fight against the minutes that remained before the plot to kill Hudson was carried out, he fed real time data to Tarka.

The area was closed to vehicles, and Washington's normally rigid air traffic restrictions had been tightened to a military-enforced no-fly zone. More than one million attendees had entered through six public security checkpoints around the National Mall and Reflecting Pool. The weather had cooperated with a crisp, sunny day of fifty-two degrees—rare for Washington, DC, in January. Everything seemed perfect and perfectly safe. It was hard to imagine anyone getting near enough to harm the future president.

Hudson stood behind the bulletproof glass panels and smiled at his wife, Melissa. She had on a deep blue dress that matched his tie, and he wondered if that had been on purpose. He wondered a lot of things. First among those rapid thoughts was when would any of this actually start to feel real? That only led to a more frightening question—was *any* of it real?

The answer would have to wait, as the Chief Justice of the Supreme Court now stood in front of him, ready to administer the oath of office. Hudson took a deep breath and placed his left hand on the Bible held by Melissa. She smiled and met his gaze. They'd made it.

Nearly two miles away, well concealed in a rooftop ventilation system, a man known only as Kniike, also took a deep breath. He had been there for days—living, eating, sleeping; two containers in the corner held his waste. He couldn't wait to get back out into the fresh air, the light of day, the payday, once he killed Hudson Pound.

"Please raise your right hand and repeat after me," the Chief Justice said.

Kniike wrapped his right hand around his MacMillan TAC-50 long-range rifle.

Hudson didn't need the Chief Justice to utter the words. The oath was something Hudson had long ago memorized. It meant a great deal to him, but tradition dictated the order of things. Every moment of the day had been choreographed according to those long-ago established customs. Perhaps he could make some changes for his next swearing-in ceremony.

Tarka listened to Rex, Vonner's top lieutenant and "fixer," in her earpiece as she raced up the stairs. If his information was right, it might already be too late. If it was wrong, it was definitely too late.

"I do solemnly swear," Hudson repeated.

Kniike said a silent prayer as he sighted the president-elect in his crosshairs.

Tarka took the last twelve steps three at a time.

"That I will faithfully execute the office of president of the United States . . ."

The sniper had taken everything into consideration—wind speed, air temperature, humidity, even the rotation of the earth.

Tarka hit the door to the roof. Locked. Chained. Alarmed. Damn!

There would only be one chance at the shot. If Kniike missed, Hudson Pound would be inaugurated as president of the United States. Of course, that did not mean he'd live long enough to serve. There were contingency plans, but Kniike wouldn't get the big payment. He'd have to make do with the two-hundred and fifty thousand he'd already received. That wouldn't last as long as he needed, not long enough to disappear. But he'd make the shot, and collect the final million. Kniike had never missed a hit.

"And will to the best of my ability," Hudson repeated.

The key was the timing of the shot. They wanted Hudson dead before the oath was complete. The .50 caliber rifle cartridge would travel at approximately three thousand feet per second, meaning it would take almost three seconds to reach his target. At that distance, the level eight glass–clad polycarbonate panel could not be penetrated. Kniike knew this, but he also knew that the panel was supposed to have been replaced with an ordinary two-point-five-inch sheet of glass, which would shatter like cascading diamonds—a shower of glitter as the body fell. It had been arranged.

Tarka, out of time and options, fired three shots, blasting the chain, the lock, and the automatic alarm, then kicked the door open and darted onto the roof.

Kniike, finger on the trigger, heard the shots and blinked. Whoever it was, he would kill them in a few seconds, but first the president.

Kniike pulled the trigger.

"Preserve, protect, and defend . . . "

## CHAPTER TWO

The explosion, visible from the Capitol, muffled by distance, came at the same moment that Hudson uttered the words, "... the Constitution of the United States, so help me God."

"Congratulations, Mr. President," the Chief Justice said, shaking Hudson's hand as both men looked to the distant rooftop, where flames and smoke smoldered in what might have been a small building fire. Yet, in the age of NorthBridge, and on Inauguration Day, they knew more nefarious elements were at work. Neither noticed the sniper's bullet that had sailed forty feet above them and lodged into one of the massive columns which supported the capitol's dome.

Cheers and roaring applause had drowned out any sound the bullet's impact had made. The United States Marine Band, located on the tier below the president, played "Hail to the Chief." Hudson turned and kissed Melissa, then hugged his beaming daughter, Florence, and slightly dazed-looking son, Schueller. He knew his childhood friends, the Wizard and Gouge, were out there in the sea of onlookers celebrating, but he didn't know where.

A loud report of gunshots startled him, and everyone else—several people actually ducked for cover—but it was just the first round of the twenty-one-gun salute. Still, it reminded him that the tension and stress of the campaign had been magnified a thousand times by the oath he'd just taken. After several more minutes of excited good wishes from those gathered, Hudson stepped up to the podium.

"My fellow Americans, I stand before you today a humble, common man, one of you . . . and I came here to serve you. Our country is as divided as any time since the Civil War. More than one hundred fifty years ago, Abraham Lincoln stood here, having ascended to power on the eve of that bloody conflict, and implored, '*We are not enemies, but friends. We must not be enemies. Though passion may have strained it, it must not break our bonds of affection.*' Today, thankfully, we no longer argue over the cruelty of slavery, and yet we find ourselves nearly as intolerant of our neighbors' ideas and beliefs. Even before the scourge of terrorism burried its brutal fists into our daily peace, we were at each other's throats—right versus left, conservative versus liberals. We seem to have lost our way." He paused and made eye contact with some of the everyday-Americans watching. They were his people, he came from them.

"There was a place, throughout our history, where we always met, and got things done. That elusive common ground is still there, and we must return to it. Two hundred some years ago, Thomas Jefferson, at his first inauguration reminded us, and I paraphrase, '*Every difference of opinion is not a difference of principle. We have called by different names brethren of the same principle. We are all Republicans, we are all Democrats.*'"

The applause gave him a moment to reflect. There were four things he promised himself he would do as president: Free Rochelle; expose and stop the wealthy elites known as REMies who controlled world events; defeat NorthBridge; and restore the federal government to what the Founders had envisioned. Only the latter two could he cite here, but between the lines, he silently pledged to do the others.

"We must change . . . " Hudson began, and then spent several minutes explaining how he believed that could be done before turning to the topic of NorthBridge. "This group of terrorists, who have been so destructive with their illegal and hideous tactics, enjoys far too much support from many of you out there. This speaks more to the failing of our system than the rightness of their so-called cause. Yet we cannot give in to the anger and frustration which overwhelm us. Instead, we must overcome it, and overcome it we shall.

"Franklin Roosevelt, taking this office in the midst of one of the darkest times in our history, said, 'This great Nation will endure as it has endured, will revive and will prosper. So, first of all, let me assert my firm belief that the only thing we have to fear is fear itself — nameless, unreasoning, unjustified terror which paralyzes needed efforts to convert retreat into advance.' FDR showed us what could be done as we rose up from the depths of poverty to defeat the most evil regime the world has ever known: Nazi Germany, a country ruthlessly commanded by terrorists."

The president looked out over the sea of faces looking up at him and suddenly shivered, worried about a NorthBridge attack. He pushed his fear aside, paused only a second, and continued in a determined tone.

"The terrorists who infect our communities now have done more to defy our way of life, more to threaten our pursuit of life, liberty, and happiness, than all the challenges we have faced since the signing of the Declaration. And it cannot continue. It will not continue. We are better than this. We deserve more."

Applause.

"I pledge to you today that we will fix these things," the president continued. "We will find and defeat NorthBridge, and any others like them. We will do this together, standing on that common ground, basking in sunlight, working under the starlight, until it is right again. Because alone we might be lost, but together . . . we are the change."

Several blocks away, Vonner's fixer, Rex, watched the ceremony on television. Quite surprised that Hudson had lived through the event, he pushed the button on his communicator and waited for his boss to pick up.

"We got ourselves a president," Vonner said.

"Just barely," Rex responded, staring at an array of twenty-six dice in various colors arranged on the table in front of him. "Tarka made it there with less than a second to spare."

"Close call."

"No, I mean literally two tenths of a second later, and Hudson would have been history."

"She'll have a full-time job, shaving those fractions of seconds for the next few years," Vonner said, panting slightly on a stair climber. He was in Washington, but had chosen not to attend the inauguration. Although everyone knew he'd backed the rookie candidate, Vonner was sensitive to the appearance that Hudson would be a puppet. After all, the people had "elected" a man with no political baggage, beholden to no special interests, to change things.

President Pound was still reveling in the pomp and circumstance of the inaugural and readying himself for the parade in a pope-mobile-like car fitted with bulletproof glass, blast resistant armor plating, and sixty-six more of the latest security measures. He shook hands, waved, smiled, and acted as if everything was wonderful, but his mind was elsewhere. Hudson already felt like a zoo animal, trapped and on display. There was much to do, and he only had the vague outline of a plan.

DC was a pressure cooker capable of swallowing the biggest and most powerful. Many had come before him planning to make major change. He recalled Trump's call to "drain the swamp," but in the end, the brash billionaire found himself fighting through the muck and mire which had, in different ways, ensnared all who had come before.

President Pound's mission was different. The left and right were at war with each other, and the extremists on both sides had run out of patience, wanting nothing less than revolution. That climate had given rise to NorthBridge. Like Lincoln, Hudson faced the real prospect of a divided nation going to war with itself.

While trying to stop that from happening, Hudson's primary objective was to pry control away from the REMies. He believed that if he could do that, the reasons for NorthBridge would go away, and with it, the group's support. Without the REMies manipulating everything to their own selfish, greedy ends, the American people could win the final CapWar.

Riding down Pennsylvania Avenue with Melissa, both waving and smiling to the masses, Hudson wondered how he could possibly do what needed to be done with so few allies. If Vonner was truly on his side, it might be possible, but that "if" had kept him awake many nights since the election, and he was no closer to the truth. He didn't know how he was going to stop the REMies and stay alive. He wasn't even sure how to be president. The only thing he knew for sure was that he was in way over his head.

# CHAPTER THREE

Hudson, finally alone in the Oval Office, walked across the plush blue carpet, careful not to step on the inlaid presidential seal. The room, by design, exuded power. He could feel Kennedy's tension during the Cuban missile crisis, FDR strategizing the swings of World War II, Lincoln wrestling over the fate of the union as the Civil War raged.

He strained his eyes, nearly able to see the great men's ghosts. Every president going back to John Adams had been in that very room. As he thought of those Founding Fathers, he couldn't help but think of NorthBridge and how they had bastardized the use of those historic names in their pursuit of power through terror.

His mind wandered to Nixon, and his decision to resign, and of the paranoid president taping meetings in the office. *What did old tricky-Dick know about the REMies?* He took a step to the window and looked out over the south lawn. *Now I'm here. What great history will I make? Will I make any at all? Will they let me?*

President Pound turned back to the intimidating room and stared at the desk made from the timbers of the HMS Resolute. He recalled that the Queen of England had presented the desk to

President Rutherford Hayes in 1880, and that nearly every Commander in Chief since then had used the desk. *What secrets does it hold?*

He was about to find out. Hudson knew the legend that each president left a note for his successor inside a desk drawer in the Oval Office. At the inauguration ceremony, Hudson had wanted to ask the outgoing president if there was a note waiting, but he didn't dare. He wanted to discover it himself. He was counting on its being there, containing a hint or a clue as to how he could bypass the tangled influence and crushing presence of the powerful elites who ran the president and seemingly everything else.

For most of the country's history, the tradition of the presidents' passing letters was not known. Only in recent decades had word leaked, and, now, after demands from the media, a public letter from each president to the next was released. But those were simple, magnanimous notes intended to make people feel good. The true letters, which everyone denied even existed, had been the subject of great speculation among conspiracy theorists. Hudson had read they could be pages long, and always contained instructions that the letter be burned immediately after reading.

*Do they exist? What information could be so dangerous to require the letter's destruction?*

Hudson paced around the desk, not wanting to be disappointed, not wanting to know, but needing to find out. Finally, he sat in the leather chair, pulled open the center drawer, looked down, and saw two envelopes, in the unmistakable handwriting of the former president, bearing his name. One was note card size, the other a standard business envelope. He opened the smaller one first and read what he knew was the public message, "Congratulations . . . Good luck . . . I'm rooting for you . . . God bless you . . ."

He left that one on top of his desk and slowly opened the

other envelope. Hudson withdrew the three typewritten pages on White House letterhead, quickly checked the end to see the president's signature, took a deep breath, and began reading.

*Dear Hudson,*

*With Arlin Vonner's backing, there is a very good chance that you already know some of what I'm going to tell you, but in case you don't, please don't shoot the messenger. I know you think you fought hard, and, in fact, in your case you did survive bullets and battles to get here. But there was never any doubt that you were going to be the next president. I wasn't at the meeting when they decided it would be you, but be assured there was a meeting, and they did decide. It's not important how they do it; some of it is even legitimate in a kind of crazy, modern, capitalistic, democratic kind of way. Yet I imagine that somebody like you, with no background in politics, a man of apparently great honor, is shocked at how this all works.*

*That being said, you have still been given one of the greatest opportunities of life, one that only a relative handful have ever known. Assuming you cooperate with them, there is much good that you can do. They do allow many pet projects, causes, a tiny bit of "reform," and there are the ceremonial duties that are actually quite rewarding. You will spend the rest of your life in great wealth, privilege, and respect.*

*Just do the four years (or eight, if you'd like) and try not to make waves. I know you're a student of history, and therefore you can look back and see the ones who made mistakes by trying to buck the system; a system that has become entrenched not just in our great nation, but across the globe. This system keeps things going, and it is everything. I hope you won't make the same mistake that Jack Kennedy and some others have made.*

Halfway through the first page, he could not read anymore. Hudson got up from his chair, walked to the other side of the desk, and found himself standing exactly in the center of the presidential seal. He glanced down at the olive branch and arrows in the eagle's talons. War and peace, at the direction of whom? He stepped over to one of the credenzas and ran his hands across the Frederic Remington sculpture, The Bronco Buster. It could not be a coincidence. Frederic Remington was a cousin to Eliphalet Remington, founder of the Remington Arms Company. The Wizard had said that perhaps the best theory for the origin of the name REMies was Eliphalet Remington, who helped manipulate wars and skirmishes around the world beginning in the latter half of the nineteenth century.

Taking a deep breath, Hudson returned to the desk and continued reading the letter.

*It's not such a bad thing to have a country run by committee, run by very successful people, by those with more knowledge of events and the truth of those events, than you or I would ever know. Think of the bad presidents, the ones that you have disagreed with. Some of them had grand plans and made bold promises as candidates. However, once they got into office, it turned out they were not that much different than their predecessors. There's a* *reason for that, obviously. It's because they <u>are</u> their predecessors. Continuity has served us well.*

*I'm sure you're thinking you're going to just be a puppet, because that's what I thought, but you'll be pleasantly surprised. You won't feel controlled. It's nothing like being a puppet. In fact, after they surround you with the people they want you surrounded with, it's much the way you imagined it would be. Those advisors, generals, cabinet secretaries, give you advice and counsel. You're the team leader, and get to make the decision—more decisions than you'll even want. Sometimes you might make the wrong decision, regardless of all that wonderful advice, but don't ever do it intentionally. They'll know.*

Hudson dropped the letter as if it might injure him and swallowed hard. It sounded worse than he thought. Surely a sinister "committee" wasn't playing the planet like a chessboard? Whomever the last president answered to must have been far more corrupt than Vonner. Had it been Bastendorff? Booker? One of the other ones?

He picked up the letter again, handling it as though it were a dirty diaper.

*I think you'll agree things are going along as well as can be expected, given the challenges and dangers of this modern world. They've managed to keep us safe, happy, and prosperous. What would've happened to the United States of America had it not been for their sage guidance, their money, their power, their influence, their ideas, their connections? I shudder to think. So, while you may be disappointed, disillusioned, even worried, or scared, don't be. This is a good system. It works, and you are now an important part of it.*

Hudson couldn't believe what he was reading. *What if I hadn't known before I walked into this office? What if I'd been like Reagan or Clinton, finding out for the first time after the inauguration? Would I have believed it? Would I have been shocked? Would I have called the FBI? Would I have found out the hard way that they're also in on it?*

He checked the time. His schedule was packed. If he wanted to finish reading and then destroy the letter, he'd better get back to it.

*You ran on a promise of change. It may not go as you had planned, but there are many ways to change things. Always start with the preamble and go about it as if handling a photograph in a dark room. Careful and conscientious resolve will produce good results. With your love of history, I know you'll find solace in the knowledge that all your predecessors have been where you are now. The key, my friend, is* <u>*your*</u> *intelligence. As for my remaining advice: keep the Constitution handy. The framers were incredibly wise. Just look at Article II—that is how to proceed. And rely on the Father. His will be done.*

Amazingly, a person he used to respect had written these outrageous words! Hudson studied the signature again.

*Could this have been written under duress?*

He felt suddenly hungover, headachy, nauseous. He realized he'd been hoping the letter would say otherwise, that the former president would have offered some sort of trick or answer as to how to fix it all, how to get the REMie leeches off, but no. This letter was the opposite of hope, telling him to "just take it" and "do what they say."

Hudson stood up, his eyes following the trail of portraits and busts. Great men had agonized in the Oval Office, the White House. They'd grappled with this same dilemma and more. How could they have not shaken off the REMies?

He gazed up at a portrait of George Washington, a man who had defeated a king, a king who had certainly been one of the elites, a forerunner to the REMies. General Washington had fought for, and then rejected, the spoils of victory. Washington had insisted on giving the people the power rather than taking it for himself or vesting it in the office of the president. And suddenly, thinking about that great man, Hudson realized there might be a path, probably the only one with a chance of overcoming the REMies' stranglehold on world events.

## CHAPTER FOUR

The next morning, after a fitful night, Hudson began his first full day as president, still tired from the festivities and balls. He rubbed his eyes and shared a Coke with Fitz.

"Apparently, the hitman was taken out at the very last second," Fitz said, finishing up the reviewing of the day's agenda with an update on the Inauguration Day assassination attempt.

"Secret Service found him?" Hudson asked.

"No," Fitz said, opening another Coke. "One of Vonner's people."

Hudson raised an eyebrow. "Really? I'd like to meet him, thank him."

"Her," Fitz corrected. "I doubt that it'll be possible. She's part of his shadow-squad. They don't exist, if you know what I mean."

Hudson wasn't sure he did know, but he couldn't spare any brainpower at the moment with his overloaded gray matter. He'd ask Vonner himself in a few minutes. The billionaire would be his first meeting of the day, but it would not appear on the president's official schedule.

"If that'll be all, Mr. President," Fitz said, heading toward the door, "I'll see you in a couple of hours."

Hudson nodded and thanked his chief of staff, a man he had learned to like, but still didn't trust. Fitz always made him laugh, and had taught him enough about politics and the legislative process that Hudson could almost pass for a seasoned politician. Still, Fitz was one of Vonner's people, and that meant he was probably one of the enemy. One day that would have to be faced, but in the meantime, Hudson wasn't sure he could do without his very able chief of staff.

Melissa told Hudson she also liked Fitz; the three of them had developed a good chemistry on the campaign trail. As the chief of staff took charge of the legislative agenda and executive team, the first lady would start getting to know the household staff. It was a smooth-running operation, with some people having served three or four first families. She wouldn't need to make too many changes, but would insist on implementing a one-hundred-percent recycling system after seeing one kitchen worker in the middle of throwing away a banana peel during her welcome tour.

"Hey, save that! It's good dirt!" the first lady had said impulsively, and she immediately made plans for composting to be mandatory. Ever since the election, Melissa had been planning on implementing a project to expand the 2,800-square-foot White House vegetable garden started by Michelle Obama. Recycling and the environment would definitely be Melissa's "first lady causes." She also wanted more beehives and a larger pollinators' garden to attract birds and butterflies. Melissa had her own mission to change the world.

Vonner looked more at home in the Oval Office than Hudson did. The billionaire seemed as if he'd be comfortable anywhere. Hudson pictured Vonner with his sleeves rolled up, working in the slums of Calcutta, or pulling victims from a Central American mudslide, maybe driving a bulldozer in a massive landfill of garbage.

Vonner had that air. He could handle anything, master every situation, take charge, make it work, win.

Hudson told Vonner about the former President's letter. "That's not quite how you painted it," Hudson said. "I'm not sure I can do this."

"Yes, you can," Vonner said, smiling.

"I thought I was going to be president, not taking orders from a group of greedy elites and banksters who believe they know what's good for everybody. Damnit, the REMies don't even give the people a chance to do what they want!"

"We've been through this," Vonner began. He and Hudson had met many times in the ten and a half weeks since the election. "You're the president, and every president has advisors."

"Every president has REMies pulling the strings. You assured me that I would not be a puppet," Hudson said, pacing the room. "Remember, you promised that we could change things, we could fix the system—the system that is fixed."

"And we will," Vonner said, leaning back against the surprisingly comfortable sofa as if he were in his living room instead of the White House.

"How? When?"

"I'm sure you think that with all my billions of dollars, I can do whatever I want," Vonner said. "I wish it *were* that way. Then I wouldn't have needed to get you elected president, I could've just done what needed doing. But it's not that way, Hudson. The world is filled with rich people who think they know best. Money does that, you see. It infects people in a way where one thinks because he's accumulated that kind of money, he's smarter than everyone else. He wants to keep the money, the power, all of it, and he'll do anything to make sure he does."

"But it doesn't affect you that way?" Hudson asked.

"Oh, it did. But once I looked around and realized there were approximately two thousand billionaires in the world . . . "

"Surely they aren't *all* REMies?"

"Oh, goodness, no," Vonner said, suddenly looking alarmed. "REMies are a small minority of maybe a few dozen."

"You don't know exactly how many?"

"Forty-eight."

Hudson leaned against the Resolute Desk and stared at Vonner. "Forty-eight people control the world."

"It's not that simple," Vonner said. "All those billionaires I mentioned earlier, they each have a certain amount of sway on world events. As I said, money breeds power and vice versa. However, many of them inherited, or otherwise lack ambition. Even the REMies, the elite of the elite, are divided, each influencing his own sphere, but there is a network, a constant negotiating going on as each vies for more wealth, power, and control."

"And the CapWars?"

"That's where everything gets complicated," Vonner said, pursing his lips for a moment before taking a sip from a glass containing lemon juice and scotch. "The REMies who want ultimate control—Bastendorff, Titus Coyne, Booker Lipton, and a handful of others—men like that made me sober up and realize I might be the last hope against these would-be emperors."

Hudson wanted to believe him. Vonner *seemed* sincere. *Why else would he have selected me? Surely there were others who would've cooperated more easily?*

He thought of the past president's letter: *"Just do what they say. Don't make waves."*

"Then tell me how it's going to work," Hudson said, sitting

down on the sofa opposite Vonner, staring at him closely. "I want to know exactly how we're going to do this."

## CHAPTER FIVE

The Wizard pulled his hair into a ponytail and smiled at Hudson through the computer screen. With the new USB drive the Wizard had created, they could now see each other.

"This is fantastic, but will it really work?" Hudson asked. "I mean, is it secure?"

"It's fitted with a scrambler, which essentially renders our voices an unrecognizable mess of static to anyone who's monitoring. But if you're not alone in the room, we can still type."

"So, they can't hear what I'm saying right now?"

"As long as you stay within six feet of the drive."

"Amazing," Hudson remarked, feeling the first sense of security he'd had since walking into the White House on Inauguration Day a week earlier. "Can you send me about a hundred of these?" Hudson laughed.

"I'd love to, but that one's custom-made, based on the quantum sound waves and proton explorations, ions, and reversing harmonies, plus . . . " He noticed Hudson's blank look. "Anyway, I call it the 'SonicBlock.' It'll work on any computer with a USB drive. It even has a wireless feature."

"I'm glad to hear that, because they already made my personal laptop unable to connect to the Internet."

"They only want you using machines they control. Don't lose that drive, and if they ask you about the static, play dumb."

"That's easy for me," Hudson said with only the hint of a smile.

The Wizard stared into the screen. "Now, it's been a week. When are you going to pardon Rochelle?"

"I'm still negotiating."

"I'll bet you are. With Vonner?"

"He says if I pardon her, the ensuing scandal will bog down any hope we have of stopping the REMies."

"He might be right." The Wizard stared at Hudson. "But that begs the question—is he really going to help you go after the REMies?"

"He's promised a strategy soon, but it's going to take years to get their tentacles out of everything."

"Start with the federal government."

"That's the idea."

"Is Vonner really on board with this? Because it doesn't feel right. It never has. You know it's encoded, all the information of the whole universe in a single instant. It's constantly flowing through all of us. And Vonner, he can't hide from truth. It's very probable he's just playing you."

"I know that. It keeps me up nights, but his first test is coming in a few weeks, when most of the REMies are meeting secretly in Panama. Vonner has promised to share the agenda with me. It lays out the overall plan for the year ahead—coups, wars, elections, economies, industries, and currencies, rising and falling, as they try to leverage themselves to the top of the pyramid."

"It's so interesting that the REMies use the pyramid as their symbol and goal. Do you know about the golden ratio?" the Wizard continued. "Da Vinci knew it."

"Does it have anything to do with what we're talking about?" Hudson asked impatiently.

"Of course. The golden ratio is in everything, although sometimes it can't be seen or proven. But when you consider geometric relationships, and express forms algebraically—"

"I'll let you know when Vonner gives me the agenda," Hudson said firmly, letting his friend know that he wanted to stay on topic.

"If we get that, we can feed it into Gypsy," the Wizard said, sounding deflated.

Zackers, a college friend of Hudson's daughter, Florence, had been murdered just after he'd given Schueller a flash drive containing encrypted information about Vonner, other REMies, and the cryptocurrency digiGOLD. The drive also held a program coded by Zackers dubbed "Gypsy," because of its ability to predict future events. It could take a single event such as a Federal Reserve interest rate hike, a terrorist attack, or the outcome of an election in Germany, feed it into a data field, and produce an outcome based on everything else already entered, including constantly updated live feeds from the internet.

Through Zackers' drive, they'd located his partner in the hacking world—Crane, another twenty-something misfit, who looked like a burned-out druggie with his long frizzy hair, scraggly beard, and mustache. But Crane could run through the DarkNet like a jaguar through the jungle at night. He'd come on board in part to avenge the death of his friend and because he basically felt "the world sucks the way it is."

"Has Crane finished modifying Gypsy?" Hudson asked. Crane had come up with the idea to add all the major news feeds into the program, which would then allow it to spot trends and REMie manipulation not apparent to human detection.

"He's close." The Wizard held up his hands as if in prayer,

smiled, and then narrowed his eyes. "REMies will take time for sure, but Rochelle can be free with a stroke of your pen."

"It's gonna happen."

"If Vonner thinks the pardon puts everything else you want to do in jeopardy, then what does he suggest?"

"He offered to break her out of prison, relocate her to an island somewhere."

"Cool! Maybe he isn't the evil bastard I thought he was. Do you believe him?"

"Of course not. And even if I did, she deserves a full pardon."

"But that brings a firestorm."

"So?"

"I just wish Rochelle had only killed the jerks that did this to her instead of a guy who wasn't even there. He was such a popular governor."

"Yeah, well I wish they'd never gang-raped her, killed her brother, and covered it up!"

"We helped cover it up," he said quietly.

Hudson ignored the comment, but knots formed in his stomach. "I'm going to give Vonner a few days. I need that time anyway to get my bearings and figure out if I have any power here at all. My biggest problem is I don't know if I can trust anyone."

"You can trust me, Dawg."

"Thanks, but I need people *inside* the White House I can trust. Right now, it's just Melissa and me. Speaking of which, I've got to go."

"Mr. President," Melissa said in a flirting tone as she walked into the Oval Office.

"How did I get so lucky?" Hudson said, walking around the desk to greet her.

"To be the president?"

"No, to have the most gorgeous first lady in history."

After a long kiss, Melissa caught him up on her official duties, and then they turned to the REMies.

"It doesn't seem as bad as the letter implied," Melissa said, referring to the letter from the former president, which he'd shown her but still hadn't burned.

"Too soon to tell," Hudson said.

"Don't be a pessimist," Melissa replied quickly. "Be the problem solver."

"I admit, there have been moments when I think the whole REMie thing is overblown and that I might actually have the power to improve the world . . . "

"You never know," Melissa said. "The truth usually lies in the middle."

Her words echoed in his head that night while he wrestled with sleep. *The President's letter . . .* he thought. *There's a truth hidden in those lies.*

Hudson felt certain his predecessor had left him a hidden clue. He got up quietly, retrieved the letter, and took it into the bathroom so he wouldn't wake Melissa. He skimmed the pages quickly until he got to the last paragraph.

There it was. A secret message, meant only for him.

## CHAPTER SIX

Hudson and his daughter, Florence, made a joint public appearance at a gathering of healthcare professionals. On the way back to the White House, Florence, sensing her father's stress, asked him now that he knew what it was like to be president, was he still glad he'd won the election.

"In some ways, no," Hudson said. "Because it is much worse than I feared. The layers of conspiracy run much deeper than anyone knows."

"Someone must."

"Most Americans have never even heard the word REMie, and yet their representatives are acknowledging privately that the REMies are out of control. We have a few friends in Congress who have been bought by the elites. They see the REMies fighting each other for the CapStone as a greater risk to our country than NorthBridge."

"I still don't understand the CapWars," Florence said.

"I'm not sure I do either," the president admitted. "But I know this much: history is a lie. The CapWars have been going on behind the scenes for more than one hundred years. Picture a pyramid. Each time, the victor builds upon the level below, consolidating their wealth, power, and control, until the present, when they're finally at the top of the pyramid—the CapStone. The winner will either rule with absolute impunity, or the pyramid will collapse, and, along with it, civilization as we know it."

Florence shook her head, trying to fathom such corruption and greed.

"The REMies use what they call MADE events," Hudson continued. "Manipulate And Distract Everyone."

"How?"

"They're experts at it. Wars, riots, scandals, natural disasters, financial meltdowns, epidemics, mass shootings, terror attacks, anything. It doesn't matter if they're occurring naturally, or are contrived. REMies will use them to consolidate wealth and power."

"Contrived? So Schueller was right?" Florence asked. "They create these crises?"

"Yes, often they've manipulated events to make something happen. Most wars during the past century were created by the REMies, and the closer they get to the CapStone, the more ruthless they get. But believe it or not, there are some REMies who are not interested in CapWars. They think those going for CapStone are reckless, and risk ruining the system for all the REMies."

"Is Vonner one of those?"

"I'm really not sure yet. I hope so."

"Can you work with those to help you defeat the worst ones?"

"Maybe," Hudson said introspectively. "The CapStone gives a single REMie ultimate control—where the system, the money, and the power all go through one place, one person—and that is the winner of the CapWar. For a while it was Rothschild,

Morgan, Rockefeller, but even they never had it all, so their power slipped away, or at least decreased. When the global elites meet at the World Economic Forum in Davos, Switzerland every year, the Bilderberg Summit, and other secretive gatherings of the powerful, REMies and other billionaires conspire to push an agenda through, ultimately using politicians and bureaucrats to steamroll and advance their ambitions. That's all part of the CapWars."

"Can you really fight that kind of power?"

"I guess we're going to find out," he said as the president's armored limousine, affectionately known as "The Beast" rolled through the open gates at the White House.

After several weeks packed full of briefings, executive orders, negotiating with Congress, and navigating the confirmation process for his cabinet picks, Hudson had grown frustrated by a system that seemed designed to slow everything. The one thing that he *could* get done without approval from Congress was freeing Rochelle, but however impatient he was with Vonner, he decided it would be prudent to give him a heads up that he was going ahead with the pardon.

"You cannot pardon this woman!" Vonner shouted into the speaker phone while jumping off a stationary bike on the patio of Sun Wave, his Carmel, California estate.

"Oh, yes, I can. Article Two, Section Two, of the US Constitution gives the president—that's me—the power to remove a conviction, commute a sentence, grant reprieves and pardons for a given crime. Fortunately for Rochelle Rogers, the man she killed wasn't just the governor of Ohio, he had been appointed Secretary of Education, therefore making his assassination a federal crime."

"Oh, yes, that's very convenient for the late governor," Vonner said sarcastically. "Look, Hudson, I know I told you that you could do this, but that was before the attempt on your life during the inauguration. Now there's just no way the public will deal with the president pardoning someone who assassinated a political figure during a time when political figures are being assassinated every few weeks! We've done polling. Hell, Fonda Raton will personally burn you at the stake."

"I'm not required to explain or justify my actions to you, or Congress, or the media, Fonda Raton, or anyone, for that matter. The power to pardon is left solely to the discretion of the president; it cannot be reviewed or overturned by anyone!"

"Dammit, Hudson! You claim you want to make changes, that you want to go after the REMies, but you'll throw it all away for this woman?"

"The point is, you cannot stop me," Hudson said, wondering who was monitoring this call. "All I have to do is walk into the briefing room and announce that I'm pardoning Rochelle Rogers."

"There'll be repercussions."

"I'll just have to take it as it comes."

As it turned out, it wasn't as easy as walking into the briefing room. He needed to first notify and consult with the Federal Office of Pardon Attorney, the Department of Justice, the Bureau of Prisons, and the victim's family. That would all take a day or two, and *then* he could walk into the briefing room, but the Attorney General recommended that they simply issue a statement rather than subjecting the president to the fury of the media. Hudson set it into motion.

The White House press secretary was briefed, and asked if there was any positive spin they could throw out to the "wolves."

"No spin," Hudson said. "She's served nearly twenty-five years—a quarter of a century—behind bars. That's enough."

"We need a better reason," the press secretary warned. "Otherwise, the next time you're in front of a microphone, they'll pummel you."

Hudson nodded. "I'll give it some thought."

"Please do," the press secretary urged. "The woman went to your high school while you were there, then she killed the governor of your home state, a beloved man who was a Cabinet Secretary designate for Education. This has 'congressional hearing' written all over it. There are dozens of ways this story goes bad, and I can't think of one way it doesn't."

Fitz, who was also in attendance, spoke for the first time. "Mr. President, you do realize that the Democrats are looking for anything to derail your agenda? Do you really want to hand this to them?"

"It isn't a matter of wanting to . . . I *have* to do this."

Leaving the meeting, Fitz called Vonner. "He's going forward."

"I heard," Vonner said, eyeing his scotch. "Then be ready."

# CHAPTER SEVEN

That night, Hudson told Melissa he would be pardoning Rochelle the next day. She was disappointed, thinking it would derail his ambitious agenda, but understood what it meant to him.

The following morning, Hudson received his typical President's Daily Intelligence Briefing (PDB), which, as usual, was filled with terrorist threats—domestic and foreign—increasingly more "chatter" about unrest in Asia, and the China "threat." Normally he'd speak longer with his National Security Advisor, but he had to give a talk to a constituent group, then do a meet-and-greet. After that, a legislative strategy staff meeting, a few phone calls to congressional Republicans, two briefings, and, finally, a video conference with NATO. All before he could meet with Justice Department officials and sign Rochelle's pardon.

On his way to the staff meeting, he stopped by to see Hamilton, his favorite young campaign staffer. Hamilton, from Iowa, always seemed able to enthusiastically handle more work than anyone else. The clean-cut, skinny twenty-something looked up from his small desk in a lower level bullpen and smiled. It had been several weeks since he'd seen the president.

"Nice work space," Hudson said.

"It's not quite the Oval Office," Hamilton said with a laugh, "but I like it."

Hudson nodded, smiling. "Good, good."

He was about to leave and continue his way up to a meeting when Hamilton said, "Sir, I just wanted to show you something." He held up a note that he'd written. Hudson started to read it.

*A few days ago, Fonda Raton requested an interview. She asked me to please deliver her message this way in writing the next time I saw you. I guess she's worried about the place being bugged or something.*

Hudson finished reading and looked at Hamilton, who rolled his eyes as though the idea that somebody would be able to bug the White House was ridiculous.

"Yes, that is an original painting," Hudson said, pointing at the note. "Everything at the White House has some kind of historical context." Hudson took the piece of paper, which also contained contact information for Fonda, folded it twice, and put it in his pocket.

Hamilton nodded, suddenly not as sure that Fonda was being overly cautious.

"I promised you a tour of the Oval Office," Hudson said as he walked away. "Don't worry, I won't forget."

Hudson asked his personal secretary if he had any free time.

"You have ten minutes, between three-forty and three-fifty this afternoon."

"Hmmm, I need something a little sooner."

"When? I could try to rearrange the ambassador at two, or—"

"How about now?" Hudson gave her his best *I'm sorry* smile. "I'll be back in ten minutes."

She looked startled and quickly started working her tablet

computer, trying to figure how to reshuffle his schedule, wondering where he was going, but knowing not to ask.

His secretary loved pizza, and the day before, the president had a chef flown in from Wisconsin to make lunch for her and other close members of the West Wing staff. The man showed up with cases of cheese, dough, pans, and other baking implements to prepare the meal. Hudson and Schueller had discovered the pizzeria on the campaign trail, and had been craving another taste ever since. His secretary had been dizzy with embarrassment at the gesture, but ate three quarters of a pizza by herself. Hudson had learned a few tricks during the campaign, and knew how to win favor.

# CHAPTER EIGHT

The President made his way up to the residence. Schueller had been staying in one of the guest rooms. He'd become an expert on the historic mansion, and was attempting to learn all the secrets of the building. Melissa and Schueller had spent hours checking out the one hundred-thirty-two rooms, all the furnishings in the White House, and had made several expeditions to the secret, 40,000 square foot warehouse in Maryland which held the thousands of furnishings that had ever been used by prior presidents going back two centuries. Schueller had even written a song called, "412 Doors," the number in the building.

"Hey, Dad," Schueller said, surprised. "Don't you have some important presidential things to be doing right now?" He thought he might be about to get a lecture. Twice Schueller had been caught playing music in the East Room in the middle of the night, claiming, "The acoustics are amazing."

"No, Fitz told me that the most important thing I could do right now is to go and harass you."

They both laughed, but Hudson pulled out a piece of paper

from the book Schueller used to write song lyrics on and scribbled a quick note.

*Get ahold of the Wizard. Tell him I need something that will allow me to have conversations with people without the REMies overhearing. Something like the SonicBlock drive I use to talk with him, but for a whole room.*

Schueller looked up at his dad after reading the words. Hudson pulled out Hamilton's note and handed it to him. Although Schueller raised an eyebrow at the prospect of his dad meeting with Fonda, he understood that the Wizard's SonicBlock drive didn't give him the flexibility to communicate in person.

Schueller wrote on the same piece of paper, under Hudson's request.

*Why not just ask the Wizard using the SonicBlock?*

*Because this is too important,* Hudson wrote, while at the same time asking Schueller out loud if he had any gigs lined up.

"I've sort of had to give up gigging," Schueller said. "Security issues are just too big a concern for all the small venues I usually play."

"Sorry about that," Hudson said. "I guess it's a good thing you took the record deal then?"

Shortly before the election, Schueller had been offered a record deal that was almost too good to be true. They believed it originated from Vonner in an effort to distract Schueller from his father's campaign. At first, he wasn't going to accept, but Hudson had pushed his son to take it. At the time, he'd hoped it would keep Vonner from finding out they were on to him, but as Hudson had already confronted the billionaire, that no longer mattered. "Either way, it'll be exciting to get your songs out there, and who knows where it could lead," Hudson had told his son. "It might even help us with the REMies. Stranger things have happened."

"Yeah, I'm going into the studio later this week," Schueller said. He had signed the contract contingent on being able to record in a facility near Washington. As it turned out, it actually had helped in their crusade against the REMies. The record label was using DC-area session musicians to back Schueller, but the singer-songwriter had been able to insist on including two of his own bandmates. Schueller had been playing with one of them for years, the other was a man he'd never met before. His name was Walt Dungan, but everyone called him by his hacker name, Crane. He'd been Zackers' partner—the Wizard had found him after he'd broken the encryption of Zackers' drive. Crane had rented a tiny apartment in the DC suburb, Silver Spring, Maryland, and would pretend to be a musician. He was digging in and relentlessly going after REMie data.

Hudson scribbled one last question: *What did you think of the letter?* He'd given it to Schueller to read the day before.

"I agree with your conclusion," Schueller said, and then wrote, *I think you need to meet with the last president asap.*

The NATO secure-live-feed (SLF) conference had been dominated by a once unthinkable topic—war with China. The rich communist government had grown more and more interested in projecting its might and influence. NATO believed an all-out conflict was unlikely, but the member states had resolved to prepare for all eventualities and to consider every contingency.

Hudson headed back to the Oval Office to sign Rochelle's pardon. Fitz was waiting. He could tell by the expression on his chief of staff's face that something was wrong.

"NorthBridge?"

Fitz shook his head. "Worse. Rochelle Rogers has escaped."

Hudson leaned back in the leather chair, disbelieving. For

several moments he said nothing, he just stared at the ornamental ceiling of the Oval Office. "She didn't escape."

"I just spoke to the Bureau of Prisons. They confirmed it."

Hudson laughed bitterly. "I don't care what they confirm, Rochelle Rogers did not escape."

Fitz let out an exasperated sigh. "Believe what you want, she's not in her cell. Rochelle Rogers is no longer in federal custody."

"Isn't that just wonderfully convenient?" Hudson said sarcastically. "Problem solved."

"Sort of," Fitz said. "But that depends on where she is."

"Twenty-five years she rots in a prison cell, and the day I'm going to pardon her, she *escapes?*" Hudson picked up his communicator, which provided a secure and direct line to Vonner.

Vonner claimed he knew nothing about the escape until Hudson told him. For the first time, Hudson hung up on the billionaire.

"I'm getting out of here," Hudson said.

"What? Fitz sputtered. "Where are you going?"

"Do you people think I'm an idiot?" He headed out the east door to the Rose Garden. A surprised but stalwart Marine guard watched as the president headed down the West Colonnade toward the residence. Along the way, Hudson called his personal secretary and informed her he needed to go to West Virginia. Without question, she immediately began the process of ordering Marine One.

Once in the private sitting room, adjoining the presidential bedroom, he turned on a computer and was about to insert the SonicBlock drive to contact the Wizard when Melissa rushed in.

"What are you doing here?" Hudson asked. "I thought you had that thing with the veterans?"

"Fitz called me," she said breathlessly.

"Did he tell you Vonner snatched Rochelle?"

"He told me BOP is saying she escaped. Fitz also said you're going somewhere?"

"She was being held at Hazelton. You know, the federal prison in West Virginia."

"Of course I know. And you're going there, why?"

"To find out what happened."

Melissa touched Hudson's shoulder. "Not a good idea."

"I'm going to find out what Vonner did!"

"Why would it be Vonner? What if NorthBridge took her?"

"What?" It hadn't occurred to him. "Why? How could they know?" Then he remembered Vonner had known, and North-Bridge seemed to be better at uncovering secrets than anyone.

*Everyone is listening in on everyone.*

"When you told me about that night Rochelle was raped, you said you saw the vacant look in her eyes."

"It haunts me."

"Maybe more than you know, because if you saw into her eyes, she could have seen into yours." Melissa paused until she saw her words register on Hudson's face. "She knows you saw it. She knows you know everything."

"My God."

"Yes," she spoke slowly, "that makes her incredibly valuable to anyone who doesn't want you to be president."

# CHAPTER NINE

For the next two days, Hudson did everything he could to locate Rochelle. Although he took Melissa's advice and did not go to the prison, he did have several calls with the warden, the head of the Bureau of Prisons, and Justice Department officials, including the director of the FBI. The director had already been a source of frustration for Hudson with the Bureau's failure to make any headway in the NorthBridge investigation. He suspected that the director, like those before him, was a REMie loyalist.

Not surprisingly, Vonner continued to deny any knowledge of Rochelle's whereabouts. And, as always, he seemed convincing, even offering his security agents' help in the search. The billionaire pressed the president on what Rochelle might know. "Can this fugitive hurt you?" he'd asked.

Hudson gave nothing to Vonner, but considered the situation desperate enough to call on the Wizard to use his connection to Booker to get in touch with Linh. As the leader of the Inner Movement, she allegedly had psychic abilities. Although he didn't believe in them, he would try anything to locate Rochelle.

The Wizard came through and arranged a video call, which Hudson took in his private study, utilizing the SonicBlock drive.

"Thanks for taking my call," Hudson said, immediately mesmerized anew by Linh's eyes. Although they had remained clearly in his memory, each time he saw her again, her eyes were always more distracting than he remembered—at once magnetic and piercing, ancient and swirling with energy.

"You're the president," she said with a soft smile.

Hudson suddenly recalled he'd seen Linh in the crowd a moment before he was shot at the basketball stadium during the campaign. Until that moment on the video call, the memory had faded into the chaos and blur of the awful attack. "You were there, at the stadium," he said, gasping the words.

"Was I?" she asked, not the least bit coy.

"Yes, you were," he replied firmly. "Were you there to help?" he asked, and then, although it made no sense to him, he added in a whisper, "You saved me, didn't you?"

"You overestimate me, Mr. President."

"I don't think so."

"I'm glad you've recovered."

He nodded, still trying to recall that moment between seeing her face and feeling the first bullet enter his body. Her expression had been filled with so much emotion. *She had to know the attack was coming.*

"Linh, do you know where she is?"

"Who?"

It was a fair question; how *would* she know who he was asking about? Yet ,somehow, he thought she might. "A woman I went to school with, from my home town. She was in prison, and now she's disappeared. Rochelle Rogers."

Linh shook her head. "There are bigger problems."

"There are always bigger problems." Hudson knew this was true, but Rochelle had haunted him for so long, and now, hours before his redemption in her release, she was gone. At the moment, he couldn't think of anything more important. He thought of what NorthBridge or Bastendorff could do with her information. "My presidency could depend on finding her," he said. *And my sanity certainly does*, he thought.

"Your life is at stake."

"Tell me something I don't know." He didn't mean to sound flippant, but he'd been targeted in at least three assassination attempts, there were bullet holes in his body, he'd sustained permanent injuries, and a powerful, clandestine terrorist group trying to spark a revolution had sworn to kill him. These were realities he had already gotten used to, at least as much as one *could* get used to assassins and coups. "Is Rochelle alive?"

"Once again, Mr. President, you're overestimating me."

"Am I?"

Linh nodded. "They are pushing the world into a catastrophic war."

*Now she's talking about China?* "We're seeking all diplomatic solutions, but sometimes war is necessary. China will back down. They cannot win."

"Neither side will win this war. You must stop it."

Hudson read the quote from the papers that Schueller had given him. The words, having come from William Casey, CIA director under President Reagan, chilled him. Hudson remembered Vonner telling him that Reagan had not known the truth about the power of the presidency, and that the REMies were really in control, until six weeks after his inauguration. But the meeting at which the Casey quote originated had taken place within just a few weeks of Reagan taking office. The new president had asked each of the cabinet secretaries to tell him what goals they had for their departments or agencies. Casey said: "We'll know our disinformation program is complete when everything the American public believes is false."

Hudson shook his head, disbelieving that the CIA director's words had been made public three decades earlier, and yet it was still going on. He recalled an interview with NSA whistleblower, Edward Snowden, in which the fugitive had said that his biggest fear wasn't for his own safety, but rather that people would find out that the US government was eavesdropping on its citizen's communications—every phone call, email, and text—and no one would care; nothing would change.

He'd been right. It had only gotten worse, with the current 3D surveillance system and who knew what else. The government not only had the ability to track every citizen, they were *doing* it. And now that he was president, he was also doing it. He had to find a way to stop it.

The Wizard had told him, "REMies use the NSA and other agencies to filter the data they collect. Three-D is bigger than just cameras in public spaces. They use your phone, computer, television, and even other appliances to track you and watch you. They know who you know, what you like, where you go, what you buy . . . They were in on the creation of Facebook and other social networks. People voluntarily signed up to be under a surveillance state. The internet is a double-edged sword; it allows you to connect and access the world, but it allows the state to track and watch everyone's every move."

*The warnings had all been there,* Hudson thought. He recalled talks and interviews he'd seen years earlier, even before 3D put it all together.

"Linkability. They use credit and debit cards, cell phones, metro cards, rewards programs, and cameras, to match you with other people; one piece of data linked to another," Jacob Appelbaum, a cyber security expert, had explained. "They can recreate your steps and who you talked with to paint a picture that is made up of facts, but not necessarily true. You may have been on the corner, but it doesn't mean you did the crime."

Hudson sat alone in his private study located next to the Oval Office. The tension and the sleepless nights kept him popping extra-strength aspirins. The job, the depth of corruption, the forces aligned against him, were all much greater than he had expected. He needed someone he could trust working with him inside the White House. So far, he'd discovered that was almost impossible. Hamilton could be trusted, but the bright twenty-four-year old was just too young and inexperienced to be of much help in any advisory role. Melissa, his most ardent supporter, was extremely busy being first lady of the United States, and wanted him to "ease up on chasing the conspiracies."

Although he did have complete faith in the Wizard, he wouldn't fit in. While laughing at the thought of the Wizard in a Cabinet meeting, Hudson suddenly thought of someone he had known almost as long, someone extremely qualified to advise him on a whole range of matters, and, most importantly, someone he would trust with his life.

Hudson went to his secretary and gave her the name. "He shouldn't be too hard to track down. Interrupt me as soon as you get him on the line, no matter what I'm doing."

An hour later, as Hudson came out of a meeting with agricultural leaders, she told him his call was waiting. Although the president suspected his secretary had timed it so he wouldn't be interrupted, it didn't matter. He was relieved and excited to connect with his old friend.

"Enapay Dranick, is that you?" Hudson asked.

"Mr. President," Dranick began. "Quite an honor hearing from my commander-in-chief."

"Dranick, it's me! Drop the formalities." It had been maybe five years since they'd last spoken, but the former army buddies had shared too much for Dranick to be calling him "Mr. President."

The two had first met in the army when Colonel Enapay Dranick was just a private, and the president was also an enlisted man. Hudson and Dranick could not have been more opposite; Hudson, a reserved, conservative, white kid from the Midwest, and Dranick, a wild, screaming, liberal, Native American from the wilds of northern Arizona. They did, however, share two things: the same humor, and a deep sense of honor and patriotism.

After forming a strong friendship, they wound up together in the wrong place at the wrong time—Iraq. After a surprise attack, Dranick, critically injured, buried in shrapnel, debris, and bodies, found himself surrounded. Hudson fought off the insurgents, pulled him out, and carried his buddy to medics, saving his life.

Dranick was upset when Hudson didn't re-enlist, but he understood. Sometimes the razor's edge-action drew a soldier back for more, but more often it repelled him, sending him home forever changed. They'd remained close as Hudson built his career in hardware and Dranick rose to the rank of colonel in the Green Berets. Then another tragic circumstance solidified their bond even more when they both lost their wives to cancer within two years of each other.

"It's mighty good to hear your voice again, Mr. Pres—uh, Hudson. How've you been, aside from the assassination attempts, becoming the leader of the free world, and that sort of thing?"

"It's a complicated business," Hudson said, relying on their friendship and history to know that Dranick would pick up the layers of meaning in his statement. "Can you come to Washington? I have something I need your help with."

"When do you need me?"

"Weeks ago. When can you get here?"

"You're my commander-in-chief."

"Then I'll see you in the morning. One of my assistants will make all the arrangements."

As president of the United States, Hudson had thousands of employees in the executive branch, and millions more technically working for him in the federal government. A shortage of staff was not the problem; knowing which ones he could *trust* was. Having Dranick on board was not only key to his ability to change things, it also might mean the difference in his survival.

# CHAPTER TEN

Having reread the letter from his predecessor for the umpteenth time, Hudson quietly asked his secretary to set up a meeting with the past president.

"Perhaps golf?" she asked.

"Perfect," Hudson replied, wondering if she might actually be trustworthy.

She'd also opened a slot in his schedule for his meeting with Dranick, which he'd decided to hold on the White House grounds in the trees between the swimming pool and the putting green. Even though Hudson was fairly certain they couldn't be overheard, he still spoke in hushed tones after dispensing with the initial pleasantries of two old friends who hadn't seen each other for several years.

Hudson gave Dranick a quick and condensed version of what he was up against while gauging his old army buddy's reaction.

"My grandfather always told me never to trust the white man's government," Dranick said with a slight smile.

"A government you spent your life serving."

"I have served the people of America, and protected its lands

—lands which my people were pushed off of, but are still part of us," Dranick said as they walked under the trees, heading toward the tennis court. "And a government that you now lead."

"I wish I led it, but I'm just another pawn." Hudson thought of Fonda and all her warnings about the REMies. "Maybe the most important pawn, but a pawn nonetheless."

Dranick nodded. "What can I do?"

"I'm going to appoint you to head the Brickman Effort."

"You want me to find and stop NorthBridge?" Dranick smiled. "It'll be my pleasure."

"I always liked your optimism, Enapay," Hudson said. "But I'm not sure you'll feel the same in a few months. I believe the REMies don't want us to get NorthBridge, or they already would have stopped them."

"You think the REMies are behind NorthBridge?" Dranick asked.

"The REMies are behind everything."

"Even if they aren't specifically sponsoring the terrorists, these REMies seem to be masters at manipulating events to fit their agenda. As you pointed out, whoever controls the media controls the minds of the masses."

Hudson stopped and looked at his friend. "I probably don't need to tell you, but I'm going to anyway. Somebody is trying to kill me. As we go against the most powerful people in the world, it's only going to get more dangerous. Accepting my offer could cost you your life."

"You know you're welcome to my life," Dranick said. "It's a good day to die."

"Then you'll start tomorrow, right after I fire the FBI director."

Dranick raised an eyebrow. "Will they let you get away with that?"

"I wasn't going to ask permission."

"Who are we going to get as a replacement?"

Hudson smiled at how easily and quickly Enapay had said "we." It reinforced his instincts that bringing him to Washington was the right decision. "I'm not sure yet, but I have a meeting with the vice president later. I'm hoping she'll have an idea."

"Can you trust her?"

"I think so," Hudson said as they turned to head back toward the White House. "They didn't want me to choose her."

Dranick nodded. On the way back, Hudson told him that in addition to running the anti-NorthBridge Brickman Effort, he was to look in all directions for corruption.

"A tall order," Dranick said. "Very tall."

"We'll get more budget," Hudson replied. "You and I may be the only ones who know it, but I just expanded the charge of the Brickman Effort not only to root out NorthBridge, but to get the REMies as well."

Vonner, wearing a black jogging outfit, paced in front of the large window overlooking the Potomac River. He had just acquired the relatively modest estate for seventeen million dollars, and had converted most of the fifteen bedrooms to offices. He didn't like traditional office buildings. One of the two dining rooms had been transformed into a workout area. Rex glanced up from his bank of computers with a questioning look on his face.

"The way they're planning to serve up this war with China is going to take a lot of selling," Vonner said while pouring himself a drink.

Rex, as usual, took advantage of the scotch distraction to roll seven blue dice. He studied the numbers quickly before collecting the dice and shoving them back in his pocket.

"Bastendorff wants the war," Vonner continued. "Rothschild

wants it, the Koch brothers . . . By my last survey, thirty-seven of the top forty-eight REMies want it."

"Booker Lipton?"

"Hard to say," Vonner said, swirling the contents of his glass. "You know he's always a tough read."

"I don't think he wants the war," Rex said, his fingers flying across the keys.

"But he would profit handsomely. With his holdings, he would make billions."

"Does he *need* more money?"

"Do any of us?" Vonner retorted. "Why do you believe Booker is against the war?"

"He hasn't made any moves." Rex checked another screen to verify his claim. REMies didn't act as one organization. They were individuals, each with their own ideas, plans, and agendas, yet they all adhered to the same grand strategy, having usually agreed on it well in advance. "Moves" were what each did to progress toward the main objective for the collective goal. This almost always resulted in a consolidation of wealth and power for all of the REMies. Sometimes an individual would make an error, but there were enough of them to cover for, correct, or even turn the mistake into something beneficial toward their ends.

War was ultimately good for the elites. That was the key reason the world had been in a perpetual state of war through all of recorded history. The wealthy always profit from war, and conflict was the best way to keep populations in line, afraid, and distracted. In the chaos, the elites continued to consolidate their power.

"Is that correct?" Vonner asked.

"I can't find any moves Booker has made toward bringing the war with China," Rex said.

"But that doesn't mean he's *against* it. We're still early into this, so maybe he still will. His moves might take longer to put into place, or perhaps they're for a later phase."

"Okay, do you want to know who else hasn't made a single move?" Rex asked while searching the data, clicking keys, scanning the different monitors. He found a few of the minor players who hadn't done anything, but they had previously expressed support for war between the US and China. "You should expect Booker to be a problem."

"Booker is always a problem!" Vonner snapped while stepping onto a mini trampoline.

"However, in this case, if he's on the opposite side, as Bastendorff is, then my enemy's enemy is my friend."

Vonner allowed a small smile as he jogged in place. "The CapWars have led us to this fractured world where a man like Bastendorff could become king, and a man like Booker is all that can stop him. Strange days."

Rex thought about the pair of twenty-sided orange dice in his pocket, but they would have to wait. "Strange indeed, when a man like you might just win the final CapWar."

Vonner took Rex's words as a compliment, but knew the fixer laced most of his statements with a heavy dose of irony. "I might just take the prize, but that depends on our president and the answer to the question keeping Hudson up at night: where *is* Rochelle Rogers?"

# CHAPTER ELEVEN

D avid Covington was a tall and imposing man, his thick
black hair showing only a slight hint of gray, and at six-
foot-four, even without his title (Director of National Intelligence) he cast an intimidating air.

Hudson didn't like him, nor did he trust him, but coming into
the federal government with no experience meant he had to take
a lot of people's advice for appointments to the more than 1,300
positions he was responsible for filling. In fact, Vonner and Fitz
had chosen most of the key cabinet positions, including
Covington as DNI. Hudson knew Vonner's behind-the-scene
involvement was going to make it more difficult for him to control
things, or even know who was really in charge, but he had no
choice; positions had to be filled, the government had to run.

Covington had requested an immediate meeting with President Pound as soon as news broke that the FBI director had
been fired.

"Mr. President, I wish you had consulted me about your decision to terminate the director," Covington said as the two men sat
alone in the Oval Office.

"David, I'm sure as DNI, you might have expected to be notified prior to a public announcement." Hudson leaned back in his leather chair. "However, as you know, I'm new to this, and there's a lot to learn. The American people wanted it this way, one of their own in here figuring it out as he goes. But at the same time, I brought in experts like yourself to help out, and to make sure we don't get in any real trouble. So, if I botched the protocol here, that's too bad. Don't let it hurt your feelings." Hudson smiled. "It's likely to happen again."

"With all due respect, Mr. President, it's not the notifying me that's the problem, it's that I don't think it was a good idea," Covington said sharply.

"Perhaps that's why I didn't consult with you, David," Hudson replied, still smiling. "The director has had nearly a year and a half to find and stop NorthBridge. He hasn't even made a single arrest. That is unprecedented, and inexcusable. The American people expect more from their top law enforcement official, and I tend to agree with that. Frankly, I'm not sure how you can possibly defend him."

"I simply don't think this is the time to change horses." Covington shifted uneasily. "Remember what happened when Trump fired his FBI Director?"

"Of course I do, but I don't see the connection." Hudson ignored what he knew was a veiled threat. Trump firing Director Comey gave his opposition a whole new platform to wage war against him. "David, you're wasting my time. The director has already been fired. Is there something else I can help you with?"

"I'd like to suggest a replacement." Covington took out a sheet of paper from his jacket pocket and handed it to the president. "Any of these candidates would be excellent."

Hudson looked at the list of five names, only three of which he recognized, and none of whom he was considering. "Excellent,

David. I appreciate your input. Now, if you'll excuse me, I'm running behind." Hudson stood.

Covington also rose. "My apologies, Mr. President, if I fouled up your schedule, but I didn't think this could wait."

At that moment, responding to a button the president had pushed under his desk, an assistant walked into the Oval Office and escorted Covington out.

Once in the back of his car, seated next to an aide, David Covington fumed. He ranted as his driver drove them back to the office. "Who does Pound think he is?"

"President of the United States?" the aide offered, smiling.

"I'm in no mood for jokes," Covington said. "Get Vonner on the line."

Covington unwrapped a package of Necco wafers—chalky, colored sugar candies about the size of a US quarter—gave a revolted look at a pink one before quickly tossing it out the window like a dead spider, and then popped two green ones into his mouth. After several minutes, the aide reported Vonner could not be reached.

"NorthBridge is a national security issue," Covington said. "How dare he not clear this with me!"

"But the president is correct; the FBI *hasn't* delivered. The public is rightfully outraged."

Covington glared at his assistant. "Are you citing structure and law to me? Maybe you should go work for Pound!"

"Maybe," the aide said, unworried. He had worked for Covington for more than eighteen years, first in the Pentagon, then for five years in the private sector, and now continuing in his new role as head of the intelligence community.

Normally Covington might have laughed, but he could tell

Pound was going to be a headache, and he didn't like headaches. In Covington's mind, he outranked the president, and, in fact, he *did*. Covington, along with the director of the NSA, the director of the CIA, the chairman of the Federal Reserve Board, and the handful of other prominent people, created policy. "Pound is unaware of how the world works. Apparently no one told him how the government is set up. Vonner better get his boy in line, because it'll be a lot easier for things to work out right if the president is on board."

"That's for sure."

"I don't have the patience to go four years holding Pound's hand. It's enough that we have to create believable situations and scenarios for the American people, but if we're also going to have to convince the figurehead that our version of the truth is the real one, then our progress is going to be greatly slowed."

# CHAPTER TWELVE

Surprisingly, the former president refused several requests to meet with Hudson.

Actually, that wasn't completely unexpected. The shocking thing was that his predecessor wouldn't even take a phone call. This worried Hudson, because the ex-president was clearly scared. Hudson knew he should also be afraid, but he didn't have time, or enough information, to worry about that. He thought back to his first day in the Oval Office, when he'd read the letter from the former president, and about how George Washington had given him the idea that might perhaps be the only way to topple the REMies. He'd been formulating the specifics ever since.

Washington had faced a choice on the eve of the American Revolution between liberty, or the colonies remaining in slavery to the king; virtue or corruption, honor or disgrace, courage or cowardice. Hudson saw the same choices in front of him, but on a grander scale. The REMies had ruled for so long, their corruption so deep, it might not even be *possible* to beat them.

NorthBridge had already started their own revolution which

seemed to be targeting the government, but for those in the know, the REMies were really railing against the REMies. Hudson believed the terrorist group was using the wrong methods in challenging the elites, yet he wasn't sure his own plan would be strong enough. He was only certain that he couldn't fight North-Bridge and the REMies at the same time.

Then he had an awful thought.

*What if the REMies are using NorthBridge to distract us from their most recent attempts at consolidating their power?*

Hudson took time out from his official duties to lead a private tour of the White House for his family, which ended in the Oval Office. All four of his brothers and sisters—including Dwayne, who still preferred living on the street, even though they had rented him an apartment in his small Ohio hometown—were present with their families.

His sister, Jenna, a widow, and his brother, Ace, both had adult children around the same age as Schueller and Florence. The cousins had shared regular visits while growing up, and the reunion of the younger generation of Pounds added to the excitement of the White House gathering.

Ace, a pilot, cheerfully reminded Hudson of his promise that if he won the election, he'd take Ace onboard Air Force One sometime.

"Don't worry, big brother," Hudson said as the group checked out the bowling alley installed at President Nixon's request. "There'll be plenty of chances to get you a ride on the plane."

"How about The Beast?" Ace's twenty-year-old son asked. The President's limousine had been built to withstand a roadside bomb, and an onboard oxygen system meant the president would be safe during a chemical attack. But the Secret Service had been adding features since the rise of NorthBridge—laser shielding, weaponized micro-drones, satellite stealth cloaking, and, of course, always carried current bags of the president's blood type.

"The Beast is the coolest," Schueller answered his cousin. "Tear gas and grenade launchers, Kevlar-reinforced tires—shred and puncture proof—night vision cameras, totally bulletproof, the fuel tank is even encased in foam so it won't explode, and—"

"And the rest is classified," the president interrupted. "Sorry. But we'll see about getting you a ride in The Beast some time."

Schueller was about to apologize for getting carried away, but at that moment, he got a text from Crane. Reading it, he whispered quickly to his father. "Trouble."

In the months since Rochelle had disappeared, Hudson had come to believe she was probably dead, and that the most likely suspect was Vonner. If Bastendorff or NorthBridge had taken her, certainly she would have surfaced by now with her damning story about the president of the United States being a coward, an accessory to murder, a facilitator to rape, and the orchestrator of a decades-long cover-up. Of course, it was possible they were saving her to be used at just the right moment, a time to blackmail the most powerful man on the planet—perhaps when the nation was waffling toward war.

Dranick had a small team of investigators looking, but the leads were virtually nonexistent. The Wizard and Crane were scouring the DarkNet for any mention or trace. Nothing. Hudson's far-flung hope that Linh would provide an answer had, thus far, proved empty.

Meanwhile, the drumbeats of war grew louder, as each week there seemed to be another incident—Chinese hacking of US government agencies, China encroaching on territorial waters of

US-Asian allies, China executing dissidents, imprisoning suspected US spies, building more artificial islands to expand their military reach into the South China sea, provocative troop movements, and the big one, increasing rhetoric toward Taiwan.

Hudson was beginning to believe he would be the first US president to engage in war with a major country since the end of World War II, and more than that, he'd have to figure out how to win a conventional war against a nuclear power. He'd ordered his defense secretary to present a plan for containment, but no one had any idea how a government with nuclear capabilities would react in the face of losing a conventional war. Even that victory was not assured, given that China's military was the fastest growing in the world, and had about a million more personnel than the US, but those numbers weren't the most worrisome. The nuclear stockpiles were the real threat, and although the US clearly dominated that category, possessing nearly seven thousand nuclear weapons to China's two hundred and sixty, even a few nukes were enough to devastate humanity.

The Wizard claimed it was the REMies pushing the world's two wealthiest countries to the brink of armed conflict, but Hudson couldn't see the angle. Sure, minor skirmishes and invading third world nations was extremely profitable. However, a direct clash between the US and China could not be good for business. International trade would collapse, Asia would be devastated and destabilized, and potentially millions would die. Surely the REMies didn't manipulate *every* event in the world? They could not, Hudson believed, control all the major governments and corporations around the globe. Constantly, he reminded himself that he *had* to believe that premise.

The president had also ordered his Secretary of State to do everything to find a peaceful solution to the growing crisis. "I'm still the Commander in Chief," Hudson told Melissa. "There isn't going to be a war without my signature."

"Not unless they shoot first," she responded before she could stop the words as the two of them sat on Air Force One en route to Florida. Vonner had provided a house on Key Largo to act as a retreat. Hudson had made the request based on wanting to escape the DC pressure cooker, but, in reality, he needed a place where he could easily get outside and beyond the reach of the countless listening devices that saturated the White House.

He didn't know about the eavesdropping drones camouflaged as seagulls and large flying insects.

# CHAPTER THIRTEEN

B astendorff left the penthouse of the massive block-wide London building which served as his worldwide headquarters, and took the lift to the fifth floor—his favorite. While the other parts of the two hundred and forty year old structure were furnished with antiques, Persian rugs, and oil paintings from prior centuries framed in ornate gold frames, the fifth floor was all done in colored plastics.

Legos. Bastendorff had collected a set of every type of Lego ever manufactured. Too busy to put them together himself, he employed two men full-time for the task. However, each new set was only partially constructed. The last ten pieces were always saved for Bastendorff.

He wandered through the cavernous space, where Lego trains wove through entire Lego cities, past volcanoes, police headquarters, airports, all sorts of crazy castles and fortresses, all constructed entirely out of Legos. Above his head hung Lego spaceships and all manner of interplanetary installations.

Bastendorff, a short, pudgy, bald man with a face that often made babies cry, turned to the two assistants trailing him and asked for an update on China. While listening, he puttered with the bricks, switched mini-figures around the elaborate displays, and contemplated his next move in the chess match he was currently engaged in with his fellow REMies. As soon as they were done with China, the aides spent the next fifteen minutes giving him the latest on President Pound.

"Thus far, he seems to be leaning slightly toward war," one of the men told Bastendorff.

"That may just keep him alive," Bastendorff said. "If he starts listening to his vice president and moves in the other direction, we can easily provoke things."

His aides knew he was referring to the plan to have a "Chinese" shooter assassinate the president. One of them handed him a report detailing the operation and the potential scenarios that would follow the death of an American president at the hands of a killer sanctioned by China's Communist Party.

Bastendorff spun the propeller on a large green and black Lego helicopter. "I hope it doesn't come to that," he said, handing the report back to the aide. "I'll read it later."

The aides looked at each other.

Bastendorff pressed a plastic button and a volley of a dozen Lego missiles launched through the air. "I'd much prefer to use our secret weapon against the president," Bastendorff said, surveying the damage his toy attack had done on their target. "In the meantime, let's intensify the war between the drug cartels in Mexico, and it might be interesting if riots break out in El Salvador and Guatemala." He twisted the tail of a four-headed Lego dragon. "Are we making any progress on the coup in Pakistan?"

"Some," the aide said, scanning a tablet computer.

"I hope so. And NorthBridge?"

"It looks like their next target is definitely going to be a Chinese container ship just outside the Port of Los Angeles."

"Perfect, isn't it?" Bastendorff's mouth formed a crooked smile, a triangle of white spit remaining in each corner. "Let's see how the president handles that."

As soon as Schueller and Hudson could get alone—they met on the White House basketball court—his son explained the meaning behind Crane's text. Gypsy, the custom-program they'd been using to discover and track events the REMies had created, had picked up some new patterning.

"Gypsy has something, Schueller said. "Although it's minor, it's a *lot* of minor. All the patterns and evidence taken together has Crane thinking there's a good chance that NorthBridge might have Rochelle."

Hudson had only recently shared the story of that long-ago night with his son as part of his attempt to try and forgive himself. Schueller, although stunned by the revelation, had handled it well. Somehow, it made him love his father even more, knowing he had big faults of his own.

"Damn," the president said, staring into the distance as a cardinal landed on a southern magnolia. "We've got to find her."

"The FBI is already looking," Schueller said, taking a three-point shot and making it.

"They're looking for an escaped fugitive," the president said bitterly. "They have no idea how important she is."

"You can't really tell them."

"No, but it doesn't appear they can do much about North-Bridge anyway. I'll have to find someone who can." The president looked out across the ellipse. "Booker Lipton."

"Isn't that kind of like making a deal with the devil?" Schueller asked, genuinely concerned. "He's a REMie."

"My father always said, 'know your priorities.' Rochelle first, next NorthBridge, and then the REMies," the president said.

"Yeah, but, Dad, don't you see?" Schueller asked. "Rochelle and NorthBridge are just distractions. It's what the REMies always do, that's why they never get caught. They keep us looking at something else."

"Rochelle is more than a distraction," the president said. "She's the reason I'm here."

"Thank you," Hudson said into his phone as he walked the shore of Key Largo, trailed, as usual, by Secret Service agents. He'd called Booker utilizing the SonicBlock, which, combined with the sound of the waves and whatever precautions Booker had in place, should ensure that no one could intercept the conversation.

After returning the SonicBlock and phone to his pocket, Hudson enjoyed the setting sun and soothing taste of salt air on his lips. He hoped Booker could use his vast resources and secret networks to discover what had happened to Rochelle, and to find out if NorthBridge really had her.

Several seagulls had landed nearby, and Hudson tossed them some bits of pretzels he'd mostly finished. Oddly, the birds ignored the offerings.

He'd considered that it might have been Booker behind Rochelle's disappearance or death, but the Wizard had argued that this was unlikely. With the new information from Crane, Hudson knew that even if Schueller was right, and this was a deal with the devil, time was running out.

Hudson, still standing with his feet in the surf, thought about something strange Booker had said when Hudson pressed for quick action on locating Rochelle.

*"Time's a funny thing."*

Hudson turned around when he heard his daughter's voice calling to him above the sound of the surf. He hugged her and then turned to the man next to her.

"Look who I found," Florence said as he looked into her smiling face.

Even behind the man's dark glasses, Hudson could recognize Secret Service Agent Trent Bond, whom they'd nicknamed "007." He'd been on duty when Hudson, still on the campaign trail, had been attacked in Colorado. Florence had kept him alive until the EMTs arrived. He'd barely made it. They'd been close ever since.

"Hey, 007, good to see you back at work," Hudson greeted, dry sand sticking to his wet feet as he walked up the beach. "I'd heard a rumor that you'd be here."

"Thank you, Mr. President," Bond said. "I'm happy to return to your detail. And *very* happy you're no longer a candidate."

"Yes, me too. Although, I have to admit that some days I wish I hadn't won."

"Tough job," Bond said, nodding knowingly.

"Oh, Dad," Florence said. "You know you love it."

Hudson smiled at his daughter.

"Mr. President," Bond began, his expression turning serious, "if I may have a minute?"

"Of course."

"Usually it's a Secret Service agent who saves the president or members of the first family," Bond said, looking from Hudson to Florence. "But in this case, you two saved *my* life."

Florence smiled, but her eyes filled with tears at the memory of that brutal day in Colorado.

"You would have done the same," Hudson said. "I just wish we could have saved you all."

"Thank you, sir," Bond said, taking off his sunglasses. "The thing is, though, I'm not so sure."

Hudson stood silent, waiting for the rest, already guessing at Bond's next words.

"The Secret Service," Bond said, looking over his shoulder, "has been infiltrated."

# CHAPTER FOURTEEN

Florence looked at 007, the man she'd kept alive with her bare hands drenched in his blood. "What does that mean? 'The Secret Service has been infiltrated?'" she asked quietly.

"There are people within the government who operate under different rules," Bond explained. "A government inside the government. A 'deep state', if you will."

Neither Hudson nor Florence were surprised, as they already knew the REMies had a hold on the US government. Hudson had first-hand knowledge that Booker had at least one Secret Service agent on his payroll, but the grave expression on Bond's face along with his nervousness told them this was beyond all that.

"They decide things," Bond continued.

"Who?" Hudson asked.

"I don't know," Bond replied. "I report to my superior, and he probably doesn't know. There are layers upon layers in order to insulate everyone, but I can tell you that the Service doesn't just protect the president. We monitor him. We watch, listen, and report everything."

"Why?" Florence asked, even more quietly than before. "How do they make you do this?"

"It's how the Service is structured."

"When did it start?" Hudson asked.

"This isn't new. I've heard from some of the old-timers that it's been like this for more than half a century, at least." Bond looked off at the other agents standing at various points up and down the beach. "I'm sorry to have betrayed you, Mr. President."

Florence turned away and stared out over the ocean.

"Is it *all* the agents?" Hudson asked.

"I don't know. It could be, but it may only be some. I can give you a list of all the agents I know about."

"Yes."

"Mr. President, I'm afraid there's something else," Bond said, looking down at the sand. "A few select agents have a classified assignment known as 'the critical move'."

"And what the hell is 'the critical move'?"

"Those agents have been trained in how to stand down in order to make their actions undetectable when they get the order."

Hudson looked at Bond, flabbergasted. "To stand down so that someone can assassinate the president?"

"Yes."

Florence gasped and turned back to Bond.

"And you were one of those agents? Trained in 'the critical move'?"

"I'm afraid so."

Florence slapped Bond across the face.

He could have easily blocked her assault, but he took it, only stepping back slightly to lessen the impact. "I'm sorry," Bond said to her. "I can help you now."

"We don't *want* your help," she hissed.

The other agents, flinched and watched tensely, but 007 waved them off.

"Calm down," Hudson told Florence. "We have an audience."

"How dare you?" Florence said to Bond in a terse whisper.

"You get me that list of agents," Hudson said.

"I'll prepare it immediately, and then, Mr. President, I'll tender my resignation."

"You'll do nothing of the sort. You owe me your life, now I expect you to earn it!"

Once back at the White House, Hudson resumed his hectic schedule, but was now armed with 007's list of rogue Secret Service agents; men and women loyal to someone other than the president, someone running the country from the deep state, hidden, unelected, and secret. He would keep some of them around in order to feed false information to the mystery man leading the shadow government, and he kept Agent Bond close by, assigned to his personal detail.

The president briefed Dranick on the Secret Service situation and directed him to investigate if NorthBridge might somehow be fueling the Chinese crisis. Dranick made his views clear—he saw no diplomatic solutions with China.

"I don't believe we can avoid this war," the Green Beret colonel said.

"Unless there's a NorthBridge connection," Hudson said.

"Maybe finding NorthBridge isn't where we should be putting our resources," Dranick said. "Perhaps the real question we ought to be asking is *why* we can't find them. How can they hide this well? Who's helping them?"

An aide interrupted and informed the president that North-

Bridge had just struck again. Hudson hurried to the situation room, where his national security team was mostly assembled, others entering just behind him.

"Mr. President," David Covington said, "they hit the UDC."

"The NSA's Utah Data Center," Fitz added, knowing Hudson would have no idea what UDC was.

"Casualties?" the president asked.

"Too soon to tell," a woman answered. "It's a large facility, a million square feet, but it's a server farm, so it isn't as heavily staffed as other comparably-sized government facilities. Still, the size of the blast—"

"There will be loss of life," a general interrupted. "Perhaps dozens. Injuries could be in the hundreds."

"How was the attack carried out?" the president asked.

"As you might imagine," Covington began, "UDC has an extensive security system. It includes an elaborate antiterrorism protection program, state-of-the-art everything, anti-aircraft defense, barrier fencing designed to stop a fifteen-thousand-pound vehicle traveling fifty miles per hour, cameras across all levels of the Three-D system, a biometric identification system, vehicle inspection station—it's a fortress."

"No need to get defensive," the president said with a quick smile, but there was no humor in his eyes.

"I'm just saying we were prepared for any eventuality," Covington said tensely.

"Apparently not," the president responded. A sharp silence followed.

The NSA Director broke in to answer the president's original question. "They flew two large, unmanned aircraft into our facility."

"So much for the anti-aircraft defense," the president said, eyeing Covington. "*Drones* did that much damage?" The president pointed to live images filling giant screens in front of them.

The two main buildings were engulfed in flames, all but obliterated.

Covington, looking on while clearly seething, popped a cinnamon Necco wafer in his mouth.

"Only one way to bring that kind of destruction with two drones," a general said, motioning to a simulation on another monitor. "Gruell-Seventy-five."

There was a brief but noticeable pause in the room. Even Hudson knew that Gruell-75, the top-secret military grade explosive, had been used in a prior NorthBridge attack on the Kansas City Federal Reserve building. A patented and classified manufacturing technique, combined with tactically engineered components, resulted in a lightweight and pliable material which packed eighty-seven times more force than any prior forms of compound-explosives. Since the KC Federal Reserve bombing investigation, and many stories on Fonda's *Raton Report*, it had become common knowledge that the extremely expensive and powerful explosive was made by only one company: SkyNok.

That corporation, a stealthy defense contractor based in Nevada, had a murky ownership trail which, allegedly, ended with Booker Lipton.

# CHAPTER FIFTEEN

In the weeks that followed the NorthBridge attack on UDC, the new FBI Director, who now kept Dranick in the loop, reported privately to the president that the Bureau was making progress. They were still trying to ascertain if the former director hadn't wanted to break the NorthBridge case for some reason, or if he was meeting some internal resistance. One thing was clear; he had not been utilizing DIRT, a secret unit within the Bureau. The incorruptible agents who formed the Director's Internal Recon Team were one of the best kept secrets in Washington, a city built on secrets.

DIRT and the new Director gave the president hope. Hudson had personally chosen the woman who now headed the FBI. It had been a tough confirmation fight, but the public's frustration and fear at NorthBridge's ability to operate and attack with impunity had bled over into their representatives. The FBI's first female director was confirmed by a single vote margin. Still, Hudson knew the REMies could "get to anyone," so he regrettably remained cautious with her, the same way he had to be with nearly everyone.

Dranick felt differently. He'd dug deeply into her background and believed the director to be solid and untouchable. "Her tenure as the Director of the US Marshals Service, combined with a high profile, leaves no doubt that she is above reproach," he'd said. However, Hudson knew power could corrupt, and the FBI was *very* powerful. Even so, she got off to a fast start, and impressed him during one of their first official meetings.

"Expect NorthBridge arrests this week," the director said.

"Incredible," the president replied. "So they don't possess super powers?"

"They are mortals," she empathetically pronounced.

"What about the SkyNok and Gruell-Seventy-five connection?"

"Booker Lipton appears safe for the moment, but two attacks using a substance only legally allowed to be sold to the US military? Sooner or later, we'll trace it."

Hudson had not seen Fonda Raton since the election. His top aides, and "anyone else with a brain," as the White House press spokesman had said on numerous occasions, regarded the internet journalist as the enemy. Her many negative pieces during the campaign made it clear she would rather have seen Newsman Dan elected, but Hudson saw something else in the rebellious reporter; a link to the *truth*. She knew about the REMies, and had a way of getting at the facts that few in the media seemed to bother with anymore.

Neither Vonner nor Fitz knew in advance that he'd agreed to meet her. They never would've allowed it. Still, he had no doubt that "his handlers" would find out within minutes of her arrival at the secluded Key Largo oceanfront compound. So far, they'd been able to keep the location of the "Key," as they called it, secret. In years past, excluding the media from the president's itinerary would have been unthinkable. However, in the days of NorthBridge, many things had changed. Security took precedence over access.

"Mr. President!" Fonda said, as if the words were a celebration. Before he could stop her, she hugged him. "Nice place you got here."

"Good to see you again, Fonda," Hudson said while nodding to a Secret Service agent. He noticed she still smelled of lavender, and favored silk blouses. He motioned Fonda to follow him and escorted her through a sunroom, out into a garden, then onto a palm tree bordered trail between the manicured lawn and the sandy beach beyond. Hudson had requested that the two Secret Service agents keep a wider distance than usual. The setting was so isolated, and the security so tight, the agents had acquiesced.

"You look good, Hudson, particularly for a man who's cheated death so many times," Fonda said as she glanced over her shoulder. "Do you really think they can't hear us?"

"Depends on how loud you speak."

"I'm not talking about the agents, I'm talking about Vonner."

"I've taken special precautions."

"Such as?"

Hudson patted the SonicBlock device the Wizard had made concealed inside his pocket and prayed it worked. "I really can't say. But speak freely, or what's the point?"

She stood back and regarded him. "Yes," she said, as if speaking about a race horse. "You might make it." She smiled. "I can see the office has already changed you."

"True. I'm not sure I even know myself anymore."

"Good or bad? I have to ask because, like you, I study history, and if one researches, it's remarkable to see the drastic transformation of every modern American president. You can check the years of their lives leading up to Inauguration Day, and then see their actions after they take the oath. The difference is startling. Have you read David Garrow's *Rising Star* about Obama? It's a good illustration of my point."

"I don't want to discuss the conduct of my predecessors," Hudson said. "You called this meeting, and I've gone to a lot of trouble to make it happen. In fact, there are those on my staff who would think me foolish to be standing here talking to you."

"Then why did you agree to see me?"

"Because we just might be able to help each other."

"Assuming we're honest."

He stopped and shot her a *don't insult me* look. "Do you notice that I'm limping? Do you know that I have constant pain in my arm? Would it surprise you to learn that sometimes nightmares wake me in the middle of the night, scenes worse than anything I had during my time in Iraq? There are assassins out there right now, planning, plotting on how they'll kill me. Within my own government, there are factions that want to see me fail, some that even want to see me *dead*. I lead a government controlled by global elites who have no alliance to anything other than themselves, money, and the pursuit of even more power, and you come here and talk to me about *honesty*? Lady, I don't have time for anything *but* honesty."

"My, my," Fonda said, smiling. "The pressure is intense, isn't it, Mr. President? All that, plus China, the economy, the CIA, leaks, the media, liberals, conservatives, and me . . . Are you going to make it?"

He glared at her.

"I think you will, so long as you remember that this is a game to them, and it's all about distractions."

"You should know, you're part of their distraction."

"Of course I am, because the distractions work, they're all anyone's talking about. The media decides the topic of conversation for the whole world every single day, and I have to report on that because it's what's happening. But who controls the media? Who makes those decisions?"

"We both know it's the REMies."

"Damn right it is!" she said a bit too loud, but, speaking more softly, she continued, "I've been on the REMies story for more than twelve years. Long before you came along."

"Twelve years and you haven't exposed them?"

"You know it's not that simple. At least, I hope you know." She faced him, squinting her eyes. "You had *better* know!"

"I do," he said thoughtfully. They'd wandered into a small grove on the property of several dozen citrus trees. Hudson pulled an orange off a tree and offered it to her.

"Love one, thanks. I need the antioxidants," she said, smiling. "You know, as soon as I met you, I knew it was all about to end."

"What?"

"That we were at the final CapWar," she said, peeling the orange.

"Who's going to win?" he asked, chuckling as if enjoying the conversation, an act he hoped would convince the trailing agents.

"It doesn't matter. Both sides are evil. The thing is, though, this is our chance . . . *you* are our chance. If we don't stop them now, we'll lose it all—control of our lives, our freedom, everything. This is a delicious orange!"

"How did you know?"

"Because I could tell that you're real."

He stared at Fonda, wanting to believe her. "What if it's already too late?"

"Don't say that." She stopped and touched his arm. "You're our last hope. If you believe it's too late . . . "

"Isn't that what's driving NorthBridge? They think the elites have taken it too far, that they can now be stopped only by revolution."

She shook her head. "I can't speak for NorthBridge, but I do think if you fail, then we're heading for a revolution that's going to be more like World War Three than 1776."

"If I fail? Aren't you being presumptuous? How do you know I'm even going to try to stop them? Vonner is a REMie, and as you're so fond of pointing out, he put me here. I guess you think he made the wrong choice. Could he have been so dumb as to choose a puppet who would try to cut the strings? Do you really believe such a rich and powerful man could make such a huge mistake?"

"Of course I do . . ." She stopped, and they stared out to the ocean over a low roll of sea oat covered dunes. "Call it divine intervention if you want, but I believe right is on our side. After more than a hundred years of deception and corruption, the REMies are fat and greedy, and they're no longer content to rob just the masses. Now they're eyeing the treasure of their fellow thieves. But there are cracks in the system. They've built their empire of empires on so many lies and distortions that even *they* are having a difficult time controlling it. Don't you feel how out-of-control the world is?"

"Even if we somehow manage to stop them, can we keep the house of cards from imploding and crushing us all?"

Fonda broke into a big smile. "See? I knew you were on our side." She reached into her pocket and pulled out a flash drive. "You want honesty? Here it is. I'm trusting you."

"With what?"

"More than you can believe."

# CHAPTER SIXTEEN

On the flight back to Washington, Hudson did a quick SonicBlock-video connection with the Wizard.

"Good timing," the Wizard said, looking as if he were sitting in a futuristic spaceship. His dark storage shed was crammed with glowing monitors, blinking LED lights, and other odd equipment. "Listen to this. Life is like a mathematical equation, and if you don't take in the disconnected frantic message fragments, it becomes clear."

"What does?" Hudson asked, almost sorry he called.

"I've been thinking. What if the reason no one can find NorthBridge is because they don't exist?"

"What are you talking about?" Hudson blurted. "They blow up something every week, of course they exist!"

"It looks that way, but what if it's not *them*? I mean, it's not out of the question that NorthBridge could just be another REMie invention. They *are* the masters of manipulation."

"Are you suggesting that the REMies have hired a bunch of vigilantes to go around attacking things? Haven't you noticed that

NorthBridge is mainly going after REMie targets? The Federal Reserve, the Goldman building, the NSA, me—"

"You?"

"In their eyes, I belong to Vonner, and he's a REMie."

"It's beyond the micro and the macro," the Wizard said. "But you have to ask what is the source of reality." He was silent for a minute, his face a blue glow as he looked off into another monitor. "It's just a theory. NorthBridge is so good at covering their moves, hiding, funding, tracking, and monitoring . . . The only other organization that's even close to that good is the REMies."

"It's still classified," Hudson said, looking through the monitor closely at his old friend. "But the FBI is going to make NorthBridge arrests tomorrow."

"Really?" The Wizard seemed genuinely surprised. "That's great, but it doesn't disprove anything. Even if the FBI Director isn't working for the REMies—which we still don't know for sure —the REMies can always find a patsy."

"It's going to be a pretty big crackdown across several states."

"Did you ever notice that before NorthBridge came along, whenever there was a terror strike, we'd know who did it, or at least have a list of prime suspects, within hours? Sometimes even minutes?"

"I guess so."

"That's because the REMies always knew who it was, because *they* are ultimately behind it all. They want us to have a boogeyman."

"Then why is it different with NorthBridge?"

"Either I'm wrong, and the REMies really don't know who NorthBridge is, which would mean NorthBridge is for real . . . "

"Or?" Hudson asked, wondering which was more terrifying, NorthBridge as an invisible-group able to pick and choose targets at will, or NorthBridge as a lethal arm of the REMies.

"If it's neither of those scenarios, then we must face the

frightening possibility that, for some reason, the REMies want us totally scared this time because this really *is* the final CapWar, and we're all going to end up dead or truly enslaved to the elites."

"Let's hope for a third possibility."

"Which would be what?"

"I don't know," Hudson said, looking out the window down at the east coast of the United States, the Atlantic seeming unusually calm for the beginning of hurricane season. He paused for a moment. His thoughts stilled.

"You okay?" the Wizard asked.

"Yeah." He took a deep breath. "But we may get some answers tomorrow, and I want to send you something else." He met the Wizard's eyes through the digital veil, and it felt suddenly like looking back through the decades. "If I transmit this to you now, SonicBlock will protect the data, right? There's no possibility of it being intercepted?"

"It's safe. It works by utilizing the same premise as life. Everything is fluctuating with intense energy, the dynamic energy of the universe . . . "

Hudson pushed the drive in and followed the Wizard's instructions. A few minutes later, the Wizard was looking at the material Fonda had given Hudson.

"Where did you get this?" the Wizard asked.

"I'd rather not say right now, but it sure does seem to corroborate Crane's work."

Zackers' former partner had been working on a program dubbed "Gypsy," which utilized bots crawling across the web, including the DarkNet, searching out trends that could prove and track REMie manipulation. The drive which Fonda had given him was a summary of her twelve-year investigation into the REMies, particularly their media influence, and what the elites themselves called "MADE events," the apropos acronym standing for Manipulate And Distract Everyone. She had

REMies links to specific media stories, trails across the web, and an incredibly intricate flowchart of which companies owned which companies, and where that ownership trail ended. Most of her sources, including hundreds within media companies, had been deleted, but Hudson had no doubt in the validity of her story.

"Is someone going to post this?" the Wizard asked after a brief review. "Because if they do, they're going to die."

"I don't think it will be posted anytime soon, but it will help us."

"Damn right it will help us! I can't believe all of this!" he said, scanning the data. "We're going to get them, Dawg. We're going to bring down the REMies."

"Let's not get ahead of ourselves, but obviously that's where we must wind up." Hudson checked his watch. They would be landing soon. He had to go. "In the meantime, get it to Crane."

"Hell yes. He'll fold this all into Gypsy, and then we're going to have a very clear picture of how the REMies play—one we might be able to actually prove."

Back in the Oval Office, the president had a surprise visitor. David Covington was quietly ushered in, yet somehow, he still made his entrance appear as if he were storming through the door. Hudson could almost see the chip on Covington's shoulder as the Director of National Intelligence immediately began to pace in front of the president's Resolute Desk.

"Your pal Dranick is interfering with national security," Covington said, chewing on a clove-flavored Necco wafer.

"Colonel Dranick is director of the Brickman Effort, and as such, has wide latitude to investigate. You know this, and I expect full cooperation from all federal agencies, including the sixteen intelligence agencies that you oversee."

"With all due respect, Mr. President, in addition to North-Bridge, we've got Islamic terrorists increasing their brazen attacks around the globe, Russia acting up, Iran, North Korea, and, of course, China. And with your limited experience, you may not realize this, but each one affects the others. ISIS has been emboldened by NorthBridge, as have the Chinese. There's been an 1,800% increase in cyber-attacks since you took office. There's so much chatter about an ISIS attack on the homeland that I fear we'll soon have NorthBridge competing for space in the head-lines with radical Islamic terror groups on a regular basis."

Hudson was irritated in so many ways, he didn't really know where to begin, but he stood and hammered the DNI. "Last time I checked, it's *your* job to make sure that doesn't happen. Let me know if you can't handle the responsibility. Never doubt that I am fully aware of the threats facing our nation."

"I'm glad to hear that," Covington said, softening his stance slightly. "Because I expect you're going to be leading us into what may become the largest war in our history, on a scale we've not seen in three quarters of a century."

"Rest assured, I am prepared to do whatever is necessary against China, NorthBridge, ISIS, or any other adversary that mistakenly challenges us."

"It'll be China." Covington paced across the carpeted presi-dential seal. "And it's time." He pulled a map up on his tablet computer. "Look at this." It showed the state of freedom world-wide, with free nations expressed in green, partially free in yellow, and not free showed in red. "Look at this blight. Russia and China—half the damn world is red. And while I wouldn't advocate going to war to bring democracy to those regions, if communist China's government is knocking on our door and asking for it, then it should be viewed as a grand opportunity."

Hudson studied the map. A huge swath of red covered the majority of Africa, Saudi Arabia, Iran, and most of the rest of the Middle East. "We may not see eye to eye on a lot of things, David, but I agree the world would be a much better place, and considerably safer, if we can flip that red to green." The president tapped China on the map and purposely traced the largest red section—Russia.

Covington smiled. "Nice to see we have some common goals. If you have no problem with it, I'd like to meet with Colonel Dranick. He and I may be able to collaborate. I believe I could save him a lot of time."

"I think that's a fine idea," the president said, knowing it wasn't at all what he wanted. He needed Dranick operating completely independently. It was the only hope to get past the REMies in the deep state and find the truth. He had no doubt, though, that Dranick could navigate a meeting with the DNI. However, he had learned that the deep state, consisting of REMie-connected entrenched upper-level bureaucrats, had, for decades, wielded more power than the president. Finding and stopping them could be his greatest challenge.

As the president indicated their time together had ended, Covington thanked him and walked to the door, where he stopped. "Oh, one last question, Mr. President. Any luck finding Rochelle Rogers?"

Hudson sucked in a breath as if he'd been gut punched, but did his best to appear unfazed. "What do you know about it?"

"Mr. President, please forgive me, I keep forgetting you're new to all this." Covington waved his arms around, indicating the Oval Office, the White House, the government in general. "I'm the Director of National Intelligence, there really isn't much I don't know."

Hudson ignored Covington's smug smile. "Then perhaps you can tell me what happened to her. Do *you* know where she is?"

"Not yet, but you can bet I'll let you know as soon as she's located," Covington said as he turned to leave. "Good day, Mr. President."

As soon as the door shut, the president flipped him off vehemently, smiled, then looked down at the seal. Shaking his head, Hudson's thoughts flew in all directions at once, and he whispered to himself, "What the hell am I doing?"

# CHAPTER SEVENTEEN

The Wizard had been right. Although seventeen NorthBridge suspects were arrested in a nationwide sweep by the FBI, none of the "terrorists" seemed impressive enough to have eluded capture during the intense investigations and biggest manhunt in US history which had consumed most of the prior two years. The president questioned the FBI Director, asking if she believed those in custody were really part of NorthBridge, or had been set up as decoys. The director insisted they were legitimate members, and pointed to NorthBridge's demands that their people be freed, or the nation should prepare for severe retribution.

Dranick was not convinced. After having an opportunity to question the "NorthBridge Seventeen," he could glean no actionable intelligence from any of them.

"Not one bit of useful information," he told the president.

"The director claims NorthBridge has evaded arrest all this time by keeping its members in isolated cells," Hudson said, "saying that they don't know who their superiors are."

"Too easy," Dranick muttered. "Two years and nothing but a bunch of low-level nobodies?"

"It took almost ten years to get Bin Laden."

"The leaders of NorthBridge aren't in some lawless, third world, border region. They're in America."

"Just because they say they are?"

"No, because NorthBridge is fighting a revolution, and a revolution cannot happen without revolutionaries on the ground." Dranick suddenly looked like an older version of himself, perhaps a Native American chief from long ago. "Where are the revolutionaries?"

Congressional hearings began on NorthBridge. Lawmakers wanted to know why more arrests hadn't been made, and demanded to see what information and evidence the intelligence agencies had on the terrorists. The president saw it as another distraction from his crusade against the REMies, which was frustratingly slow even on its very best days.

The Wizard and Crane, using Gypsy and a number of other methods, had gathered petabytes of data on the REMies' practices, structure, and holdings. However, Hudson's plan to destroy the REMies (code named "Cherry Tree" in honor of George Washington, whose portrait had sparked the inspiration) wasn't even close to ready.

He finally broached the subject with Melissa over dinner in the residence. "I think I know how to beat the REMies," he said while cutting into his filet mignon.

"Are you sure you want to have this conversation in the White House?" Melissa asked, dabbing a bite of chicken into some incredible sauce—so delicious, she'd already asked for the name and recipe.

"I've got the SonicBlock on," he said.

She nodded. "Good. Maybe I better have more wine."

He smiled. "Maybe we should order something stronger." He laughed. "Anyway, it was George Washington who gave me the idea."

"Do you two speak often? Perhaps in the Lincoln bedroom?"

"Washington led the revolutionary army against Great Britain," he began, ignoring her questions. "After doing the impossible by defeating the most powerful military on earth, he served as the first president. They tried to make him King of America, but he'd have none of it."

"Still a history teacher," Melissa said, moving some broccoli into the remaining sauce on her plate.

"But the most important thing old George ever did was stepping down from power."

Melissa nodded. She'd heard part of this lecture before, and knew nothing could stop him now.

"For the first time in the history of the world, a revolutionary leader voluntarily gave up power after winning it." Hudson's face lit up whenever he told the story, his awe for the country's first president very evident. "King George once famously asked his American painter, Benjamin West, what Washington would do after winning independence. West replied, 'They say he will return to his farm.' King George responded incredulously, 'If he does that, Washington will be the greatest man in the world.'"

"And how does this help us defeat the REMies?" Melissa dutifully asked.

"Washington gave up power because he wanted the people to be in charge," Hudson said, as if it was obvious. "The great American experiment!"

"Let me see if I'm following you," Melissa said, pouring more wine for both of them. "The REMies are King George, and you're George Washington?

"We don't have enough power to stop the REMies. They control too much, but we have one massive advantage. They're outnumbered by more than seven billion! If the people learn the truth, they'll take the power back from the REMies." He raised his glass to her triumphantly. "A repressed people will *always* revolt."

# CHAPTER EIGHTEEN

For the next several months, there were no additional NorthBridge arrests, but the terror group struck against three Federal buildings in separate incidents, in different cities. NorthBridge claimed they would continue to attack until the seventeen were released. The US population was increasingly fractured, and the economy had fallen into a downward spiral fueled by fear of terrorism and the increasing possibility of war between the world's largest trading partners—the US and China.

Dranick was making more progress in identifying the shadow government and Deep State than he was with NorthBridge. At the same time, the Wizard, utilizing Fonda's REMie files and Crane's Gypsy work, reported to Hudson that they "might be only weeks away from cracking the CapStone conspiracy wide open."

Hudson himself was exhausted. No sign of Rochelle, North-Bridge striking with impunity, ISIS more active around the world, the domestic economic woes beginning to affect the global economies, and all of it seeming to push the US closer to war.

"When you're up to your ass in alligators, it's difficult to remember your initial objective was to drain the swamp," Melissa said to him on the morning he was heading to Portland, Oregon, to give a major foreign policy speech, making the case for war to an international peace conference.

Hudson forced a laugh. He was too agitated to see much humor these days. "And I'm about to walk into the lion's den," he said, thinking of his upcoming speech.

"At least you'll get some time with Florence."

It had been months since he'd seen his daughter more than fleetingly, but she and his brother, Ace, as well as his sister, Jenna, would be riding along on this trip. It had been Florence's idea that her dad needed more "family time." The week before, it had been Schueller and Hudson's sister, Trixie.

"I'm looking forward to it, but when is it your turn?"

Melissa gave him a flirty smile. "I get Thanksgiving weekend."

"Good call," he said, knowing they would be taking five days off and spending the holiday in the Virgin Islands. "No work."

"Exactly." She blew him three kisses.

*Two weeks*, he thought. *I sure need it. Being president is so much harder than anyone knows.*

It had been strange for Hudson, because he'd expected the REMies to be telling him what to do, but no one had. Now, he almost wished for someone else to make the tough decisions. Almost, but not quite.

"That was quite a speech," Linh said, "but I still don't understand. If you're trying to make the case for war, why speak at a peace rally?"

Hudson wasn't surprised to see her this time. After all, he knew that the Inner Movement, as a major proponent of peace, opposed a potential war with China. There was no point in trying to explain to her all the complicated nuances of why the United States would have to stop communist China's aggressive expansion. Linh was one of those naïve people who believed there was always a peaceful solution. Hudson certainly wished there was another way, but sometimes bullies and despots only understood force and retaliation.

The reception was crowded, and not exactly friendly territory. Most of the people there had not voted for him. This was simply a public relations tour to drum up support for the impending conflict, which he no longer thought could be avoided. Yet, despite their differences, he still believed Linh was an ally.

"The discussion of ideas, debating, and discourse are the pillars on which democracies are based. We must listen to each other, even when—and *especially* when—we disagree," Hudson said.

Linh's face reflected his own frustration. He stared a little too long, until an aide interrupted with just the word, "Sir?"

Hudson turned and saw there were more people waiting to talk to him. There were always so many people waiting.

Linh took half a step back, as if acknowledging the others, then stopped, started to speak, paused again, and finally said, "Your remarks reminded me of Dr. King's mountaintop speech. Do you know it?"

"Of course," Hudson said. "'Well, I don't know what will happen now,'" he began, delivering King's famous words in an evangelical tone. "'We've got some difficult days ahead. But it really doesn't matter with me now because I've been to the mountaintop. And I don't mind. Like anybody, I would like to live – a long life; longevity has its place. But I'm not concerned about that now. I just want to do God's will. And he's allowed me to go to the mountaintop. And I've looked over. And I've seen the promised land. And I might not get there with you. But I want you to know tonight, that we, as a people, will get to the promised land. So I'm happy, tonight. I'm not worried about anything. I'm not fearing any man. Mine eyes have seen the glory of the coming of the Lord.'"

Applause broke out from those gathered near enough to hear his rendition. Linh smiled, obviously impressed he could recite Martin Luther King Jr.'s words from memory. "Then, of course, you know when he gave that speech?"

Hudson nodded, the significance dawning on him. "The night before he was assassinated," he said softly, almost to himself. Hudson recalled seeing Linh in the audience before the attempt on his life at the stadium. He looked into her eyes. She had the same sad, concerned expression as she'd had that day. He stared hard, in that fleeting moment, as the crowd was pushing him one direction and her the other, as if to ask, *Is it going to happen again?*

She was swept away before he got an answer. As he tried to visually follow her in the crowd, he felt burdened with an inexplicable sense of loss. Suddenly, three young women were in front of him, singing a medley of John Lennon's *Imagine* and *Give Peace a Chance.*

*Imagine there's no countries*
*It isn't hard to do*
*Nothing to kill or die for . . .*
*All we are saying is give peace a chance*
*Imagine no possessions*
*I wonder if you can*
*No need for greed or hunger*
*A brotherhood of man*
*Imagine all the people sharing all the world*

*All we are saying is give peace a chance*

Another ten agonizing and awkward minutes later, he was in the motorcade, heading to the airport. Fitz was on the phone.

"Great speech," his chief of staff said. He had pushed for Hudson to speak at the peace event to justify the war amidst his biggest critics, when most others in the administration were against it. "The first round of comments from the media are looking good. One of the cable news anchors even compared you to Kennedy during the Cuban missile crisis. They're eating it up. They love you."

"Trying to sell a war to the country," Hudson said, still preoccupied by the exchange with Linh. "If we have to sell it, is it really the right thing to do?"

"Come on, Mr. President, no one *wants* to go to war. They have to be convinced that it's worth all the blood and money. Look at World War II, Mr. History Teacher. It took Pearl Harbor to convince Americans it was time to stop Japan, and Roosevelt used the anger about the attack to declare war on Germany at the same time. There will always be peace demonstrators, but public opinion is shifting, and your decision to walk right into the opposition and confront them head on is going to convince a lot of people."

The night before, he had debated one of the leading peace activists in the country, and although his opponent made a few good points, Hudson, a master debater, clearly won.

Florence, who had attended the peace conference with her father, believed the war could, and should, still be avoided. She told him about a presentation where she heard a talk by three former Nobel Peace Prize recipients, but before Hudson could comment, his brother Ace and sister Jenna, both veterans, took over the conversation.

"So many people don't understand," Ace said. "The relative peace and prosperity we've enjoyed in this country is because we're always prepared to go to war."

His sister echoed Ace's sentiments. "Sometimes the only way to have peace is to go to war."

## CHAPTER NINETEEN

The nineteen-vehicle motorcade rolled across the tarmac, with The Beast stopping in front of the stairs attached to Air Force One. The president spoke for several minutes to VIPs, including a general, the Mayor of Portland, and a few other dignitaries. At the same time, staff, and certain members of the media, were boarding the plane using the rear stairs.

As Hudson climbed the steps, the larger crowd, gathered beyond the rope line, cheered. He felt guilty for not having gone over to greet them, but the schedule was tight. Although the peace conference had publicly been the main reason for his trip, he would now be flying down to San Francisco for an international banking conference that would include a secret meeting concerning the implications for the US and world economies in the event of war with China.

At the top of the staircase, President Pound stopped, turned, and waved to the crowd gathered on the tarmac. Almost ten months into the job, he was finally feeling like the president; like he could—maybe—change things. He gave a last enthusiastic wave.

The first bullet entered through his neck. The president's body crumpled as if all strength and rigidity had instantly left its form. Hudson never felt the second shot, which hit his lower back. Blackness surrounded him and took hold as his consciousness surrendered.

Secret Service agents scrambled into action immediately. "Teacher down! Teacher down!"

The interval between the two shots had been less than a second, but by the time the third and fourth followed three seconds later, agents were dragging the president's body through the door. "Red-seventy! Go airborne! Now, now, now!"

There were procedures and protocols long-established and indelible in the agents' training. However, the confusion of the moment blurred it all into a chaotic disaster. "Close it, damn it! We're under attack!"

An agent's head exploded, spraying blood across the presidential seal on the door as two other agents fought to pull it closed. One of them took a bullet in the leg, but they managed to get the heavily armored door closed.

The Secret Service Counter Assault Team (CAT), wielding SR-16 carbine assault rifles and other heavy artillery, began laying down suppressive fire. They were located around the motorcade vehicles, which were to be loaded into the C141 Starlifter cargo carrier plane. The armored vehicles provided good cover, and a blazing firefight ensued.

Several Phoenix Ravens, part of the US Air Force elite security commandos who traveled with Air Force One, exited the rear door and began laying down fire to protect the aircraft. Other Ravens, still onboard, started a systematic search of the jumbo jet looking for enemy combatants and explosives.

"Repelling coordinated attack," a CAT agent radioed. "Hawkeye-Teacher, Red-seventy. Bring whiskey, hard!" His report that POTUS was in eminent danger, and the request for air support, would unleash an immediate and furious military response.

The crowd of well-wishers and onlookers had dispersed into screaming panic while two agents continued to return fire from the steps. Random explosions, ricocheting bullets, and wailing sirens turned the extreme scene apocalyptic.

Inside Air Force One, three agents, carrying the president's body, rushed down the corridor to a small medical suite. The physician to the president, who always traveled with him, pushed through his stunned shock at the sight of Hudson's injuries and quickly began prepping for surgery. His training also kicked in as he pulled down the surgical table and slid it into place. Almost simultaneously, the agents laid the lifeless body of the president onto it.

One of the protective detail agents, still outside defending the aircraft, got hit in the chest. The impact of the high-powered bullet sent him over the railing, crashing down to the concrete. Air Force One began to taxi. The lone agent remaining on the steps searched desperately for a target. Canisters of colored smoke and teargas rained down.

Inside the plane, agents had secured "the football," the brief-case which held the codes for nuclear deployment and always traveled with the president. Agents pushed three members of the president's family toward the rear entry. Only about a third of the reporters and staff made it on board before agents got the rear door closed and secured. The remaining people took cover in and around the motorcade vehicles.

As the plane slowly rolled toward the taxiway, Secret Service agents locked down the press quarters, guests, general staff, and dining crew areas. Ravens continued their search. Another

Special Agent had assumed command of the communications room, where they were already trying to reach Vice President Brown. Air Force One had only moved seventeen feet since the attack began.

Outside, CAT agents engaged the enemy with a full arsenal of advanced weaponry until six simultaneously fired rocket-propelled grenades, "tank busters," demolished their position, leaving only two CATs alive—barely. Two Secret Service snipers, stationed several hundred yards away on an airport building roof, and another atop a truck, searched desperately for targets. Nothing.

The president's physician, singularly focused on reviving Hudson and saving his life, had already concluded his injuries were so grave that it might not be possible. They had plenty of the president's blood type on board, and all the necessary equipment to complete the operation, but bullets into flesh were massively destructive. Even if they'd been at a top hospital in a major city, survival would be doubtful. A trauma team was the only hope. The real enemy had become time.

"We need to transport him to the University Hospital in Portland, *now!*" the physician said to one of the agents, who relayed the information into a microphone on his wrist.

The response came back immediately.

"Negative."

# CHAPTER TWENTY

Police on the ground ran toward the bullets, looking for shooters. Another missile impacted, blowing the stairs apart and taking out the last Secret Service agent.

"Multiple shooters! NorthBridge attack!" one state trooper called in before he was hit. Three Ravens died instantly when something else exploded.

"Where'd that come from?" a Raven, who'd been far enough away from the flash point to survive it, shouted.

The only other surviving Raven shook his head. They didn't know if it had been a bomb, a missile, or some other improvised explosive device.

"Must have been an IED," the first Raven speculated. "This has gotta be NorthBridge, no one else could bring this much havoc!"

A second later, they were both dead.

Just as the plane began picking up speed for takeoff, it veered and came to an abrupt halt. Dozens of police and bystanders lay injured on the bloody tarmac as emergency vehicles roared down the runway. More officers stormed into the crossfire, trying to find the source of the attack. An agent on board, looking out the window at the mayhem, called Washington. "This isn't just a shooter. There is an undetermined number, but multiple hostiles are attempting to prevent us from taking off. Repeat, we are under heavy fire, receiving artillery fire."

The Special Agent in charge (SAIC) rushed to the cockpit, wanting to know why they weren't moving. As he ran, he spoke into his wrist directly to the crisis center at Secret Service headquarters in Washington DC, relaying the situation. Horrified, they were already watching the whole thing live via the 3D System. Smoke had enveloped Air Force One, shots were still being fired outside, and the agent was thinking only two things —"NorthBridge" and "Get. Into. The. Air!"

Secret Service agents were trained to always expect multiple attacks, and, as he reached the cockpit and saw the navigation officer and radio operator pulling the unconscious pilot and copilot from their seats, he knew this was a coordinated event. He quickly conveyed the scene to his superiors while also asking the navigator what happened.

"I don't know," he said. "They both just went out, like someone turned off the switch."

"Can either of you fly this plane?"

"I could probably keep it in the air," the navigator replied. "But I can't get us off the ground."

The radio operator shook his head.

Just then, a missile emerged from the smoke and exploded under the nose of the plane.

"We're under attack!" the radio operator shouted.

"You're just now realizing that?" the SAIC snapped. "They're trying to destroy the runway so we can't take off."

"Preparing countermeasures," the navigator said.

"While on the ground? At *this* range?" the SAIC yelled.

"Whatever is necessary."

The SAIC ran from the cockpit in search of the solution he wasn't sure existed. He knew there was armor plating on the plane which could withstand a nuclear blast from the ground if they were airborne, but he wasn't sure how it would react while sitting on the runway. The windows were also armored glass, but Air Force One had never actually been attacked before today. Just past the dining room, he ran into the president's brother and sister with the first daughter, Florence. The three had just talked their way out of the secure area and were heading to the president.

"Why aren't we in the air?" Ace, Hudson's brother, asked. "We're sitting ducks here."

Secret Service agent Bond came up behind the SAIC. Bond's eyes met Florence's. "We need you," he said. "Now!"

The SAIC moved as she passed while also answering Ace. "Pilot and copilot are down." At that moment, he remembered from advance work that Ace was a pilot. "Can you fly this thing?"

"Yes," Ace replied. Without hesitation, he began jogging toward the cockpit. "As long as they don't knock an engine off before we get up. Come on, Jenna, I need a copilot!"

The president's sister knew Ace had logged more than twelve thousand hours flying 747s, but other than some minor flight experience in the military a long time ago, she had none. Yet Jenna was a firm believer that great things can be accomplished, and incredible courage can be found, when one is without options and there is simply no other way.

Another explosion sent a shocking vibration to the fuselage as Florence stumbled into the makeshift operating room. The horrifying sight of her father, almost unrecognizable, greeted her.

Hooked up to an IV, oxygen tubes clipped into his nose, excessive blood, and the absence of color in his skin told her how dire things were.

*He looks dead,* she thought.

"Florence," the doctor said. "I'm sorry."

"Sorry?" Florence asked. She had met the doctor on several occasions, and knew him to be a competent and efficient man, so she couldn't understand why he had just said he was sorry.

"He was gone before he even made it to the table."

"No," Florence said, now understanding what the doctor was telling her. "No!"

"His heart has been stopped for four and a half minutes."

Another agent in the room looked at Bond and said, "The continuity of government plan has been deployed." Bond knew this meant that the Secret Service was in the process of locating and staying with the Speaker of the House of Representatives, the President pro tempore of the Senate, and the Secretary of State. The vice president, of course, already had protection. But at that moment, Bond didn't care about the crisis in the government. His only concern was for Hudson and his daughter.

Florence looked at Bond for a fleeting second, her eyes reflecting back on the attack in Colorado as if to say *not again.*

"What have you done?" Florence screamed, without knowing she had, at the doctor, while beginning to administer CPR.

"I defibrillated, did CPR," the doctor said. "A bullet nicked his carotid artery before it exited past and damaged the second vertebrae. Another large caliber bullet is lodged near a spinal nerve in his lordosis."

"One, two, three," Florence said, pumping the president's chest. "Come on, Dad!"

The doctor didn't interfere. He knew it was too late. The President of the United States was dead.

## CHAPTER TWENTY-ONE

W atching live coverage of the attack on Air Force One from the office at his Sun Wave estate in Carmel, Vonner held the communicator in his clenched fists. No answer. His voice, a combination of fear and anger, trembled as he yelled for Rex.

Rex had been in the server room, mining the DarkNet for digiGOLD data in his obsessive quest to find a way into the hidden realm of NorthBridge. Accustomed to Vonner's demands and tirades, the fixer detected something a bit more urgent in his employer's tone.

"What is it?" he asked, jogging into the Pacific room.

Vonner just pointed to the gigantic screen.

"What the hell!?" Rex shouted as he watched the smoky images of Air Force One under siege. "Is Hudson on that plane?"

Before Vonner could answer, the network split the screen and showed a replay of the president getting shot as he waved from the door.

"What in the fangdangled world does NorthBridge think

they're doing?" Vonner asked, trying to find his drink without taking his eyes from the screen.

"It looks like they've decided to declare war," Rex said, heading to his workstation and immediately beginning to type. "Assuming it's them."

"Who else would do this?" Vonner wiped a tear from his eye, hoping Rex hadn't noticed. "There must be ten or twenty shooters. It's an all-out attack. No one other than NorthBridge could pull off a military operation like this on American soil."

"I can think of someone," Rex said, fidgeting with five black dice. "Booker Lipton. His private army, the BLAXers could do it."

"Yes, but why?"

"To win a CapWar."

Bastendorff had been called up from the Lego floor. "I got an alert," he said, walking into his office, reaching into a silver bowl for a handful of pretzel sticks.

"President Pound has been shot. Air Force One is taking hostile fire," his assistant said.

"Excellent," Bastendorff replied, licking his sweaty hands. The strange habit was one of the reasons some of his employees called him a "troll" behind his back. "Now we're getting somewhere. Is the useless pillock dead?"

"No one knows."

"How can no one know if the American president is alive or not?"

"His plane is trying to take off," the assistant said, pointing to a monitor.

After watching the replay of President Pound getting shot,

Bastendorff said, "He's dead. No one survives that, especially if they don't get him to a hospital immediately."

"What if you're wrong?"

"Wrong?" Bastendorff laughed, reaching for his third jelly doughnut. "If I had a dollar for every time I'd been wrong, I'd be broke. Instead, I'm the richest man in the world! Now, with Pound dead, Brown becomes President. Then we just need to make sure Senator Russell is appointed Vice President. I've already got that in the works. Then we simply produce a scandal to force our new president, Celia Brown, to resign, and presto! Our boy Russell is the new president! Just like Nixon-Agnew-Nixon-Ford all over again. It worked once, it'll work again. Boy, I love this stuff!"

The Wizard sat tensely, watching the horrifying images on his television. Medical analysts, weapons experts, military personnel, and other contributors had been rushed on the air by cable news producers, all speculating that it would be next to impossible to survive injuries like those sustained by the president. Slow motion replays, enhanced video, and ultra-close close-ups showed every drop of blood and tearing flesh as the bullets ripped into Hudson over and over. The coverage included details of the Colorado and stadium attacks during the campaign, and the failed attempt during the inauguration.

"While it is the job of the Secret Service to protect the president, the FBI conducts the investigation if the president is attacked," the announcer said over footage of the Secret Service counter assault team fighting back at the airport before being overwhelmed. "The prior attacks against President Pound are all assumed to be the work of NorthBridge. There is no reason to believe this full-scale assault on Air Force One is any different. We can only hope this time they apprehend the culprits."

The Wizard didn't think so, but at that moment he didn't care who did it, or if they got caught. He just wanted his friend to live. He'd always known that the odds were against Hudson surviving his presidency, but actually facing his death now left him feeling vacant and confused. The Wizard, a student of metaphysical and philosophical principles, including Booker Lipton's Universal Quantum Physics, believed in fate, destiny and a trusted force which governed the universe. But, in that moment, he couldn't get it to reconcile with the horrors he saw on TV.

"Come on, Dawg, don't be dead," he whispered determinedly.

Booker Lipton had often said, "You can't just trust the universe when it's convenient." The Wizard tried to hold that thought, but his tears were washing it away.

The news reports continued speculating how such an attack could happen in America, in broad daylight, against the president and Air Force One.

"The Secret Service counter assault teams, or CAT, have been beefed up considerably since NorthBridge launched its reign of terror nearly two years ago," the anchor began. "They were in full deployment, the spectators had gone through two magnetometers, as well as other screening, and yet this happened."

The footage of Hudson being shot replayed on a split screen, the other half showing live coverage of the crisis. The Wizard was suddenly brought out of the real-life nightmare by a call from Crane.

"This has all the markings of a REMie action," Crane said in lieu of a greeting. "As soon as I first saw the news, I ran it through Gypsy, like always, but this time I added a few new filters I've been working on, and it shows up REMie."

"The news and government officials are already saying NorthBridge," the Wizard said.

"No surprise."

"Yeah, but why would the REMies assassinate the president?"

"Why did they kill Kennedy? Why do they do *anything*? Because they can," Crane said bitterly. "Anyway, this could be the link to NorthBridge being under REMie control."

"Is Gypsy showing that link?" the Wizard asked, realizing his hands were trembling. His mind was taking leaps and making connections even before Crane could answer.

Booker Lipton was a REMie, Arlin Vonner was also one, and although the group of elites didn't act as one, they shared a common goal of protecting their power. They'd rather fight amongst themselves than let the masses have any power, any chance at true freedom, anything at all . . . other than distractions.

"Yes," Crane said quietly, still reviewing the data streaming in. "I think they're what the patterns are showing us, and within a few days, maybe even hours, we'll have a clear link between NorthBridge and the REMies."

It was huge news, but as the Wizard watched the replay for the umpteenth time, he realized it was probably too late. "I'm afraid we've lost him."

## CHAPTER TWENTY-TWO

F lorence continued counting as she pressed on her father's blood-covered chest. Twenty- nine, thirty compressions . . . two breaths.

"He's gone," the physician said above the constant bursts of machinegun fire.

"Do we have an automated CPR device?" Florence shouted at the president's physician. At her hospital, Florence had seen automated chest compression system machines help prevent or lessen neurological damage by providing a steady supply of oxygen to the heart and brain. Life-sustaining circulation can be maintained only by uninterrupted chest compressions, and often the person providing manual CPR would grow tired or inconsistent within a couple of minutes. Florence had certainly fallen into that category, as the stress of pounding on her dead father's chest while their plane was under attack by armed terrorists was overwhelming her.

"Yes," he said, grabbing it from a compartment and quickly setting up the device to relieve her efforts. He then attached a monitor that showed the quality of oxygen getting into the president's brain. "He's been dead six minutes."

"Stop saying he's dead!" Florence yelled.

Agent Bond began speaking into his wrist. He was required to report that the president of the United States was dead.

Florence caught Bond's eyes. "No!" she said, punctuating her words with a flashing glare which made clear the unstated understanding that Bond owed her father.

Bond paused before quietly reporting to his superiors, "Resuscitation efforts ongoing."

"If we keep the chest compressions and breathing going—" Florence said, grabbing the physician's arm.

"His oxygen levels still aren't normal," the physician interrupted. "We're facing cerebral ischemia."

Florence knew the battle—getting blood to the brain. If they could bring Hudson back, he would still be able to function. "What about—"

*Boom, BOOM, boom!*

"They may blow us up before we—"

*BOOM, BOOM!*

"We've got the same job, Doctor . . . keeping the president alive," Bond said.

"Neither of us has done a very good job today," the physician said.

Florence shot him a hurt and angry look. "We. Are. Not. Done!"

"If we get through the next couple of minutes, we can go ECMO," the physician said as the plane jerked and swerved. Florence had seen the Extracorporeal Membrane Oxygenation (ECMO) system used at the university hospital where she worked.

"What's that?" Bond asked as the physician opened a cabinet and began setting up the ECMO.

"It restores oxygen levels in the brain to normal to help minimize permanent injury," he said. "But we have to cool his body."

"Let's get gel pads to his torso and legs."

"If you insist on continuing," the physician said.

The plane's engines grew louder as it pushed faster down the runway.

Florence nervously double checked the straps securing her father.

"I'm going to have to go in and surgically remove that other bullet," the physician said. "We'd be better off putting a catheter into the groin. That will cool the blood down as it passes through the catheter."

The sound of machine-gun fire was momentarily drowned out by another close explosion.

"We can't do surgery under these conditions," Florence said.

"You can do everything in the world to keep his brain healthy, but if we don't get that other bullet out, his heart won't be able to pump enough blood."

Florence grimaced. "Then let's prepare to operate."

Bond looked stunned. At that moment, a command came into his earpiece.

"Brace yourself. We're going to try takeoff."

# CHAPTER TWENTY-THREE

The Secret Service interrupted Schueller mid-session at the recording studio and handed him a phone.

"They're going to need to bring you back to the White House," Melissa said.

Schueller could tell she'd been crying, and recognized the strain in her overly calm voice. "What's happened?"

"Please, Schueller, I'll tell you everything when you get here."

"Is Dad okay? Tell me now."

"It's bad, honey. He was shot boarding Air Force One. We're only getting sketchy reports, but it's really bad, and the plane is still under attack."

Schueller closed his eyes for a second. He'd been dreading this news since his dad decided to run for president. "Florence is with him, is she . . . ?"

"She's okay."

Schueller let out a breath. The Secret Service agents were moving him toward the exit as he talked. "Wait, Uncle Ace and Aunt Jenna were with him on this trip, right?"

"So far they're okay. Schueller, I have to go. I'll see you when you get here."

After the call, Schueller pulled up the news on his phone and watched the disturbing video of his father getting shot, then switched to a live news feed.

*If Dad really is dead*, Schueller thought, *I'm going to* . . .

He realized he had no idea *what* he would do.

"I've got Tarka on speaker," Rex said to Vonner.

The gray-haired billionaire quickly ended another call with Fitz. "What the hell is going on? Where are you?" he asked Tarka.

"I'm here," Tarka said breathlessly. "I'm in it." Her assignment to stop any assassination attempts against the president had kept her constantly busy since the inauguration. She'd killed four would-be assassins, and blocked seven other plans that might, or might not, have been successful. It wasn't that Vonner didn't believe the Secret Service couldn't do their job, it was that he simply didn't *trust* the Secret Service.

"You're at the Portland airport, and you couldn't stop it?" Vonner slapped his desk.

"There're too many of them," the operative answered, annoyed. No one could have anticipated an attack this incredibly sophisticated on American soil.

"Who? How many?" Rex asked. "How did they get that close to Air Force One?"

"They neutralized CAT," she said with a mix of awe and suspicion.

"How?" Vonner repeated, knowing he could believe and trust anything she said.

"Ghosts!" Tarka said. "Damn impossible to see. It's like fighting ghosts!"

"Sounds like NorthBridge," Vonner said.

"If it's NorthBridge, then we're at war. A war we've already lost."

Even before the first bullet struck President Pound, and up to that very moment, as Ace was trying to get Air Force One off the ground, Linh sat alone in a dense grove of fern and Douglas fir trees located in the most secluded section of Portland's five-thousand-acre Forest Park, the largest forested natural area located within city limits in the United States. Even without cell coverage, Linh knew what was happening, yet she remained calm and still, sitting in the lotus position, meditating.

Colonel Dranick, frustrated to be trapped in Washington when his friend needed him most, had been working the phones from the instant word broke of the attack. As fate would have it, his home military installation, joint base Lewis-McChord, outside Tacoma, Washington, was just a hundred and thirty miles from the president's location. A Green Beret team from Lewis-McChord and fighter jets had been deployed. Specifically, Dranick's former group, part of the Second Special Forces Battalion, was en route to Portland International Airport.

"Tactical counter-strike team still thirty minutes out," the commander told Dranick. "A Chinook and a couple Apaches are blazing sky to PDX as we speak."

"What about ODAs?" Dranick asked, referring to Operational Detachments, the troopers who parachuted into any kind of raging hostile place and made it theirs.

"We've got a go-team on a C-17, ETA eleven minutes. They'll parachute in. Drop zone Air Force One."

"Won't it be gone by then?"

"By gone do you mean airborne, or ended?" the commander asked, iron-hard-serious. "They report both pilot and co-pilot down, and shelling incoming. Runway damage could already be a problem, if they can even get her moving."

"Damn it!" Dranick snapped. "Who are these guys?"

# CHAPTER TWENTY-FOUR

In between barking orders into his radio, the Secret Service SAIC shouted to Ace, "I don't care how you do it, but get this thing airborne!"

With only seconds to familiarize himself with the customized controls of Air Force One, Ace turned to his sister. "Can you do this, Jenna?"

"The question is, can *you?*" she asked calmly.

Ace flipped some switches, set the flaps, turned on the landing and strobe lights, enabled the autothrottle, then steered the plane back onto the taxiway. Smoke filled the runway ahead, with several vehicles burning on the tarmac, and somewhere behind him, his brother, the president of the United States, lay dead or dying.

"Commencing takeoff," Ace said, not bothering to communicate with the tower, since he didn't know who was listening. Air traffic was always prohibited for three to five miles around Air Force One anyway. "Tell Florence and the doctor to hold on. We're going for a steep ascent right through hellfire."

The SAIC relayed Ace's warning to Agent Bond and to three agents who let the other passengers know.

Ace looked over at his sister and said, "Be sure the F/D is on." He checked the runway heading, made certain the LNAV and VNAV were armed, slid the throttles forward, then clicked the TO/GA button. "Hold on, folks!"

Ace applied forward pressure to the stick and said a prayer. The plane picked up speed, but it was difficult keeping the nose gear firmly against the runway. He used the rudders to keep the airliner centered on the damaged and pitted tarmac. Just when he thought they might make it, a missile flew right across the front of the windshield, just missing them.

"Get us the hell outta here!" his sister shouted.

"Countermeasures deployed!" the flight engineer reported. Infrared flares bursts from the aircraft, shielding them temporarily in a shower of mega "fireworks" designed to confuse honing or "heat-seeking ordnances."

Ace accelerated well beyond normal taxi speed. The faster they went, the more he could feel trailing friction and the weight differential of Air Force One. He pushed the throttles past TRT (Thrust Rated Takeoff), hoping to avoid more missiles.

"Aren't you risking a flame out?" the flight engineer asked. "You're exceeding max TRT!"

"I'd rather risk that than a direct hit!" Ace replied tensely.

More shots rattled across the fuselage.

"Damn it!" Ace said, feeling several tires go. "They hit the wheels!" The jumbo jet listed to one side. He fought the controls as one of the tires completely shredded.

"Two bogies sustained damage," Jenna said, referring to the five sets of wheel bogies making up the 747's undercarriage arrangement.

Ace tensed further, knowing it would be hard to hit the tires and miss the critical hydraulics. "Get us up, come on, come on," he muttered to himself.

"Vee-one," the navigator announced. This mark, normally cleared by the co-pilot, meant they'd reached the point of no-return. They had to take off no matter what. Ace pulled back on the controls, hard.

"We've got hydraulics warnings lighting up all over," Jenna said. "Electrical, too. Uplocks, struts, trunnion link, all compromised."

More bullets bounced off the nose.

"Come on, baby, get us up," Ace repeated.

"Another bay is lighting up," Jenna said. "Downlock articulator, reaction link . . . out."

Ace, sweating and straining against the controls, twisted and pulled until, suddenly, they got lift.

"Wheels up!" the navigator sang.

Another missile buzzed by, lost in the countermeasures. "Two more incoming!" the flight engineer yelled.

"Damn it! This is more like flying out of Baghdad than Portland!" Ace barked.

"You've got to bring the gear in!" Jenna shouted. "We need the speed!"

"If I do, we might not be able to get it down when we need to land!"

"We may never get the chance to land if you don't pull it in now!"

Ace knew Jenna was right. He reluctantly retracted the landing gear, moving the switch to *off*. It was putting off a crisis for later in order to avert this one, but it was a tough bargain. Ace worried they'd taken enough damage that the controllers and hydraulics wouldn't be able to extend the gear whenever they decided to land. He'd never attempted a belly landing, but that nightmare would have to wait. He raised the flaps.

"What the . . . ?" Ace exclaimed. As they climbed steeply, several parachuting soldiers flew past, within mere feet of the plane. "Who the hell are these guys?"

Straining to get a better look, Jenna said, "I believe they're Green Berets."

"Hell yeah!" Ace said. "I damn sure hope we don't hit any of them." The jumbo jet was too big for him to maneuver around them. All he could do was continue their steep climb and try to get out of the reach of ground fire.

Everyone in the cockpit was held in tense silence, watching monitors, screens, gauges, and indicator lights. *We might make it,* Ace thought. He'd never taken off at such an angle. To the passengers, it felt near vertical. Suddenly, the airliner punctured the clouds, and a few minutes later he was able to begin to level out.

"You did it!" Jenna whooped.

"You and God," the navigator said.

"I hope you have an arrangement with Him," the engineer added, "and He'll also work with us on the landing."

The SAIC burst into the cockpit. "Damn decent flying, Ace," he said. "How bad's the damage?"

"It could've been worse." Ace wiped the sweat from his face. "Now, where we going?"

"Get us to DC," the SAIC said.

"What about Hudson?" Jenna asked. "We need to get him to a hospital."

"We can be in Seattle in about twenty-five minutes or so," Ace said.

"We've got company," the navigator interrupted. Two F-22 fighter jets appeared on either side of Air Force One.

"Air Force One, this is Rollins-eight-twenty-niner. We've got your back."

"Good to have you," Ace said. "Can you take a look underneath and give us a damage assessment?"

"Roger that," the fighter pilot replied.

"What about getting Hudson to a hospital?" Jenna pressed.

"Washington says keep heading east," the SAIC said. "There are plenty of hospitals along the way. We'll reassess as the situation warrants."

During the takeoff, Hudson, after being clinically dead for more than nine minutes, suddenly began breathing on his own.

"Thank God!" Florence said.

The physician gasped. "No one else could have saved him." He looked up for a moment. "But we're not out of the woods yet. Look at his pressure. We've got to operate."

"Can't we get into a hospital where an experienced team can do it?" Florence asked.

"I wish," the physician said. "But there just isn't time. We've got to do it now!"

Agent Bond put his face in his hand and shook his head.

"Find out from the cockpit how soon we're going to be at cruising altitude, and how long we're going to stay there," the physician instructed Bond. "Let them know that we're about to operate on the president."

Florence, with tears in her eyes, added, "And you tell them that the president is alive!"

# CHAPTER TWENTY-FIVE

The Green Berets landed as Air Force One was safely away. However, in a development described by the commander as "eerie," all the shooting had stopped. The Army Special Forces took up positions and prepared for engagement with hostiles. Yet, when the smoke cleared, there was no one to shoot at, as if the attackers had never been there—no bodies, no blood belonging to the enemy, no trace.

State and local police joined the Green Berets, but it would be hours before they found out how the terrorist had pulled off the first ever attack on Air Force One. By the time the FBI got there, the dead and injured had been catalogued; sixteen Secret Service agents killed, another seventeen injured—four of those critically—eight dead police officers and eleven wounded. The US Air Force lost five Phoenix Ravens. In total, there were fifty-seven casualties; they'd all taken bullets to protect the president.

Civilian victims were surprisingly light; twenty-six injured, and of those, only seven had been shot, likely caught in the cross-fire. The earlier stampede of spectators had ended up in the airport, the parking lot, and even spilled out onto the highway.

Dignitaries and average voters had sought cover and comfort with each other.

"Where on earth did the shooters go?" Dranick asked the Green Beret commander. "I know they call NorthBridge phantom terrorists, but they were in there heavy. People don't just vanish."

"We'll find them, Colonel," the commander said to Dranick. "Any word on the president?"

Reports were already swirling around that President Pound was in a coma, or brain-dead. High level sources had issued denials, cited classified information, and speculated about the speculation, but factual information was seemingly nonexistent.

"He's alive, that's all I know."

Amidst the smoke and explosions, Tarka had seen the last of the attackers slip away, and, just prior to the Green Berets' arrival, she followed the gunmen. In the process, she discovered what would take the government hours to figure out.

The terrorists had a tunnel network under the airport. Some of it appeared to have been for electrical conduit, storm drains, and some kind of maintenance systems. However, there were clear indications that improvements and modifications had recently been made.

"They aren't ghosts or magicians," Tarka said to herself, "but they might be psychics, somehow able to see into the future." She continued running through the tight spaces as she muttered to herself. "It must've taken them weeks to put all this together, maybe longer. How could they have known the president would be coming to Portland?"

By the time she reached the end of the tunnel, all she found was tire tracks where three of four trucks had been parked.

Although Tarka probably missed them by only a few minutes, she had no way to follow. Instead, she called in her location and waited for a pick up. There was too much heat to go back the way she came. The feds would surely find the tunnels soon. Normally, a helicopter would retrieve her, but air traffic was still restricted in the area.

She walked to a nearby hotel. It would be a good place to stay out of sight. After a quick conversation with Vonner and Rex, Tarka found out her next destination wouldn't be Washington. Instead, she was heading to Los Angeles, to investigate their best NorthBridge lead ever.

After the F-22 pilots reported significant visual damage to the undercarriage of Air Force One, the SAIC and Ace had a conference in the cockpit.

"There is an imminent risk that even if the landing gear comes down, it will collapse when the wheels and what's left of the tires touch down," Ace said.

"What will happen?"

"With shredded, incomplete tires, hydraulics shot, bad gear, and other unknown impairments . . . " Ace rubbed his forehead with his palm. "Best case, we slide and come down on our belly. But even with preparations, it could easily spark a fire."

"And worse case?" the SAIC asked.

"Engines and wingtips hit the ground, dragging, digging in . . . the aircraft cartwheels. Bigger fire, possible explosion."

"That can't happen."

"Agreed," Ace said.

"Options?"

"Not many, but we should go in empty."

"Meaning?"

"Dump all our fuel. Let them calculate just how much we need to make it on one landing. I'm told that the weather at Andrews is picture perfect . . . "

"You've never landed Air Force One," the SAIC began, "and you want to do it on one try, with no margin for error?"

"I want to get us all home safely. Dumping the fuel gives us the best chance."

The president's physician and Florence successfully completed the surgery on Hudson during the three-thousand-mile cross-country flight. About an hour before Air Force One reached Joint Base Andrews Airport, located on the outskirts of Washington, DC, agent Bond updated his superiors. "The president has yet to regain consciousness. His condition is still grave, but he is alive."

When the physician stepped out of the room for a few minutes, a weary Florence grilled Bond. "Was this part of the critical move?" She motioned to her father's barely alive body, filled with tubes and hooked up to monitors. "You tell me the truth, Bond!" She hadn't called him "007" since he told her that a group of Secret Service agents, including him, had been trained in how to stand down in order to make their actions undetectable when they get the order so that someone can assassinate the president. "Was the Secret Service in on this?"

"I don't know, Florence, but I do know that a couple dozen agents were injured or killed today trying to protect the president. I know some of them were my friends, good men."

"Excuse me for not mourning them, because I don't know who's good and who's bad anymore, but I know they took an oath to protect my father, a man I *do* know is good. How did you ever accept that training, Bond? How could you think that it was okay to let someone kill the president of the United States?"

"I'm not going to try and justify or explain it, but the preservation of the country has always been more important than the life of just one man. That's the premise of sending our young people off to die in war."

"You're equating political assassination of the duly elected leader of a democracy with a soldier dying in battle? Is *that* how you sleep at night?"

"No. Listen, Florence, there are people a lot smarter than me, who know a lot more than me. They're part of a group who have been keeping the world safe for decades—"

"Safe? Do you *believe* what you're saying? What they *told* you?"

"All that's irrelevant to this anyway. Clearly, the attack today was NorthBridge, and the people we're talking about have been trying to stop and capture those terrorists."

"They're sure doing a lousy job!"

The final decision was made to dump the fuel and land at Joint Base Andrews on fumes. Other destinations were considered, however, the Air Force would rather recover the airplane at Andrews than at any other location. It was secure, and fully able to handle whatever disaster might occur.

The passengers were informed of the status, and had watched as the remaining fuel had been dumped from the wings. They understood enough to realize the chances for fire and explosion had been traded for hopefully lesser risks. Much of the flight had been in silence; a communications blackout had been maintained. A list of all survivors had been relayed through the cockpit to the ground, and further relayed to family members. Traumatized staff members of the media, and various others on board, could be seen praying—

for the president, for themselves, and most of all for a safe landing.

The runway had been foamed, a practice discouraged by the FAA except in extreme emergencies, since it might reduce the aircraft's braking ability, causing it to overshoot the runway. Fire crews and other emergency vehicles were scrambled and ready. The F-22 fighters in tow, which had escorted them across the country, gave Ace a final message of encouragement before peeling off. Although he knew there was no risk of attack, Ace felt suddenly naked without their shadow. Now it was time to get his brother safely to the ground.

With virtually no fuel onboard, they had greatly minimized the risk of fire, but their main concern was that if Ace didn't get it just right, the plane could flip, cartwheel, break apart, or fold. Depending on the amount of structural loss sustained during the attack, any of those events could lead to a partial disintegration. He would have to maintain air speed and control while not landing too hard or fast.

"Bring it in straight and level," the navigator said.

*This is like landing a hotel from a third-story window,* Ace thought as he checked the crosswinds and fought unresponsive instruments. Apparently there had been more extensive damage when the tires, sensors, and hydraulics had been hit in Portland.

"You've got this, big brother," Jenna said quietly as they came down to nine hundred feet, the low fuel indicator light blinking. He had to make it on this try. There wasn't enough fuel to take it back up.

All the passengers were braced for a crash landing. The President had been secured, but in his delicate condition, if the plane cartwheeled, the results would be catastrophic. Colonel William, an experienced Air Force One pilot, coached Ace from the Andrews tower.

"Keep it level," the Colonel said calmly. "Looking good. Adjust your pitch."

Ace increased his descent. Instruments showed the airliner passing one hundred and forty knots indicated-air-speed.

"Too fast, Ace," the Colonel cautioned.

"It's fighting me," Ace said, trying to bring the speed back to one hundred and forty KIAS.

"It's okay," the Colonel said. "You might have lost some sensors when the hydraulics got hit. Just focus on the glide path."

Ace made small adjustments to pitch, trying to keep the heavy plane on target. His descent rate of seven hundred fpm was right on, but the jet was vibrating.

"Five meters," Jenna warned when the aircraft's belly was about sixteen feet above the runway.

Ace initiated a flare by raising the nose three degrees. Then he pushed the thrust levers to idle. "Brace!" he shouted.

Air Force One hit the runway with the force and sound of trees being tangled and ripped from a mountainside during an avalanche. Crew members were jerked forward, then thrown back in their seats. Inside the medical suite, the heavily secured president barely moved as Florence and the physician watched, strapped in their seats.

The airliner slid fast down the foamed runways, spraying sparks and spinning sideways. Fire trucks, lights flashing, chased. Ace tried forcing the controls, desperate to get her straight. The grinding screech of metal against runway, combining with the vibration, made it feel as if they were inside a collapsing building, but Air Force One did not cartwheel or break apart, and the friction was slowing them down. Finally, after sliding sideways forty feet off the runway, the plane stopped, and for a brief instant there was nothing but silence. Then cheers from the cabin, laughing gasps from the cockpit, and sirens.

The colonel's voice came through Ace's headset, "Couldn't have landed her any better myself. Nice work, pilot."

Ace thanked the colonel, unbuckled, and headed for the medical suite to check on his brother.

Florence hugged her uncle and gave him an update. "He's going to make it," she said optimistically. But Ace thought his brother looked dead, and saw his concern mirrored on the physician's face.

Even before the fire crews cleared the area, a medically-equipped Marine One helicopter landed as close to Air Force One as it dared. Twenty-three minutes later, the president was in the Intensive Care wing of Walter Reed National Military Medical Center.

The nation came together in prayer and vigil for the young, popular president. Underlying the collective hope for Hudson's recovery was a fear and panic spreading through the population.

*Was anyone safe? Was a full revolution from NorthBridge coming? Had it begun in Portland? Could America be headed for a war with China?*

Although NorthBridge still hadn't claimed responsibility for the attack on Air Force One, everyone knew it was them; the phantom terrorists who had once again slipped away without a trace.

*How do they do it? They're going to kill us all!*

As Hudson clung to life, the FBI, as the agency responsible for investigating attempts on the president's life, was combing the Portland airport for clues and promising swift results. But people had grown increasingly more cynical after two years of such little progress against NorthBridge. The brazen attack against the most secure plane on the planet had shocked the world, especially when no culprits were immediately apprehended. Several leaders voiced publicly what many were silently thinking: President Pound, who had survived so many attacks by the terrorists, might be the only one strong enough to lead the fight against them.

The other question suddenly and unexpectedly sweeping the US, as well as the rest of the world, was: *What did the president see during the nine minutes when he was dead?* The term "near death experience" or "NDE" quickly became the most requested words across all online search engines.

However, he had to wake up first.

The doctors were cautiously optimistic, but it remained "touch and go." Still, speculation was wild, in churches, in universities, at the office water coolers, in bars, all over social media. Everyone wanted to know, *What did he see?*

# CHAPTER TWENTY-SIX

In Los Angeles, Tarka found much the same as she did in Portland—the faint evidence that a big force had been there.

"This warehouse was emptied in a hurry," she told Rex. "Probably just before, or during, the attack on Air Force One."

"Anything there to indicate who or where?" Rex asked.

"This was the work of a highly-trained unit. If it was North-Bridge, then they have help."

"Russians? Chinese?"

"Israelis."

"Really?"

"They're good," she said. "Best I've ever seen."

"There's a chance the president's going to survive."

"Happy to hear it, but that doesn't remove the problem."

"Problem?"

"There's a strike team out there capable of hitting any target, anywhere in the world, without leaving a trace. You want to talk about terror? Wait until *that* sinks in."

"They may not leave a trail on the ground," Rex said, "but it's impossible to move through cyberspace without my finding their trail eventually." He rolled twelve turquoise dice and turned back into a field of monitors rolling with data and patterns from the DarkNet.

Fonda's *Raton Report* was relentless in pressuring the government for answers. *Was it NorthBridge? If so, where were they? Did they have inside help? How big was the terrorist organization? Were foreign nations sponsoring, training, funding, and/or arming, the rebels? Or was it another organization?* She warned the government better have proof when they accused someone.

The *Raton Report*, which had become the number one news website, was the first major media organization to refer to North-Bridge as *rebels* instead of *terrorists*.

"The attack on President Pound and Air Force One, at an airport in a major American city, resulting in the deaths of dozens of military personnel and law enforcement, was an act of war," Fonda announced. "These are rebels. From their first act, they declared themselves as such with their stated goal to usher in a second American Revolution. We must not live in denial any longer. It is time to respond to the enemy and realize we are at war . . . a war unlike any we have ever known."

Her post stirred controversy and ratcheted up panic. It also increased the debate on China. Thorne, the former presidential candidate, shock-jock, and self-proclaimed opposition leader, asked at the start of his daily radio show, "If the US really is in the middle of a civil war or a revolution, how can we simultaneously fight a war with a major world power?"

But even more than the questions of war, callers still overwhelmingly wanted to speculate on what the president had experienced when he was dead. The topic would not subside. In fact, it grew into more of a national obsession. Experts appeared on every major talk show, the morning news programs, countless radio shows, and online forums, to discuss near-death experiences.

As many as 200,000 Americans a year had an NDE, and an estimated five percent of the population had previously reported an NDE. Many believed that consciousness separates from the brain at "death" and glimpses the spiritual realm. Then, when the "deceased" person is resuscitated, they can often recall what was seen. The experts explained that the experiences could vary widely, but there were twelve common themes: an awareness of being dead, a sudden sense of well-being, an out-of-body experience, a sense of entering or being in a tunnel moving toward the light, encountering deceased loved ones and/or beings of light, an overwhelming feeling of unconditional love, recounting one's life experiences, learning secrets of the universe and/or learning one's life purpose, facing a decision on whether or not to return to life, being back inside one's body, and a renewed sense of faith.

Melissa didn't care about the NDE hysteria; she just wanted Hudson back. It was reported that the first lady hadn't left her husband's bedside since he'd arrived at Walter Reed Hospital. The military had accommodated the first family by providing rooms for Schueller and Florence as well. They, and the nation, held their breath and prayed to whatever or whomever they believed would listen.

And then one day, more than a week after Ace had landed at Joint Base Andrews, President Pound woke up and spoke.

Headlines blazed across papers around the world, and banners topped every news website: "The President is Conscious!" "He's Awake!" "President Pulls Through!" "Pound Speaks!"

## CHAPTER TWENTY-SEVEN

Hudson stared at his daughter as if she were an angel. "You brought me back," he said, tears in his eyes. "I was dead, and you brought me back to life."

Florence smiled through her own tears. "Now I truly know why I became a nurse."

"Thank you."

She looked deep into his eyes. "Where did you go?"

He said nothing.

They stared at each other for a long time, until she realized he wasn't going to answer. But she could tell by his eyes that he'd had an incredible experience, that he knew something he might never share. And she cried, not just from that realization, but with all the pent-up emotions that had choked her since the attack. She could finally let go.

Hudson held her, and was reminded of when she cried in his arms after her mother died.

Melissa gave an interview to her favorite female journalist on one of the morning shows. She had felt it was too soon, since Hudson was still in the hospital, but he'd encouraged her to do it. The outpouring of support had been incredible, and the public's preoccupation with the nine minutes continued to be an international mania.

The interview took place in the Blue Room. The first lady and the interviewer sat across from each other in fauteuils, open wood-frame armchairs dating back to 1812. The camera zoomed out from the windows in a sweeping view of the South Lawn, and panned back around the historic room which had served as a reception hall since President John Adams, and had been the site of the only wedding of a president and first lady in the White House, when Grover Cleveland married Frances Folsom in 1886.

The interviewer asked good, relevant questions. Melissa appeared tired, but strong. She told of the thousands of letters they had received, hundreds from world leaders, most of whom they had never met, which felt even more special in a way not easy to explain. But the ones that touched them the most came from ordinary folks.

Melissa said one of her favorites was from an old woman who lived in Tang Ting, a mountain village in Nepal. "She sent prayer flags. They had been hung on the ridges above her home, so that the prayers for the president would be blown with the wind and spread compassion and goodwill into the world, because people all over the planet needed President Pound to recover and make peace." Melissa's eyes were teary.

"The old woman is right," the interviewer said, compassionately touching Melissa's hand.

Melissa nodded, rubbing her eyes. "It's amazing to me that someone in such a remote place—I'd never heard of it, but I looked it up, this tiny village with no roads leading to it, set in the

Annapurnas, some of the highest mountains on earth—knew what had happened and cared enough to reach out to us. Beautiful ... "

The interviewer asked a series of questions about the president's condition before zeroing in on the one thing everyone wanted to know. "Has he told you about the nine minutes?"

"It's a very private thing, as I'm sure you can imagine," Melissa said. "That kind of profound experience takes a long time to process within one's self."

"You are no doubt aware of the fascination everyone has with just what he saw or felt during that time. Do you think he will speak of it publicly sometime in the near future?"

Melissa shook her head. "I cannot answer for the president. However, he is grateful for all the prayers, and deeply believes they are what made the difference."

The interviewer tried the same question a few more times in different ways, but got no further, and finally began to wrap up.

"Before we end," Melissa said, "there's one more letter I need to mention. A nine-year-old boy from Oregon wrote to apologize since—"

"Oh, because it happened in his home state?"

"Yes," the first lady said. "He thought it was his fault. I just received his note today, and haven't yet had a chance to respond, but I want to tell him right now that this was not his fault. This was bad people who did this. And we *will* find them." Melissa stared, unblinking, into the camera until it was turned off.

After three and a half weeks in the ICU, and another month recovering in the residence at the White House—several of the rooms had been converted to hospital-quality facilities with round-the-clock medical staff—Hudson was finally back on the job, running the country full-time. During the first twenty days of his recuperation, Vice President Brown was effectively in charge of the nation, and the two had grown closer due to the extreme circumstances.

All of this had not gone unnoticed by the REMies. Through Gypsy, Crane had picked up a substantial increase in REMie activity around the vice president. In the early days after the attack on Air Force One, the REMies, along with everyone else, believed Hudson would die, and Brown would become President permanently. As Hudson's recovery progressed, the REMies still saw a potential problem with Brown, believing the vice president's role in the administration would forever be more important.

Hudson pushed the SonicBlock drive into the computer and waited for the Wizard to appear on his screen. The two old friends had only spoken briefly twice since the Air Force One attack. The Wizard could already sense the change in Hudson; an intensity in his eyes, and at the same time, a lightness in his being.

"How are you feeling?" the Wizard asked. "You still look like two-month-old garbage."

"At least with me, it's only temporary," Hudson joked.

The Wizard laughed, then his expression changed. "Normally, the hope in life comes from knowing we're not separate, we're all connected, but when you died, I did too."

Hudson nodded silently.

"Dawg, you saw past the void. You gotta tell me . . . "

"Some day."

"Yeah," the Wizard whispered, looking away. He rubbed his face and turned back to the monitor. "We've got problems."

Hudson had called to get caught up on Crane's progress with tracking REMie MADE events and financial operations through

Gypsy. But with the Wizard's words, he assumed one of his biggest worries had come to pass.

"Did they get to Brown?" Hudson had an important private meeting with the vice president coming up, and wanted to be sure she had not been compromised by the REMies.

"No. As far as we can tell, Brown is still clean." The Wizard shifted in his seat, pulled his ponytail out, and narrowed his eyes. "This is about Rochelle."

"Have we found her?" Hudson asked, afraid the answer might be that they had found her body.

"I wish," the wizard said. "The week before Air Force One was attacked, Ross Corbett was killed."

"Too bad," Hudson said, recalling his uncle's friend, who'd been there the night Rochelle had been raped. "Can't say I'm sorry. Never did like the old cuss. But what happened?"

"It's not that simple, Dawg. It's not just Corbett. Hundley was found dead the week after you were shot, and then Marco's body turned up in Lake Erie twelve days after that. Last week, it was Bowers."

"Damn." Hudson felt his stomach tighten. All four of those men had sexually assaulted Rochelle and taken part in the killing of her brother. "Someone knows."

"Yeah," the Wizard said. "And they know who was there that night. Which means . . . they also know what happened."

"What if Rochelle's doing it? Finishing what she started with the governor? What if she really did escape, and now she's finally getting her revenge?"

"Do you really believe that?" the Wizard asked.

"No, I guess not."

"Gouge said someone followed him one night, two weeks ago, and took shots at him."

"You talked to my uncle?"

"I'm not talking about old man Gouge. They tried to kill *Tommy* Gouge!"

"Oh, no . . . " Hudson closed his eyes, trying not to think back on that awful night. Rochelle's rape, and the murder of her brother, had taken place in Tommy Gouge's father's tire shop. Gouge's father was also Hudson's uncle. Whoever was going after the people who were there could easily destroy his presidency. But, as he recalled the face of each person who was in the tire shop during those horrific hours, he suddenly wondered if justice wasn't finally being done.

The Wizard's eyes went wide. "That's right. You, Gouge . . . It ain't just about the guys that did it, it's about *us*, too. The guys who *saw* it. The guys who didn't *stop* it."

"The guys who didn't report it," Hudson added. "Who didn't say a damn thing."

"Yeah, so maybe the Air Force One attack was part of this. The timing is crazy coincidental."

"The attack on Air Force One was a military operation, not the work of a bitter victim, some other vigilante, or a common blackmailer."

"That's my point," the Wizard said. "Corbett, Hundley, Marco, and Bowers were professional hits. If it was NorthBridge, or a REMie like Bastendorff, or any REMie . . . I think it's a good bet that whoever tried to kill you also has Rochelle."

Hudson and Celia Brown walked the manicured trails through the woods at Camp David. He purposely kept the conversation on light issues until they were a sufficient distance from any structure from which they could be monitored. However, the Wizard had warned him that even in nature, the NSA could hear him. Satellites, drones, telescopic microphones, camouflaged surveillance stations, surveillance drones disguised as birds and insects, and a myriad of other high-tech devices were at their disposal, and certainly deployed against the president.

There really hadn't been time to form a personal relationship with his vice president. Hudson had to trust his instincts more than ever, as he knew an enemy from within was trying to stop his efforts. He and Celia Brown were in a life raft together, whether they liked it or not.

He knew she was married to the CEO of a $30 million construction company, and had three grown children. She'd been a doctor before the politicization and soaring costs of healthcare drove her into politics; first to the House, and then the Senate. He'd always considered her an inspired speaker, with a voice like a gospel singer. A woman of conviction. Hudson believed that if not for the REMie control over the elections, she might have made it to the presidency instead of him.

He looked over at her and saw the small, heart-shaped, amethyst brooch she always wore, every day without fail. Someday he would ask her about it.

Someday . . . would they even *have* a someday?

"Celia, I invited you here today because I wanted to ask you something."

"Something you can't ask me at the White House?"

He stopped to look at her and nodded. It was apparent in her knowing expression that she understood. "You're an African-American, yet against affirmative action. You're a woman, yet pro-life. You're a Republican, yet you are one of the most outspoken antiwar activists in the nation. How do you reconcile these views?"

"Shouldn't you have asked me all this before you chose me as your running mate? Before we won the election?" She smiled. "I wouldn't have pegged you for one who applies stereotypes."

"Maybe those are stereotypes," the president said, "but the

majority of women are pro-choice, the majority of African-Americans are for affirmative action, and the majority of Republicans are not antiwar."

"I suspect it's the 'antiwar' part you're most interested in," she said with no trace of drama in her voice. "Seeing how the media and their corporate masters seem intent on pushing us *toward* war with China."

"They make a compelling case. The latest polls show the majority of Americans now see war as necessary."

"The late Howard Zinn once said, 'We need to decide that we will not go to war, whatever reason is conjured up by the politicians or the media, because war in our time is always indiscriminate, a war against innocence, a war against children.' He could've been talking about this war, but, of course, he was talking about *every* war. They are all the same." Her voice had a soothing tone to it, even when talking about catastrophes.

"As you know, I've been to war, and I believe there are times when it is necessary. I just don't think this is one of those times."

"I'm glad to hear that, Mr. President. But . . . "

"What?"

"Can I speak candidly?"

"Of course."

"Although you are the Commander in Chief, I'm afraid it isn't entirely up to you."

Hudson wondered if she knew about the REMies. He wasn't sure if he trusted his vice president enough yet to bring them up. "What do you mean?"

"With all due respect, Mr. President, you must be aware that there are those within the Pentagon and the intelligence community who wield more power than you."

He stared at her, surprised at the matter-of-fact tone in which she summarized his dilemma. "I plan to oppose this war."

Her expression wasn't what he expected. Instead of a satisfied smile, she looked suddenly worried, even a little scared. "Are you sure? I believe that position invites great risk to you personally. It reminds me of what happened to Donald Trump, who, as a candidate, had a long list of maverick ideas and aimed to drain the Washington swamp. Like him or not, once he got into office, many of his radical ideas mysteriously and suddenly changed to be much more mainstream. At the time, I recall former ultraliberal Congressman Dennis Kucinich, from your state of Ohio, warning us against the deep state, the pure permanent bureaucrats who comprise the intelligence community and the Pentagon. He said they were out to destroy the Trump presidency, and he went on to say that our country itself is under attack from within, saying that those in the deep state with their leaks to, and manipulation of, the media, represent a clear and present danger to our country."

"I remember when Kucinich came out with all that. It was surprising that more people didn't heed his advice, especially since he was no fan of Donald Trump."

"Kucinich is a patriot, a defender of the Constitution. The deep state has long been after him. In 2011, the Obama administration wiretapped his Congressional office. Kucinich also stated that the intelligence community was trying to re-ignite the Cold War between Russia and the United States. That's why the media continues to marginalize him."

"Then how do you get away with being an anti-war Republican?" Hudson asked.

"I choose my battles carefully. I absolutely oppose all war. I believe there's always another way to resolve differences. A peaceful way. Otherwise, I try to avoid controversy."

Hudson nodded. Some might consider the vice president's method to be cowardly, but standing next to this woman and staring into her fiery eyes, he knew she was no coward.

"What did you want to ask me today, Mr. President?"

"For your help."

She stared at him for a long moment. "What would you like me to do?"

"Figure out a way we can stop this war." He paused, found her eyes again. "And still live to get reelected for a second term."

# CHAPTER TWENTY-EIGHT

V onner and Rex were at the estate on the Potomac River, monitoring what had become an increasingly volatile situation. While his boss was on a conference call with several other REMies, Rex had forty-two tiny dice of various colors spread across his desk. He rolled them in groups of three and memorized the results. In between rolls, he checked the monitors that surrounded him.

A few days earlier, he'd spotted Crane on the DarkNet. He didn't know who he was yet, but he knew that he was working on behalf of the president. Rex could tell by where he was going, what he was looking at, and the trails he followed and left. Even more than the surprise that Hudson had a DarkNet expert helping him was the program they were utilizing. Rex didn't know it was called Gypsy, didn't even know much about it, but he was impressed, and extremely curious. He'd been able to see it in action quite a few times as it vacuumed and filtered normally unprocessable data. Rex had not been able to pinpoint where Crane was operating from, and probably never would, but now that he knew the person was out there, he would follow him—at least the virtual him—and learn what Crane was learning. Rex had immediately written his own program to watch and track Crane, and to mirror and record everything he did.

Vonner, who had taken his conference call outside, stormed into the grand room and caught Rex scooping up his dice. "What is it with you and those dice? A man with so much intelligence, someone who looks at everything so precisely, with such an appreciation of facts . . . what in fangdangle do you *get* out of these damn dice?"

"Numbers." Rex said the word as if it were a prayer. "The universe is made of numbers. All of the answers can be found in the numbers."

"But rolling dice is nothing but chance."

"I don't believe in *chance*," Rex said, emphasizing the word chance as if it were a profanity. "What may appear as random to you is actually part of a greater pattern. Numbers always form patterns. If you see the patterns, the right ones, you can notice, trace, and anticipate things. The patterns form on top of each other, around each other, over, under, through, again and—"

"Oh, shut up!" Vonner snapped. "We've got real stuff to deal with. Hudson is about to come out in opposition to the war."

Rex already knew this, he'd seen it in the patterns, but he didn't say that to Vonner. He did, however, add another problem. "It's not just his opposition to the war. It seems the president's near-death experience had quite an effect on him."

Vonner poured himself a drink and glared at Rex with a confused expression. It was the confusion that irritated him more than another potential problem.

"We picked up some conversations the president's been having during the last few days," Rex said. "The president wants to push for term limits for Congress. He's looking at a massive tax reform that would essentially eliminate the IRS by taxing on consumption rather than income. Your boy Hudson even wants to abolish fossil fuels. And the kicker, wait for it . . . he plans to propose *slashing* military spending."

"What the hell?" Vonner said, adding more alcohol to his drink. "Is he a damn Democrat now?"

"I guess he died and saw the light," Rex said with a smirk.

"If that's the case, the next time he gets assassinated, he might as well stay dead."

Rex raised an eyebrow. "There's going to be a next time?"

It was no secret that David Covington didn't have much respect for Hudson Pound. He did, however, believe the office of the president was, if not sacred, at least critical to the security of the world. He argued that the FBI had wasted nearly two years on the NorthBridge investigation, and that the Brickman Effort, led by Colonel Dranick, had fared no better.

"Unprecedented events call for unprecedented actions," Covington said, testifying before Congress. "We cannot let these terrorists get away with this. Their attack on President Pound and Air Force One was an attack on our very way of life, on freedom itself."

He was seeking authority to assemble a team to go after NorthBridge, similar to the team of US law-enforcement agents Eliot Ness formed in 1929 to bring down legendary gangster Al Capone. The team of nine agents became known as "The Untouchables" because they were incorruptible, aggressive, fearless, and smart. Covington told an aide in private, "I plan on liking the next president, and I want a country left for him to lead."

Congress granted broad authority to Covington under Article I, Section 8, Clause 15, of the Constitution, and the Intelligence Reform and Terrorism Prevention Act. The new authority for the

Director of National Intelligence meant that Covington's Find and Stop Terrorist squad, his "FaST" agents, would now lead the hunt for NorthBridge. It also meant Covington would have a nearly unlimited budget and unrestrained power to do whatever he deemed necessary to stop any threat to the United States.

It seemed that the president would not be leaving the White House for a while, which temporarily freed Tarka from her dangerous and covert mission of keeping him alive. But when Rex gave her a new assignment, she realized that saving Hudson Pound came in many forms. There wasn't much to go on, but Rex explained that finding the woman no one else had been able to find might be a tougher job than keeping a president alive.

Yet Tarka had resources that others didn't.

The operative, a classic Greek beauty, was as tough as she was smart, possessing the useful ability of obsessive precision. Everything had to be checked, and considered. An avid chess player, Tarka hadn't lost a game since age nine. Another asset she held was a list of contacts which included some of the world's most powerful people, as well as many two-bit criminals, and everyone in between. She was particularly well connected in the seedy underworld of hackers, blackmailers, smugglers, and spies.

When Tarka's regular network of rogues came up empty, she wasn't surprised. If Rex hadn't been able to locate Rochelle Rogers, she must be either dead, or else nearly everyone who *knew* her location was dead. There was only one person who could help her, perhaps the last person Vonner would ever want her to contact.

The enemy—Booker Lipton.

# CHAPTER TWENTY-NINE

Melissa stared a little longer than usual at her husband as he dressed. He was thinner and scarred, his hair grayer, with a lame arm, and a permanent limp—a soldier back from the crusades. It had only been a year since he took office, yet he seemed a different man. Indeed, he *was* a different man, not just from the batterings, the pressure, or the brutal wounds. It was because of those nine minutes. She knew it, but he'd refused to speak about it, even to her. He'd journeyed to the dark side of the moon and been altered by the experience.

Melissa had been reluctant to press in those early weeks, but his silence on the topic hadn't just fueled frenzied worldwide speculation. It had also stolen something from their marriage—a bond of trust, "for better or worse, 'til death do us part."

"I'm sorry, Melissa, I'm just not ready to talk about it," Hudson said, buttoning his white cotton shirt.

"Why?" she asked, teary-eyed. "You're not too fragile to lead the free world, you aren't too weak to reshape the entire government, to defy the REMies, to push peace with all the force of war. Why can't you trust me with what happened in those nine minutes? Tell me what you saw."

"I can't," Hudson said.

"I don't understand why you want to keep something like that secret from me. Was it so terrible?"

"Try to understand . . . it may look like I've healed, you may think I'm no longer fragile or weak, but it's only those nine minutes that are holding me together."

She stared at him, confused, then full of caring concern. "That's exactly *why* you should share it with me."

"If I share it, even with you, it will be gone."

"What will?"

"Everything."

Melissa wiped her eyes, gave him one last pleading look, then turned away. Hudson reached for the back of her shoulder, as if to pull her into his arms, but then dropped his hand before she saw.

She handed him a bright blue tie.

"You know I don't wear those anymore."

"You're about to give your first State of the Union address," Melissa said. "Wear one tonight."

He shook his head.

She sighed quietly. He wouldn't tell her about the nine minutes, but she had seen plenty of its results. He wouldn't wear ties anymore, had become a vegan, refused to kill bugs, and the greatest secret of all was his stance against war.

*How could the president of the United States be unwilling to engage in war? How was he going to stop NorthBridge? What about the ever-looming war with China? What if that news got out that the president had become a committed pacifist?* Melissa shuddered.

Suddenly, she whirled around. "Damn it, I'm your wife!" she said, grabbing his hand. "*Talk* to me. Tell me what happened!"

Hudson pulled her into a hug, but shook his head.

Melissa pulled away. "I don't understand why you can't talk to me."

"I know you don't, honey," Hudson said. "And I'm not sure how to explain it."

She stared at him for a moment longer, then turned and walked across the room to a window, giving up on the nine minutes, at least for now. "Maybe a little more time," she said, not loud enough for him to hear.

These worries about Hudson were not just her own. The Twenty-Fifth Amendment to the Constitution had been mentioned several times in the media. After the attack, it guaranteed the government could continue to run and power would be returned to Hudson, but now it might be used against him.

*Whenever the vice president and a majority of either the principal officers of the executive departments or of such other body as Congress may by law provide, transmit to the president pro tempore of the Senate and the Speaker of the House of Representatives their written declaration that the president is unable to discharge the powers and duties of his office, the vice president shall immediately assume the powers and duties of the office as Acting President.*

Melissa had read his State of the Union speech. Hudson was smart enough to know how dangerous it would be if he announced his new-found pacifism. He could say a lot of things about changing the government and the world, but that was one secret he needed to keep at all cost.

Still, she knew he might go off script. Ever since he'd "died," Hudson had become unpredictable, even a little strange. Fitz had asked her if she could get Hudson to cut back on some of the philosophical ramblings during cabinet meetings, and many on the White House staff had found him in a kind of "thoughtful trance." He explained to Melissa and Fitz that during those times, he was simply meditating.

"Presidents don't meditate," Fitz had said.

"I'm certain that if prior presidents had meditated, we wouldn't be in the mess we're in now," Hudson had calmly replied.

Melissa noticed, not for the first time, that in spite of his beleaguered body, his eyes burned with a fire hotter than ever. *At least there's that*, she thought, but Melissa didn't know how to handle the "new" Hudson. She was too practical for all his "love and light" ideas. Yet one thing was clear; he had to stick to the message, and not try to use this speech to take the pressure off NorthBridge or China.

"What did Vonner say about the speech?" Melissa asked.

"He liked it," Hudson said casually as he pulled on his sports coat.

"Won't you even wear a suit?" Melissa asked.

"No."

"Have you told Vonner about your plan to oppose the war?"

"No, but I'm sure he's aware of my views. Vonner misses nothing. He's probably listening to us right now," Hudson said, waving a hand in the air. "Hi, Vonner, we're still not sure if you're friend or foe, but—"

"Sometimes, it's not about who's good or bad," Melissa began.

"Really?" Hudson asked, checking his appearance in the mirror.

"Come on, you know it's rarely that simple. Someone can be bad for the right reasons, just as someone can be good for the wrong reasons," she said tensely.

Hudson smiled at his wife. He always liked how she could quickly sum up a complex issue.

"Vonner may seem like a bad man," Melissa continued, not returning the smile, "but his cause is good."

"Manipulating world events to keep the population controlled is a *good* cause?" he asked, recalling a long list of REMie MADE events, the acronym's meaning, "Manipulate and Distract Everyone," echoing in his head. *How long have we been manipulated? Distracted? Too long.*

She sighed, frustrated. "No, but manipulating them for other reasons might—"

"It depends on the reasons?"

"Exactly."

## CHAPTER THIRTY

I n the back of a limousine driving down K Street, in Washington, DC, a REMie, affectionately referred to as "the Shark," and a powerful US senator discussed their dilemma.

"The assassination attempt and his near-death experience have made the damn president more popular than ever," the senator said.

"If we can't kill the president's popularity," the Shark replied, "we'll just have to kill the president, for longer than nine minutes."

"Pound seems to have nine lives," the senator muttered.

"Oh, don't worry about that," the Shark said, smiling maliciously. "There's more than one way to skin a cat."

Tarka thought it was an odd place for a meeting, but she'd never been to the redwoods before, and Booker Lipton was an odd man, not to mention it would be better if Rex didn't know about her receiving help from one of Vonner's most bitter rivals. She knew

Rex tracked her as best he could. However, his best was not equal to her abilities to vanish, which she did often for short stretches, while "in the field."

The towering trees hushed out the entire world, even the demons in her head. Raised in Greece until her parents were killed by terrorists, followed by six—or was it seven?—foster homes across Europe, Tarka had plenty of demons. Normally she kept them at bay by focusing on the mission, whatever it might be. Keeping a president alive against terrorists, amongst other threats, had done the job nicely for the past year. Today, though, the trees had taken over, and she couldn't get over the realization of how much she loved them.

"They take your breath away, don't they?" Booker said as he stepped out from behind a huge trunk.

Normally, surprising Tarka's "hair-trigger" reflexes would have made her pull a weapon, or at least one of the seven martial arts disciplines she'd mastered would have kicked in, and Booker would be on the ground, most likely dead. Instead, the trees calmed her.

"They certainly do," Tarka replied. She suspected he had bodyguards stationed behind nearby trees, maybe even up in the high branches, protecting him, even if she hadn't been one of the top assassins employed by his main nemesis. Booker Lipton, an African American with more money than anyone on the planet, had made countless enemies while accumulating his fortune. She doubted he went anywhere without some of his BLAXers—a private army rumored to be as large, and better trained and equipped, than those of most small countries.

"Thank you for agreeing to see me," Tarka added, shaking his hand.

"Interesting that Vonner doesn't know you asked for my help," Booker said, amazed that the stunning woman in front of him was also a lethal killer.

"All he cares about is getting the job done."

"Oh, I suspect Vonner cares about a great deal more than that."

"I'm sure you're right."

Booker nodded, regarding her carefully.

"Is Rochelle Rogers alive?"

"Yes, she is."

"Do you have her?"

He seemed surprised by her question. "No."

"But you do know where she is?" Tarka asked, assuming he would not have taken the meeting if he had nothing to offer.

"Yes."

"Then why haven't you rescued her yourself?"

"Why are you trying to find her?" Booker asked.

Tarka smiled at his avoidance of the question. She was a fighter, not a negotiator, and Booker was both. She decided to stick to the point. "Will you tell me where Rochelle is?"

"Perhaps," Booker said, beginning to stroll down a narrow trail through lush ferns. "What are you offering?"

"Nothing," she said, following him as the trail wound among the giants.

He stopped and looked at her, laughing. "Do you know who she is? That the president plans on pardoning her? That she apparently has some kind of dirt on your employer's puppet president? That she killed—"

"I know all that."

"She sounds like a valuable pawn in the game, doesn't she?" Booker said, still smiling. "Yet you're asking me to just hand her to you, to *Vonner*, a man who has never missed a chance to try to screw me over? In fact, he goes out of his way to cause me harm."

"You're here, aren't you?" Tarka had reasoned that if Booker knew where Rochelle was, and wanted her, he would already have her.

"How big is your team?"

"Big enough."

"Not for this mission."

"Where is she?" Tarka asked, trying to spot Booker's people among the massive redwoods. She couldn't see anything, but she could sense them.

Booker shook his head. "You're pretty damn sure I'm going to tell you."

"I am, because you *want* me to get her."

"True," Booker said, starting to walk again. "And doesn't that worry you?"

"Not at all."

"Yes, it does," Booker mused.

"Vonner wants her," she said. "If you're setting him up for something, Vonner's a tough guy, he'll deal with that. My job is to rescue her."

"Does the president know about this mission?"

"I think you're in a better position to know that answer," she said.

Booker nodded. "She's being held on a tiny island in the Philippines."

"Which one?" Tarka asked. "There are more than seven thousand islands in the Philippines."

"Quite right," Booker said, impressed with her knowledge. "It's in the Mindanao group, but it's unnamed." He handed her a flash drive. "GPS coordinates and other pertinent details."

"Who's holding her?"

"That's on the drive as well. A well-armed group. Seventeen men, four women. Concrete bunker at the center of the island. Heavy jungle canopy. You'll see lots of photos."

She nodded. Everyone knew Booker had access to the best satellite imagery. His companies supplied the intelligence communities, including the NSA and CIA, with most of their high-tech equipment. "Anyone else on the island?"

"No."

"Who pays the bills?"

"Can't you guess?" Booker asked, stopping again, this time to lean against a mammoth log.

Tarka knew it was likely one of six or seven people, and she wouldn't have been surprised if it was Booker himself, but she went with the obvious. "Bastendorff?"

Booker, impressed again, nodded slowly. "You be careful, Tarka," he said, meeting her eyes. "You're a smart woman, hopefully smart enough to know you're not *that* smart. You may think I'm setting a trap for Vonner, but Bastendorff is the spider in this story. Try not to get caught in his web."

"I think there are many 'spiders' in this story."

Booker smiled. "True enough, but he's the worst of them." He paused. "The webs are everywhere."

# CHAPTER THIRTY-ONE

Linh had been trying to get an appointment with the president for weeks. Even if his schedule hadn't been crushing, he hadn't been ready to see her before now. The morning after Hudson delivered the State of the Union address to a joint session of Congress, he found himself walking in the trees on the White House South Lawn with the one person he believed knew of the Air Force one attack in advance.

"I'm happy to see you, Mr. President," Linh said.

"I believe you. Really, I do," Hudson replied. "Yet your actions say otherwise."

Her eyes squinted as her face expressed pain.

"You knew it was coming." He stared at her, trying to understand, trying to answer so many questions, trying to see into her thoughts, but all he saw were mysteries. "You knew I was about to be killed," he said, his voice full of anguish. "Why didn't you *warn* me?"

"How could I have known?"

"Don't." Hudson pointed a finger at her. "I have been through too much. You know that I know that you knew." He lowered his hand, looked up at the sky, then back into her eyes. "So, please, tell me."

"I did try to warn you."

"Well, no offense, but you didn't do a very good job."

"You chose."

"I chose what?" Hudson looked at her incredulously. "To get *killed*?"

"Yes, we all choose our paths, but that isn't what I was referring to," Linh said. "I meant that you chose not to believe me, chose not to pursue it."

Hudson shook his head. What he really wanted was to shake her, to yell that he felt betrayed by her, that he needed her to tell him all that she knew, about everything, but he felt no right to do any of those things. "Then why are you here?" he finally asked, trying not to sound desperate.

"I thought you might need to talk about it," she said. Her face held a soft, tranquil serenity that nearly made him cry.

*Of course I want to talk to you. You're the only person who would understand it. Ever since that horrible day, I've been waiting to see you again, to tell you what happened, to ask you so much!*

He stared at her, thinking all the wild thoughts that had been tormenting him. It was like having a conversation with just their eyes. It left him feeling at once invigorated, drained, and like he wanted to weep. "You know . . . What do you think I want to talk about?" he asked, not intending it to come out as the whisper it did.

"The nine minutes."

He gazed at her for a long moment. "I can't." But it was all he wanted to do.

"Why not?"

He scanned the area, wanting to make sure no one was too close. He knew there were fifteen agents nearby, but he had faith in the Wizard's SonicBlock. Fear of being overheard wasn't the problem. "I'm afraid," he said, ashamed.

"Don't be."

"If I start, I'm afraid I won't be able to stop."

"It will be okay," she said, never taking her eyes from his.

"Not if it unravels me."

"Would that be such a bad thing?"

"Yes," he scoffed. "Maybe if I weren't POTUS, I could . . . "

"What?"

"Maybe I could explore dreams and rainbows, chase ghosts, wonder about fate, the meaning of life . . . and things beyond."

"You can."

"I can't," he said, breaking her gaze for the first time. "I'm the president of the United States."

"Those are exactly the type of issues our leaders should be concerned about."

"Really? Haven't you ever heard about the separation of church and state?"

"Church? You know this has nothing to do with religion."

He nodded, and was about to speak when he saw Fitz walking briskly across the South Lawn toward them. "Give me a second," he said, jogging off to intercept Fitz.

"Two-minute warning, Mr. President," Fitz said while looking over Hudson's shoulder at Linh.

Hudson recalled the top-secret video conference with the leaders of India, South Korea, and Japan. Although everything in his being now wanted to avoid war with China, preparations still had to be made. Separate calls with Russia and Pakistan would take place later in the day. "Can you give me three or four more minutes?"

Fitz stared at him as if he were crazy. "War, international leaders—these things don't wait, especially for some controversy waiting to happen," he said, nodding toward Linh, whom he'd previously called a high-class psychic, somehow making the word "psychic" sound more like "hooker".

"Do it anyway," he said, heading back to Linh.

"You're out of time," Linh said.

"In more ways than one."

"Do you believe in destiny?" she asked.

"I don't know. Maybe, sometimes . . . "

"You should."

He stared at her for a long moment.

"Whenever you need to talk . . . " she offered.

He nodded.

"In the meantime, I have some news about your friend."

His first thought was of the Wizard, afraid he'd been the next victim of whoever was killing the people who'd been there that tragic night at the tire shop. Even when she said "Rochelle," he was still confused.

Linh looked around. "Rochelle is alive."

"Rochelle? She's alive?" Hudson expected himself to be elated at the news, but instead, a sick feeling overtook him.

"A man named Bastendorff has her." She waited until Hudson caught her eyes before continuing. "Vonner is about to send one of his VC agents to attempt an "extraction", I think they called it."

"Vonner knows where she is?" Hudson said, his voice rising.

# CHAPTER THIRTY-TWO

Any other meeting he would have cancelled and called Vonner immediately to find out why he hadn't been told Rochelle had been found. Hudson suspected they were never *going* to tell him, or were planning to use her against him.

But the call would have to wait, because as much as he wanted to see Rochelle finally free, there had to be a world left for her to enjoy. War with China could make that impossible, and his video conference with the leaders of India, South Korea, and Japan might help prevent it.

The countries were all on edge with China's expansion and aggression in the area. However, war between the two biggest economies in the world—Japan was third, India seventh, and South Korea was also a big player—would destabilize not just the region, but the entire global financial system. He needed to calm their fears and get them onboard with his peace plan.

Director of National Intelligence, David Covington, was waiting when the president returned to the Oval Office prior to the conference.

"Mr. President, I have a report you need to hear before your call," Covington said, swallowing the final remnants of a lemon Necco wafer.

"Can't it wait, David? We start in . . . " He looked to Fitz.

Fitz held up three fingers.

"You have to delay for ten minutes," Covington said after watching the exchange. "There's a critical national security issue which directly relates to the conference you're about to convene."

Hudson didn't care for the man, but knew Covington understood the stakes, and wouldn't make the request lightly. "Okay."

At the president's assent, Fitz sprang into action, began speaking into his cell, and headed to his office. Redirecting three world leaders wasn't fun, but it could be done.

Hudson gave Covington a *"start talking"* nod.

Covington handed the president a folder and began summarizing the report. "The NSA picked up some disturbing communications, and the CIA was able to corroborate it with several sources, including a mole we have inside the MSS."

Hudson knew MSS was the Ministry of State Security of the People's Republic of China, one of the most dangerous intelligence services in the world. With more than 100,000 intelligence personnel and agents worldwide, the MSS had replaced the KGB as the CIA's most formidable foe.

"What did we learn?" the president asked, wanting Covington to get to the point.

"The Chinese were going to invade Taiwan the day you were attacked boarding Air Force One," Covington said.

The bombshell hit Hudson as the ramifications of that statement swirled in his already overburdened mind.

"The Chinese see the vice president as a peacenik," Covington continued as the president rose and began pacing in front of the windows. "They believed she wouldn't retaliate."

"But then why didn't they take Taiwan anyway?" Hudson

asked, momentarily pausing to lean on the Resolute Desk. "I was as good as dead for weeks."

"We kept the extreme direness of your condition a closely guarded secret," Covington said, remaining unmoved, like a soldier. "They believed you would recover quickly, and, fulfilling our obligations under the Taiwan Relations Act, intervene against them. A safe assumption based on your record and your rhetoric."

Hudson nodded, thinking about how before those nine minutes, he'd been ready to go to war with China for a variety of reasons. Had the PRC invaded Taiwan, it would have been an easy decision for him based on treaties and strategic interests alone. But the timing was extremely troubling.

"You understand what this means?" Covington asked. "That the most likely sponsors of the Air Force One attack were the MSS?"

Hudson stared at him. Although his thoughts had gotten that far, he hadn't quite allowed the conclusion to form completely.

"The Chinese government tried to assassinate the president of the United States," Covington reiterated the shocking news.

"An explosive accusation," Hudson said, trying to digest it. If true, war would be impossible to avoid. "What's our proof?"

"As I said, we have the communications intercepts, and several sources," Covington explained, pointing to the folder still on the president's desk. "It's all detailed in the report."

Hudson glanced at the folder, and then back to Covington. "I'm sure it is, but if I'm going to start World War Three, I'll need a little more."

"Should I convene the Council in the Situation Room?" Covington asked while surreptitiously rubbing the powder off an orange Necco wafer between his thumb and forefinger.

"We're not there yet," the president said as Fitz returned to the room. "Do the satellites show any PLA movements toward Taiwan?"

The PLA, or People's Liberation Army, was the largest military force in the world. With more than two million personnel, and with the second largest defense budget, it was also the world's fastest growing military.

"Not yet," Covington said tensely. "But that could change at any time."

"And so can my response," the president said. "Get me more intel on this. I want a clear, visible line from Beijing to that runway in Portland."

"The leaders are waiting," Fitz said, pointing to the door. "We need to do the conference."

"I'll see what else we can get," Covington said. "But when you read the report, I'm sure you'll agree it's already fairly conclusive."

"*Fairly* isn't good enough," the president said. "If I had died, that would have been one person. If we do this, we're talking about tens of thousands, perhaps even *millions*, dead."

# CHAPTER THIRTY-THREE

Vonner listened calmly while Hudson ranted about not being informed about their locating Rochelle. When he finally paused to take a breath, the billionaire cut in.

"I'd like to know your source," Vonner said dryly. "I've only just been informed myself. I instructed one of our top agents to find her at any costs. She has, and now she will lead a rescue."

Once again, Hudson couldn't decide whether or not to believe him, but that question ultimately held far more consequences than he could contemplate at the moment. "Bastendorff isn't going to let her go easily," he said.

"No, but he won't be expecting us."

"Assuming they get her out, where will they take her?"

"I'm not going to return her to the Bureau of Prisons, if that's what you mean." Vonner smiled, taking a slow sip of his single malt scotch. He stood on the edge of a bluff overlooking the Potomac River. There were many places he wished he could send Rochelle Rogers, one of them being the bottom of that raging water, but that would be too much of a strain on his relationship with the president. It would also be too obvious if she died during the extraction. He'd given the matter a great deal of thought, but still hadn't resolved anything concrete. Vonner let the silence linger another few moments before asking Hudson, "Where would you suggest we send her?"

The question caught Hudson unprepared. "You, uh, you once mentioned a little hideaway somewhere. Can we keep her safe there? Can we keep her safe anywhere? I was originally thinking about something like the witness protection program. I'm sure she just wants some peace. But that was before Basten-dorff . . . I still can't—"

"Are you going to pardon her?" Vonner interrupted.

"I'm not sure it's wise at the moment," the president said, surprising both himself and Vonner. "It seems best for everyone if we can just keep her safe and out of sight."

"We can do that," Vonner said, trying to dampen the pleasure from his voice and resisting the urge to say, "Good boy."

"A nice place," Hudson added. "Some luxury."

"Of course," Vonner said.

"I'll be waiting for updates."

"Sure. Now, can we discuss your plan to remake the world into some kind of Utopia you evidently dreamed up while you were recovering?"

"You sound irritated," Hudson said, thinking he was the only one in the conversation with a right to be annoyed with anything. "You knew we were going to go after the REMies. You promised help, said it was your plan to do it. That's why you chose me."

"Yes, yes, but this isn't the way to go about it."

"The REMies rule by utilizing the system, which includes politicians spending decades in congress, the complex and oppressive tax system, having the might of the US military at their disposal, and a corrupt banking system anchored by the Federal Reserve Board."

"It's not that simple."

"Of course not, it's intentionally insanely complicated," Hudson said. "That's why we need radical tax reform, term limits, a major overhaul to campaign finance laws, significant defense spending cutbacks, and most of all, a complete reorganization of our banking system."

"You really are trying to get yourself killed."

"Is that a threat?"

"Hudson, how many times do I need to tell you that *I'm* not the enemy?"

"Ask me at the end of my second term."

"Look," Vonner said, "I'll support your opposition to the war with China, even though I believe it's a wasted stand, but—"

"Why do you say that?"

"Because the REMies don't really want war with China, they want the *buildup* to a war with China."

"They're playing a dangerous game."

"That's nothing new for them," Vonner said, trying to sound as if he wasn't one of them. "The China confrontation is all part of a strategy to shift manufacturing and economic activity to a group of other Asian countries—Indonesia, Pakistan, Bangladesh, the Philippines, Vietnam, Thailand, and Myanmar."

"Why can't they just do it without the threat of war?"

"The elites who control the world are constantly struggling with each other for supremacy."

"CapWars."

"Exactly. Nothing is ever simple. There's no money in simple. The more complicated a thing is, the better the opportunity is for bigger profits."

"It also means less chance they'll get caught."

"The REMies are so far beyond getting caught. They're the only ones who really do the catching."

"That's why we have to go after them."

"We will," Vonner said. He noticed Rex leaving the house

and starting toward him. "But you have this all backward. You think, 'Hit them fast with everything at once!' That will *not* work. We go slow, and get one victory at a time, until the momentum builds. So, please, start with the war, save that other stuff until we win that one."

"Okay," Hudson said. "I'll think about it." But he had no intention of slowing down. He couldn't, because he absolutely believed he wasn't going to live long enough to wait for the victories to pile up.

# CHAPTER THIRTY-FOUR

O ther than Camp David, it was the president's first trip away from the White House since the Air Force One attack. The Florida beach house had become an armed camp, with choppers patrolling the air and gunboats offshore. Normally Tarka would be there, lurking just outside "the protection bubble," the Secret Service name for the secure space around the president. She'd shadowed him for more than a year, working to keep him alive, neutralizing any threat—and there'd been many— by any means necessary. But now, she had to keep him safe in another way, and Vonner had sent another Vonner Security agent to Florida.

Even before the attack, being president could often seem like being a prisoner—always in that bubble of protection, never really alone. But now, with his movements limited to the White House, Camp David, and the Florida beach house, known as the "southern White House," he felt especially trapped and smothered; not just from the NorthBridge threat, but also knowing the REMies were out there, watching, listening, and manipulating everything. Hudson was a puppet, and he never stopped wondering who was really pulling the strings.

Hudson and Schueller walked barefoot up and down the beach, discussing ways to avoid a military conflict with China. Based on the latest reports from Crane, no matter from what angle they viewed it, it seemed war was inevitable.

"I can't help but wonder," Schueller said, as a flock of seagulls landed nearby, "the attack on Air Force One, war with China, the recent NorthBridge strikes, all these things, all these *distractions* . . ." He raised his eyebrows at his dad. "What are they doing?"

"What do you mean?" Hudson asked, watching the seagulls take off as they got closer.

"Is it really the war? I don't think so. I don't think that's their endgame. They're doing something else."

Hudson raised his eyebrows back at his son. "Ever since I got into this, people have been telling me—Fonda, the Wizard, Linh from the Inner Movement, you—that they are distracting us—the elites, the REMies, whoever— and I've come to believe that it's true. My question is, why haven't the American people, or, for that matter, why haven't the citizens of the world, figured this out? Why can't they see they're being manipulated, controlled, used?"

"A lot of us do see it," Schueller said angrily. "Thorne talks about it every day on his radio show."

Hudson stopped and faced Schueller, a comical look of disgust on his face. "You listen to Thorne's show?"

"Occasionally," Schueller said, laughing at his dad's expression. "He may be a jerk, but he sees what we see."

Hudson nodded. "Maybe, but he's no fan of mine."

"He's no fan of *Vonner's.*"

"Vonner owns the company Thorne works for!"

"That's gotta just make him hate Vonner more."

"Probably, but Thorne didn't like losing to me in the primaries."

"No doubt. Still, he's using his platform to wake people up to the way the elites are screwing everyone."

"We need many, many more to realize what's happening."

"They will, but that's not the big problem," Schueller said, scooting out of the way of a surprisingly aggressive wave. "Most of the people who *do* see it aren't in a position to do anything about it."

"We are."

"Are we? You may be the president, but can you really stop a war?"

"I thought we decided this wasn't really about a war with China. Even Vonner insists the REMies don't really want the war. They want the threat of it, the buildup to it."

"That's a risky game," Schueller said, scanning the dozen Secret Service agents behind them.

"Exactly what I said. They're risking World War Three."

"Unless they control the Chinese government as well."

"They might."

"Follow the money," Schueller said. "It's always about the money."

"A greedy race, we are," Hudson said, repeating something Linh had said during their last conversation. "Crane's working on tracking all the financial schemes of the REMies, but the program can only do so much. We'd need thousands of people, working fulltime for years, to sort it all out."

"True," Schueller agreed. "I'm talking to Crane later today."

"It's time to call the Wizard," Hudson said, pulling out his secured tablet and inserting the SonicBlock. He scanned the area, knelt down, and asked Schueller to help shield the screen from both the sun and any distant probing eyes. His regular Secret

Service agents had almost grown accustom to this kind of strange behavior from the president. Their expressions did not change.

The Wizard appeared shortly after the scrambled matrix finished its patterning. "Daaawg!" he said, turning into the camera as if he'd been in the middle of something. "It's getting hot. It's not just the new NorthBridge attacks. There's a lot of stuff heating up on the DarkNet."

After an initial lull following the Air Force One attack, NorthBridge had become more active. They employed smaller attacks on government facilities across the nation. Even with all the heightened security, it was looking more and more like a guerrilla war, with NorthBridge seeming to have the advantage against the giant military industrial complex of the United States. The US was not used to fighting wars on its home turf, nor going against such a well-funded, organized and invisible foe who seemed to be able to do anything and get in anywhere. They'd locked down a number of power plants from inside the computer systems that ran them. Many secure networks on military bases had been infiltrated, the terrorists using the access to discharge troops, cancel requisitions, and generally wreak havoc.

"Fear or beauty, it's always a hard choice . . . every day we face it over and over again," the Wizard said. "I think another major attack is coming."

Hudson instinctively looked over his shoulder, having been the target of so many of the attacks. Although he was as determined as ever, he wasn't sure he could physically take another one. He didn't trust the Secret Service, the FBI, and certainly not the CIA or the NSA, but he sure hoped on that day they were protecting him.

The president looked out to sea. Other than two Secret Service gunboats and a tanker in the distance, everything seemed clear. Then he imagined that instead of oil, the tanker was filled with terrorists ready to strike, just minutes away.

*They could overwhelm the gunboats and wipe out the whole beach. Kill Schueller and me in an instant . . . Everything has gotten so dangerous. What if . . .*

"Dad," Schueller said, touching his father's shoulder, "are you okay?"

"Yeah, sorry." He took one last quick glance at the tanker, then focused back on the screen. The Wizard was in the process of braiding his long ponytail and putting on some sort of ornamental silver band to hold it in place.

"All the chatter and trends on the DarkNet point to Washington, DC," the Wizard said. "Crane has Gypsy following it, but they may surprise us."

Hudson immediately thought of the White House, the last remaining place he felt remotely safe.

*What if NorthBridge attacks the White House!?*

"We know where she is," the president said, changing the subject, knowing the Wizard would know just whom he meant.

The Wizard looked at him, speechless and stunned. "Is . . . is she . . . " he finally stammered.

"We believe she's still alive," Hudson answered. "Vonner is sending someone to get her. I'll let you know."

"Vonner?"

"I can't very well send the Marines, can I?"

The conversation shifted back to NorthBridge and how to find out who they were, debating if NorthBridge really had orchestrated the Air Force One attack, or if it was someone else. And if so, who? They also discussed the REMies and how to stop them. Schueller was less interested in Air Force One and North-Bridge, making it clear he'd like to know those answers, but he believed, and his father agreed, that the REMies were the real issue. Stopping the REMies was what they had to do. Ultimately, they were the greatest threat, because NorthBridge was fighting against the status quo that the REMies held and wanted. North-

Bridge was, therefore, the enemy of the REMies in some ways. Although Hudson did not agree with him on this point, North-Bridge *was* an ally to the president's efforts to take back world control from the REMies.

"NorthBridge will never be my ally," Hudson said bitterly.

The Wizard, who agreed with Schueller, looked unblinking into the camera. "The end of the world makes for strange bedfellows."

# CHAPTER THIRTY-FIVE

While getting dressed, Hudson caught a clip on one of the morning news shows. Thorne was giving yet another interview about the "true populist movement" that was happening in America. The show's host asked him if he was leading it.

"This revolution doesn't have a single leader. It has millions of them."

"What do you think President Pound would have to say about that?"

"Is Pound still president?" Thorne replied. "I hadn't noticed."

The host couldn't help but laugh, then held up Thorne's best-selling book, *Don't F*ck With We The People*.

The book's title made Hudson think about Cherry Tree, the name he'd given his plan for using the people to rid the world of the REMies. He needed someone on the outside to rally the masses. Maybe Hudson could make sure the truth got out, but getting large numbers to take to the streets, boycott certain institutions, and galvanize all the diverse factions to demand change with one voice, would be almost impossible to do within the confines of the office of the president.

*Could Thorne help? Am I insane to even think of asking him?* He smiled at the thought. *Don't F\*ck With We The People.* Hudson knew he was right. Thorne could help.

After a report reviewing the little progress made on the investigation of who was responsible for the attack on Air Force One, the next segment featured two former officials from previous administrations talking about White House leaks. Many presidents had leak problems. In Hudson's first six months, there'd been almost no leaks from the executive branch, but in the past few months they had started springing up, and in recent weeks they were almost daily. Crane had run them through Gypsy, trying to discover the source, but so far the sophisticated program had failed to produce anything conclusive. It did verify what they already suspected; that the leaks were an attempt to sway opinion to support war with China.

*The damned REMies,* Hudson thought. *Vonner wants me to take it slow and not push. The hell with that, I'm going forward anyway. Let's see how many fronts they can fight on at once.*

Melissa walked in the room, putting on an earring.

"Wow, you look fantastic," Hudson said, seeing his wife adorned in a white and green dress designed by Martinus Andreas. As First Lady, it was no surprise that she'd graced countless fashion and political magazine covers, but Melissa had appeared on the front of just as many business publications. "Beauty *and* brains, how did I get so lucky?" Hudson had often said.

While trying to decide what to wear, he told Melissa about his latest idea to use Thorne to implement Cherry Tree.

"You're crazy," Melissa said, sitting on a sofa. "The man wants you dead or destroyed."

"Do you remember the letter from the former president?"

Hudson asked, ignoring her statement while pulling on a pair of dark jeans.

She gave him a look that said, *How could I forget?* It had been a rhetorical question. Hudson knew his wife never forgot even a syllable she'd heard. He often joked that Melissa remembered things she'd never even been told.

He pulled out the letter from a locked drawer and read the last section.

**You ran on a promise of change. It may not go as you had planned, but there are many ways to change things. Always start with the preamble and go about it as if handling a photograph in a dark room. Careful and conscientious resolve will produce good results. With your love of history, I know you'll find solace in the knowledge that all your predecessors have been where you are now. The key, my friend, is your intelligence. As for my remaining advice: keep the Constitution handy. The framers were incredibly wise. Just look at Article II—that is how to proceed. And rely on the Father. His will be done.**

"When I first read this, I thought that "Father" meant God. It doesn't. It's the Father of our country, George Washington."

"So?" Melissa, a good listener, had a talent for giving the appearance of enthusiastic interest to something she'd heard before, even many times before.

"And the 'Article II, that is how to proceed' I assumed meant Article II of the Constitution, which deals with the president and the executive branch, where the framers laid out the structure of the government."

"Makes sense." She looked for a necktie, hoping he'd finally wear one again, but then noticed they'd all been cleared out.

"Yeah, but what we call 'Amendments' are written in the

Constitution as 'Articles'," Hudson said, pacing the room. "So the Article II in the letter is talking about the second Amendment. 'A well regulated Militia, being necessary to the security of a free State, the right of the people to keep and bear Arms, shall not be infringed.'"

"Why didn't the president just write that?"

"Because the REMies read the letter. Don't you see? The president was trying to help me!" Hudson's arms were flailing as he spoke excitedly. "And that's not all. Remember, it was the portrait of Washington that made me think of using the people to fight the REMies. Well, I checked. The former president had that portrait of Washington put up there just before I took office."

"That does seem odd to change the portraits in the final days," Melissa said, pausing to look closely into his eyes.

"And it wasn't just one portrait changed. Lincoln and Kennedy were also put up. Before that, Roosevelt, Jefferson, and Truman had been hanging. It's no accident, Melissa. It was a message." He buttoned up a light gray collared shirt.

"What's the message?" Melissa asked, getting up and walking over to a tray where she poured herself some orange juice. "I could see Washington, but why Lincoln? Kennedy?"

"The message is that it's possible to beat the REMies. Lincoln presided over a civil war—"

"Lincoln was assassinated."

"The REMies killed him."

"Oh, how encouraging," Melissa said. "Kennedy was also assassinated."

"Yeah . . . You know what I think? He tried to defy the REMies and they had him ambushed in Dallas."

"It sounds less like a clue to encourage you, and more like a warning to keep you in line."

"Maybe if Washington wasn't there, maybe if the letter didn't point me toward the Constitution and specifically the Second Amendment."

"I don't know," she said, handing him a charcoal-colored sport coat.

"'A well regulated Militia, being necessary to the security of a free State, the right of the people to keep and bear Arms, shall not be infringed,'" he repeated, putting on the coat and looking approvingly in the mirror.

"You want Thorne to help you sell an armed uprising?" Melissa asked. "Isn't that what NorthBridge is doing?"

"No one has ever proven a connection," Hudson said, taking a sip of her orange juice. "And I'm not talking about an uprising. I just want the people to say 'enough!' I wish it could happen with people just gathering by the thousands, standing silently night after night and shaking their keys."

Melissa looked puzzled.

"That's how then Czechoslovakia freed itself from forty-one years of communist rule and oppression."

"Shaking their keys?" she asked, hearing something new in his voice.

"The people had finally had enough. Without benefit of newspapers, radio, television, and before the internet and social media existed, solely by word of mouth, they began to gather in mid-November 1989, and by December twenty-ninth, it was all over. They were free!"

"What did they do?"

"Like Mandela in South Africa, the man they wanted as their leader had been in prison. They petitioned for his release, and in the early days of their new freedom, the poet, Vaclav Havel, became their elected president in the first democratic election since 1946."

"Amazing," Melissa said. "But I still don't understand about the keys."

"They symbolized the unlocking of doors for them and saying 'goodbye, it's time to go home,' to the communists."

"Great story, but things are much different here."

"The fact that the people are armed just means the REMies will have to listen," Hudson said.

"I think the letter was a warning. Don't wind up like Lincoln and Kennedy."

"Sure, it's also a warning, but it's mostly an answer—revolution, civil war. The people will topple the tyrannical government controlled by the elites."

# CHAPTER THIRTY-SIX

Tarka measured the remaining moments until she would drop into the warm ocean. Counting seconds was something she did automatically. Every mission came down to seconds, or, more precisely, fractions of seconds. She knew everything she could do measured in the tiniest slivers of time—how long a muscle movement would take, a breath, a sprint to cover, to reach a target. Success or failure, living and dying, all came down to the timing. She could also calculate the remaining darkness prior to dawn, or in daylight, she'd gauge the flow of shadows, the sound of a breeze through the trees.

In this case, the moonless night would provide most of their cover for the operation. The jungle, the tides, wind direction, ocean depths, all had been taken into account.

Her entire life was the mission. Whatever the current one was, it acted as friend, lover, work, relaxation, *purpose*. However, this one was even more important to her. Not because it meant so much to the president of the United States, whom she'd already spent more than a year protecting, but because the woman she was seeking to rescue was a member of Tarka's sisterhood. Like her, Rochelle Rogers had paid so much for events of their youth which were beyond their control.

As Tarka dropped into the dark water, she worked to release the distractions. Like Rochelle, Tarka learned young the desperate agony of losing a loved one, to be crushed under the weight of being a victim. The two women also shared the empowering feeling of taking matters into their own hands, quenching a thirst for revenge so raw that one could kill easily and often. Having read Rochelle's file, Tarka had been horrified at the events leading to the assassination of the Ohio governor, and impressed by the woman's determination to want to make the perpetrators pay.

And now a man Tarka despised was making Rochelle suffer yet again, imprisoning her yet again, and doing who-knew-what to her yet again. Tarka considered Bastendorff the devil incarnate, and not just because he was a master manipulator. Vonner, the man she worked for, shared that ugly trait. She considered that an unfortunate fact about her employer, yet Vonner's version seemed somehow far more palatable than Bastendorff's. Each man had used riots, lies, conjured news, fabricated causes, financial enslavement, coups, assassinations, whatever, to advance his agenda.

After leaving Tarka and the rest of the extraction team, the boat set off to their rendezvous point, careful to keep a safe distance from the island until the VS agents had Rochelle. As she SCUBAed toward the beach, she was having difficulty clearing her mind. This was the closest mission she'd ever had to Bastendorff, whom she referred to as "sinister". The REMie billionaire had a long history of sponsoring terrorists like those who had killed her parents. In fact, although she didn't have all the evidence yet, she had enough to conclude that Bastendorff had been the "master" behind the murder of her parents.

*He robbed me of my childhood*, she thought as she adjusted

the speed of her Underwater Propulsion Jet machine, or "UPjet", the seconds still counting off in her head. She knew Bastendorff would never be at this remote island in the Philippines, but taking Rochelle from him would strike the first blow, help to undermine his grand scheme, and move her closer to revenge.

Right now, though, she had to banish those thoughts, to forget Bastendorff even had anything to do with the mission. The island, anything but a fortress, was still well defended by cold and battle-hardened soldiers the billionaire had recruited from the vast network of mercenaries regularly used by REMies to do their dirty work. There was no backup for her team, no armed helicopters on standby. This was a lean, stealth operation that must remain invisible.

The team emerged from the water twenty-five feet apart from each other and joined into a single unit only when they were sure they had not been detected. This part of the island was not monitored by electronic surveillance due to the impenetrable jungle. That meant they would have to navigate around the perimeter, sticking to the shoreline until they reached more open beaches, almost a mile around the rocky waters. The high tide left the beach non-existent, and the rocks, roots, and other hazards in the water meant their UPjets were useless.

Utilizing night vision goggles, the team pushed on, and thirty-three long minutes later, they reached the first solar panel-adorned com-tower. Tarka spoke in hand signals. One agent peeled off and found the door. The tower, located at the beginning of the surveillance area, also told them they were less than five hundred feet from a guard station.

They hit silently, in fast, practiced motions that gave the man no time to react. He wasn't killed because there was no need. Instead, he was injected with a fast-acting sedative and bound. He'd likely awaken in a few hours, by which time Tarka and her team would be long gone.

Picking up speed on the well-maintained trail, they were rejoined by the agent who'd remained at the first solar tower to sabotage the monitoring equipment. The team successfully repeated the procedure at the next two com-towers and guard stations. Advanced intel had shown there would be no other obstacles between them and the main compound, located a quarter of a mile inland. They would ignore and avoid the two remaining com-towers and guard stations located on the island's northeast coast.

The last guard station they'd hit had been located at a long pier, where two small powerboats were moored. After searching the entire area, the team put a series of small explosives in place. They moved silently onto an area they called the "crossroad." One trail continued around the shore to the two remaining com-towers. The other, bigger trail, more like a narrow dirt road, went to the main compound.

Tarka then led them swiftly, but cautiously, down the edges of the narrow dirt road toward the main compound where Rochelle was being held. After the extraction, the plan called for them to retrace this part of the route back to the pier. One of the powerboats would be their transport out to the rendezvous point.

As they reached the end of the road, the team spread out and took up position on the edge of the jungle, where they waited and silently watched.

"I don't like it," Tarka said to her second in command as she looked through night vision binoculars.

"Why not?" the man asked. "It's exactly as we expected. Three exterior guards in front, two of them look asleep. Two more should be in the rear. They sure don't seem to be expecting trouble."

"I know. It all matches the satellite data," she said in a quiet, tense voice. "There should be a total of thirteen soldiers on the island, we've taken out three, there are two more at the other stations, we're looking at three—"

"That's eight," the man said, finishing her tally. "Plus two in the back and three inside. Let's do this and pull our target before the sun blows our cover."

Tarka scanned the trees, the roof, even turned the binoculars back up the road they'd just come down. "It seems too easy," she muttered. They could take out the three soldiers in front in a matter of seconds . . .

"Come on," her second in command urged. "There's no option to abort this one," he reminded her. Most missions were go or no-go, at least to a point, but as soon as they'd slipped into the water, this one was a go. She knew international ramifications, the fate of Pound's presidency, the lives of her unit, and, of course, the freedom of Rochelle Rogers, all rested in her actions over the next few seconds.

She took one last quick scan of the area. "Okay, go." She pointed to three of the VS agents who had already been designated. Those three would skirt the perimeter, take out the two rear guards, and come in from the back of the structure at the same time Tarka and the other three hit the front.

One hundred and forty seconds later, they fired the first muffled shots.

Moments later, they were inside.

Eighty-two seconds after that, Tarka's team had taken out the inside men and found their target.

"Rochelle Rogers?" Tarka asked for verification.

In the glare of Tarka's flashlight, Rochelle awoke, startled, looking older than forty-six. The skinny black woman could have been sixty, but Tarka knew it was her, and didn't wait for an answer.

"We're here to rescue you," Tarka said, trying to force a smile, wanting to be as gentle as possible, but knowing they weren't safe yet. In the dim glow of her flashlight, the house looked like an upscale vacation rental. *Nice prison if you had to be in one.* "I need you to cooperate. We've got a quick walk to the pier and a short boat ride. Can you do it? Are you okay?"

Rochelle nodded, looking around. Tarka spotted shoes and handed them to Rochelle, who was pulling on a sweater over her night clothes.

"Let's go," Tarka said to the two team members who'd gone into the bedroom with her. They picked up the rest of them as they moved through the house and back out onto the road.

Rochelle managed to keep up as the team moved swiftly through the darkness. Tarka, with her night vision goggles, watched every tree they passed with suspicion. She simultaneously counted steps and seconds, constantly calculating contingencies and fallback positions. Near the end of the road, Tarka sent two agents ahead to be certain the pier was still clear and to ready the boat. Another was sent to watch the beach leading to the northeast side of the island to make sure soldiers from the remaining outposts didn't show up.

She paused to give her agents a head start to their assignments and let Rochelle catch her breath. That's when the trouble began and Tarka stopped counting.

## CHAPTER THIRTY-SEVEN

I t was unlike the Wizard to send word for a call. Usually he waited for Hudson to check in with him, so when Schueller gave his father the message that the Wizard needed to speak with him right away, Hudson knew something big had happened.

"What is it?" Hudson asked as the matrix pattern ended and the Wizard came through, staring into the camera with an expression of dread. Hudson's small hope that the Wizard had some good news crumbled.

"Garland is dead," the Wizard said.

Hudson felt an involuntary shiver. "That means there's only four of us left," he said, wondering if the Wizard's expression was closer to fear than dread. "You, Gouge, his dad, and me."

"That's right," the Wizard said. "We're the last men standing. There's no such thing as an isolated system anywhere in the universe, you know what I'm saying? How do you explain that? It's space. Space is what connects us all, touches each of us. One proton joins the next, and the next, and so on until there's you."

Hudson shook his head. "Who's next?"

"Nobody knows where I am," the Wizard said. "I'm impossible to find. You're the most protected man on the planet. Gouge has been in hiding ever since Zackers was killed, but Gouge's dad is a sitting duck. Seems likely they'll hit him next."

"We can't just let them die," Hudson said, staring at the keys on his laptop. Gouge's old man was also Hudson's uncle. They'd never been close, even before that night Rochelle was raped and her brother killed, but after that, Hudson couldn't stand the sight of him. Part of Hudson thought the mean bastard actually *deserved* to die. "Should we warn him?"

"What, and admit we were there when it all went down?" the Wizard asked. All those years, they'd never let the perpetrators know they'd been there and seen what happened.

"It's a little late to be worried about that now. What's he going to do if he finds out we know?"

"It's probably not a good idea for anybody to know you were there that night."

"Somebody obviously already knows," Hudson said. "Bastendorff had Rochelle, so he must know. And who knows who else?"

"What are they going to do with that information?"

"I'm afraid to find out," Hudson said, feeling himself breakout in a clammy sweat.

"I'll call him," the Wizard said. "It's too dangerous coming from you."

Later that night, Melissa and Hudson resumed their conversation about Cherry Tree, the plan to bring down the REMies.

"It's too dangerous," Melissa said.

"I've been hearing that a lot lately," Hudson replied, slipping into bed. He explained the call with the Wizard.

"When were you going to tell me someone's been executing everyone who was there?" Melissa asked.

He was about to say that he didn't want to worry her, but caught himself before walking into that minefield. "We don't know for sure they're going after the Wizard, Gouge, and me."

"You said yourself they went after Gouge."

"That could just have easily been REMies. They've been looking for him ever since he took off with the drive Zackers gave him. And they can't get to me."

"Maybe," she said. "But killing you isn't the only way to harm you. They can put out the whole story about that night and Rochelle . . . "

"I know, but it doesn't matter," Hudson said. "There are three things I must do as president: correct the wrongs that were done to Rochelle by making sure she's free, find and stop NorthBridge, and, most important of all, expose the REMies' system of control and bring down their empire."

"*All* of those things are too dangerous," Melissa repeated.

"There's that phrase again."

"NorthBridge has tried to kill you *repeatedly*. In fact, you may recall that last time, for nine minutes, they succeeded."

"We don't know that the last time was NorthBridge."

"Who else would it have been?" Melissa asked, scowling. "Let the FBI, Covington's FaST squad, and Dranick take care of NorthBridge. You don't need to go on some crusade against—" Her eyes went glassy. "I don't want to lose you again."

He started to speak, but then saw the tears running down Melissa's cheek. He leaned over and put his arms around her.

"How do you think I feel each time you take a bullet?" she asked.

"I do think of that, but when I was elected . . . I don't belong to just you anymore. I belong to the American people. I have to get this country right again. I have to stop the terror . . . if that's even possible."

"That's not fair."

"I know," he said, pulling her close. "But it's true. We have to be brave. This isn't just about the future of our country and our freedom, the REMies have made a system that is unsustainable. Can you imagine if the economy collapses? If law and order break down? It's closer than we think . . . the end is just a few bad decisions away."

"The REMies won't let you win."

Hudson nodded. "I wasn't going to ask their permission."

"That's a far tougher fight than NorthBridge," Melissa said, gently holding his head and looking intensely into his eyes.

"We can't let the REMies continue to rule the world because the problem is too big to solve."

"They are sooo big," she said, kissing his forehead. "Talk to Vonner, he knows. The REMies are huge beyond anything. We can't even fathom the trillions of dollars they control. We'll need more than fifty million Americans with guns. How can we stop them?" She smiled through her tears. "I don't think jingling keys will work."

When Hudson saw her familiar pattern of bravery, it almost broke his heart. "We're working on it," he said softly. "We're accumulating proof of their existence, proof of everything they've done, and when we have enough, and the timing is right, we'll release it. When we show the proof to the country, to the world, everyone will know that they've been manipulated, and that millions have died and suffered and toiled for the benefit of a few hundred wealthy elites who imagine themselves kings or emperors, who think they can rule better than we can, who think they're above the masses and that they deserve more."

"NorthBridge might not have succeeded yet in killing you, but the REMies, they won't miss. You know they have Secret Service agents who could murder you in your sleep anytime they want."

"I'm sorry, honey. As you said, it's not fair, but you've got to get used to this and realize that I believe some things are worth dying for."

He knew instantly that he would always regret saying that to her, giving her an inestimable burden, but he couldn't do otherwise. He had no choice.

# CHAPTER THIRTY-EIGHT

Thorne's visibility and popularity had been increasing ever since he lost the primaries to Hudson, but it had grown even more radically since the inauguration. And with each NorthBridge attack, the shock-jock seemed to somehow gain more stature among the tens of millions of Americans dissatisfied with the current system. In recent months, he'd become the de facto opposition party leader. Some were actually calling him the public face of NorthBridge. Although he denied any knowledge or affiliation with the terror group, many in the media believed otherwise. The FBI had investigated and found no link, but that didn't stop the speculation. The Director of National Intelligence, David Covington, with his new authority, had assigned a FaST squad to Thorne, hoping, once and for all, to clear or condemn the shock-jock.

The Find and Stop Terrorist squads, with their catchy FaST acronym, were a popular subject among journalists as progress was finally beginning to happen in the battle against North-Bridge. Covington himself made an impressive and authoritative guest on news shows. FaST was proving to be far more successful than the Brickman Effort, Dranick, previous FBI initiatives, or even those of the military. In fact, over the course of the previous twelve days, FaST had rounded up hundreds of NorthBridge members. Covington claimed much more was coming, with an even larger crackdown in the works. The media began selling Covington as a hero, and it seemed that NorthBridge might finally be getting some resistance.

On his highly-rated radio show, Thorne declared that he didn't believe FaST was arresting real NorthBridge members. "Instead," he said, "Covington is using NorthBridge as an excuse to send his storm troopers after dissenters, which includes anyone who doesn't agree with what the elites want, and specifically those opposed to an illegal war with China. A FaST agent couldn't find a real NorthBridger if one was standing next to him."

The same day that Thorne was making headlines with his controversial claims, Dranick and the FBI Director made similar suggestions to the president in private.

"Covington is going after normal American citizens," Dranick told Hudson in the Oval Office. "Albeit we're talking about Americans on the fringe—conspiracy theorists, groups wanting to abolish the Federal Reserve, tax protesters, militia members, Tea Partiers, etcetera."

"People who might have been sympathetic to NorthBridge," the president said.

"Yes, but with no known connection, no history of violence, and, in most cases, no criminal record at all."

"Covington has turned an abandoned military base into a large prison camp where there are already rumors of extreme interrogation methods being utilized," the FBI Director added.

"How is that possible?" the president asked.

"He's had them deemed enemy combatants. That gives him

the authority, at least until the appeals and challenges work their way through the federal court system."

"I'm not going to allow my administration to be part of suppressing the Constitutional rights of American citizens," Hudson said. "Covington works for me!"

The president buzzed his secretary and asked her to get the DNI on the phone immediately.

"Did you see the *Raton Report* this morning?" Dranick asked. "She hits you pretty hard on this."

"I don't care what Fonda Raton does," Hudson answered a little too gruffly.

"Maybe you should," Dranick said. "Fonda Raton wrote the piece herself, citing sources that Covington was using the North-Bridge situation as a cover to round up Americans problematic to the administration."

Dranick's assistant, a twenty-something private in the army, sitting across the room, looked up from a laptop. "If I could interrupt?"

"Go ahead," Dranick said.

"The mainstream media is calling Thorne and Fonda Raton 'terrorist sympathizers', and pounding the message that FaST is nailing NorthBridge."

"No surprise," Hudson said. "I bet it's unanimous." He knew the mainstream media was owned and controlled by the REMies. "With all the arrests, maybe people will allow themselves to feel safe again."

"Yes, sir," the assistant said. "Most of the stories are like this one. The long national nightmare is finally coming to an end."

"The public has grown so frustrated, so scared, and so desperate for action, that it won't take much to convince them that these sweeps are a good thing," Dranick said. "There sure isn't broad support for the types he's picking up—rabble-rousers, misfits, and complainers."

"Early crosschecks into our database shows that the majority of FaST arrests are gun owners," the FBI Director added.

Hudson thought of the Second Amendment and his Cherry Tree plan. He buzzed his secretary. "Do you have Covington yet?"

"We're having trouble reaching him, Mr. President."

"Keep trying, and interrupt me the minute you get him."

"The *Raton Report* also shows that Covington has utilized the Three-D system extensively. She alleges that Three-D has been spying on citizens. If they did anything that seems counter to the state, a FaST unit shows up and either harasses or arrests the parties."

"Unbelievable!" Hudson said.

"Again, mainstream media is reporting that those allegations are baseless NorthBridge propaganda," the assistant chimed in.

"I know Fonda Raton," Hudson said. "She may be a lot of things, but she's no terrorist. She's a journalist, a real one, a damn good one."

"Ironic that you find yourself on the same side as Thorne, Fonda Raton, and even NorthBridge," Dranick said. "How do you deal with that? I imagine Fitz is going to have a heart attack."

When the president finally reached Covington on the phone a few hours later, the DNI denied Fonda and Thorne's accusations.

"Mr. President, even *you* must know that Thorne and Raton are radicals," Covington said, making the word "you" sound as if Hudson had just spilled red wine in the DNI's new car. In a flash of annoyance, Hudson was certain he could detect the sound of Necco wafers clicking in Covington's mouth in a pool of bitter saliva. "Nothing they spout can be trusted. Both Thorne and

Raton have extreme agendas, and while we still don't have any proof they're associated with NorthBridge, they have certainly never condemned them."

"That may be, but I'm going to ask the Office of the Inspector General to look into the matter."

"You do that," Covington said curtly.

"In addition, I'm going to ask Colonel Dranick to chair an oversight committee to review FaST practices," the president said. "Specifically, I want to be certain that you're not using FaST in any of the manners charged in the *Raton Report*."

Covington stifled a laugh. "Mr. President, I know you suffered . . . how do I say this? I'm not sure what damage may have resulted to your reasoning capabilities during those infamous nine minutes when you were dead, but it is extraordinary that you're seeking to impede an investigation by the Director of National Intelligence into the very people who attempted to assassinate you based on the hearsay of a known communist."

"If what you say is true, David, then you have nothing to worry about."

After the call ended, Hudson contacted Dranick to ask him to convene an oversight committee.

"I'm sure Covington *loves* that idea," Dranick said sarcastically.

"The man always seems angry to me," Hudson said. "Not sure what it is."

"NorthBridge just issued a statement, signed by AKA Franklin, insisting that several of the people Covington's FaST have in custody have never been members of their organization."

"I can hear Covington now. 'Who are you going to believe, a bunch of terrorist scum, or the Director of National intelligence with a decade's long history of patriotic duty?'"

"Tough choice, given the circumstances," Dranick said.

# CHAPTER THIRTY-NINE

Tarka didn't *see* the VS agent next to her take a bullet in the face, or his night vision goggles exploding off his head. She *heard* it. Before his dead and bloody body hit the dusty road, Tarka was already diving for cover, pulling Rochelle down beneath her at the same time. The two women rolled into a ditch overgrown with broad green leaves and thorny brambles.

"Who's shootin' at us?" Rochelle screamed.

"The people who've been holding you and don't want us to free you," Tarka whispered, putting a hand gently but firmly over Rochelle's mouth. "Now, if you don't want to die in this ditch, I need you to stay calm and do what I say."

Rochelle nodded.

"Light a fire," Tarka said quietly into her radio. A couple seconds later, an explosion ignited a section of the forest a hundred feet ahead of them. The two VS agents still with her provided cover as Tarka and Rochelle crawled through the thick vegetation. They made it thirty feet before a dozen soldiers dressed in all black emerged from the jungle opposite them.

"Bring on the sun! Bring on the sun!" Tarka shouted into her radio.

Flash bombs lit the area almost instantly as Tarka, Rochelle, and the two VS agents jumped to the road and sprinted desperately toward the pier. Just as the jungle went dark again, Tarka tackled Rochelle back into the ditch. Machinegun fire sprayed all around them. This time Tarka saw the VS agent go down, nearly cut in half. Then, unbelievably, she saw something worse.

Another dozen soldiers were coming from the direction of the pier.

"Are any of the team left?" she yelled to the last VS agent with her, after the agents at the pier and the one headed to the other towers didn't respond by radio.

He pointed to the soldiers, all coming from the direction the other three agents had gone. "Assume no."

"Obviously the intel was very wrong," Tarka shouted, her mind struggling for answers. She'd been told there would only be thirteen soldiers on the island. The most recent satellite data confirmed that count. Now she had no idea how many they were facing—certainly dozens. Tarka started counting again. There were three of them left, and only two armed. She crawled back to the downed VS agent and grabbed his weapon and extra clips. "Can you shoot?" she asked Rochelle.

Rochelle nodded. "Not that though," she said pointing to the Heckler & Koch MP5K machine gun.

"A gun's a gun," Tarka said, knowing Rochelle had killed a man. "Point, aim, fire, except this one is easier. You don't need to aim too much, just spray bullets at anything that moves." She looked at the scared woman. "Got it?"

"Yeah."

Tarka tried the radio again. "Give me rainbows. Give me rainbows."

Nothing.

She signaled her last agent. *Move.*

The man had seen covert combat in fourteen countries. He'd survived other ambushes, but this was the worst situation he'd ever been in. He kept low, and moved like a snake through the brush.

*The soldiers aren't shooting,* Tarka thought. *They must be trying to take Rochelle alive.* It was probably the only advantage she had left. Tarka still believed they were going to die, but if the soldiers really had been ordered to take Rochelle alive, they just might live a little longer.

Tarka was counting—ten feet to the crossroad. She signaled the agent. *Get into the jungle.* It was their last option. They'd never make it in the open, and even if they made it through the crossroad, it was still eighty yards to the pier. If any VS agents were still alive, they'd be there waiting to help.

*If we can get to the boat, we can blow the pier and maybe make the rendezvous.*

The ditch had been tough going, especially for Rochelle, who was just in night clothes and a sweater, but the jungle was much worse. Like a tangled wall, it was nearly impenetrable. Tarka and the other VS agent both used their hunting knives—cutting, pulling, pushing, breaking, stomping. Too slow. Much too slow.

They could hear the voices behind them. Tarka counted some angle of breaths and grunts in a formula she'd learned in many dark pursuits over the years. Her guess was the soldiers were eighteen feet behind them. Two minutes more and they would be on top of them. She thought of turning and shooting, but figured that might end the soldiers' "keep Rochelle alive" order. They might do better as prisoners, but she knew the soldiers would only keep Rochelle. She and the other VS agent would be shot immediately. Her mission was to rescue Rochelle. If she couldn't do it today, then the next priority was to keep Rochelle alive so someone else could rescue her later. Damn.

She tried the radio again. "Rainbow, rainbow."

Static.

Sixty seconds later, they'd only moved four feet. The soldiers had gone eight. *Now or never,* she thought.

She whispered to the agent and Rochelle, "Turn and fire on three, two, one!"

Tarka sent a flash bomb as the three opened fire. They took out at least nine soldiers before the shooting stopped. The agent reported "no injuries." Tarka was also clear. She checked Rochelle—all good.

At least for the moment, the soldiers had fled back toward the road. The agent and Tarka resumed trailblazing while Rochelle covered the rear.

Tarka thought they had a chance now if they could do that maneuver one more time and the jungle thinned a little. If at least one of her guys was still alive out there, just maybe, they could make it to the pier. And if the boats were still unprotected . . . A lot of ifs, but it was possible.

Then they heard the helicopter.

# CHAPTER FORTY

The jungle was too thick. She could see neither the chopper, nor where the soldiers were. Then it got loud. Really loud. Explosions.

Machine-gun fire from multiple sources—more than ten.

Screams.

Shouts.

"Keep going!" Tarka yelled. The VS agent was less than two feet from her, but he still couldn't hear. She turned and gave hand signals. All three of them began thrashing violently through the unyielding vegetation. Tarka cleared sweat from her eyes. Rochelle was panting. They pushed and climbed their way across the damp tangle until suddenly Tarka tumbled onto the beach. She slid her night goggles back on and saw the pier and the boats. The area appeared deserted. Most of the gunfire sounded as if it was coming from the area around the crossroad.

"Let's go!" There was no time for counting or waiting. *Got to get to the boat.*

Tarka held onto Rochelle's arm as they raced to the pier.

They hit the boards in full stride, but were now fully exposed. Tarka released her grip on Rochelle and began running sideways with her weapon aimed toward the crossroad. She didn't know how many of the three VS agents, who had gone ahead before the soldiers appeared, were still alive, engaging the soldiers, allowing Tarka and Rochelle to get away, but the idea of leaving them behind to die while she escaped was torture.

The intensity of the firefight at the crossroad suddenly ended, and Tarka knew her team was gone. She called ahead to the last VS agent, who was just boarding the boat.

"The soldiers are heading this way! Let's—"

The boat and the one next to it exploded into a thousand splintered shards of wood and fiberglass. The last VS agent was vaporized. A lethal fireball engulfed them in a split second and expanded outward so fast that Tarka and Rochelle were thrown fifteen feet backwards.

Tarka crashed down onto the collapsing pier, the wind knocked out of her. As she tried to catch her breath and get up, intense pain in her left arm pulled her back down. It was certainly broken. Wincing from the agony, she called out Rochelle's name, but after several attempts at yelling louder, she realized she couldn't even hear her own screams.

Forcing herself up, she scanned the area. Turning away from the extreme heat coming off the still-burning pier, Tarka saw soldiers heading down the beach toward her. The helicopter that had fired the grenades into the boat landed behind them. She frantically looked for Rochelle, thinking they might still make it back into the jungle. Every moment, Tarka desperately counted —options, seconds, the calculated steps and distance to the soldiers storming in her direction.

Suddenly, she caught a glimpse of Rochelle splashing in the water.

Tarka, her survival instincts kicking in without her consciously knowing, somehow got to the edge of the collapsing pier, braced her legs around one of the posts, and hung over. She stretched her right arm, extending her hand to Rochelle. Even in her inverted position, Tarka could see the soldiers rushing toward them. They had obviously spotted her among the fire and wreckage. Rochelle reached out and wrapped a wet hand around Tarka's wrist. They locked together. Tarka ignored the excruciating injury and hoisted Rochelle back onto the burning pier.

"Can you run?" Tarka shouted at the soaking wet woman. They could hear, but not well over the echoing ringing in their ears.

"Yes," Rochelle replied, gasping. "But where?" Both women looked from the flames on one side of them to the fast approaching soldiers.

"I don't know," Tarka admitted. "But we have to try. Come on!"

They darted down the debris-littered pier toward the beach. They might be able to slip through before the soldiers reached them, but not if the men decided to shoot. It would be the final test of whether or not the order to take Rochelle alive was ironclad.

"But there are no boats left, and we're on an island," Rochelle yelled as they ran. "We've got no way off. How long can we hide in the jungle?"

Rochelle thought of the still-hidden UPjets. "There is a way."

But ten yards from the tree line, the soldiers caught up.

"Hands on your head," one of them ordered, menacingly waving a machine gun at them. "Now!"

As Rochelle placed her hands on top of her head, Tarka's eyes darted quickly, trying to find a possible escape, any advantage. There was none.

"My arm is broken," Tarka pleaded.

"Do it now," the man barked, shooting above her head.

Tarka started to force her lame arm up, gritting her teeth.

"Kill her," another solider said. "We don't need her."

"*I* might need her," the first man replied slyly.

"No time for that, you idiot, she's trouble. Kill her!"

Tarka eyed their helicopter, the rotors still spinning. She counted the distance, saw the process of getting there. She could reach it alone, but not with Rochelle . . .

"Don't worry, I'll kill her soon enough." The man licked his lips.

"Do what you want, but make sure you kill her," the first soldier said, "because you know damned well our employer will kill *you* if anything goes wrong."

Tarka wasn't listening anymore. With nothing to lose, a plan formed in her mind.

Get to the helicopter. She'd come back for Rochelle. If she got lucky, she could kill most of the soldiers from the air. If not, it would be a better way to die.

"What could go wrong?" The man laughed. "I'll finish up with her, give her to any of the boys that want a turn, and then she's fish-food."

Before the other soldier could respond, the helicopter blew apart. Shrapnel and debris went flying as everyone dove for cover. Tarka rolled into the sand and brought down Rochelle, pushing their momentum toward the jungle. She kicked a soldier in the face and grabbed his gun in one flawless motion.

"Look!" Rochelle screamed, pointing to the sky.

Tarka shot three soldiers before looking up. She might have hit more, but shooting an assault rifle with one arm made accuracy impossible.

Another helicopter hovered above the trees, sweeping toward the beach. This one appeared more like a military gun ship than the last. *Damn it*, she thought. More than thirty soldiers were advancing on them. Tarka fired her weapon, hoping to mow down more of them, but the clip was either jammed or empty. Outnumbered and out of options again, she turned to run into the jungle, grabbing Rochelle on the way.

The helicopter swung around and opened fire with two M230 chain guns, which sent a near endless stream of lethal 30mm linkless ammunition slicing through at more than three hundred rounds per minute. Hearing the bullets tearing up the ground, Tarka finally admitted it was over. She'd failed not only in saving Rochelle and punishing Bastendorff, but now she would never have the chance to see that evil REMie die.

Yet, somehow, they reached the jungle. Tarka dropped at the base of a large agathis tree and dared a look back. All the soldiers were dead. The gun ship set down. A voice blasted from a loudspeaker mounted on the side of the helicopter.

"Tarka, this is Paul Grayson. Booker Lipton sent me."

Rochelle, who had run farther into the trees than Tarka before collapsing into the thick underbrush, stood up to look back. "Who's that?"

Tarka didn't know if it was a trap. "I don't know."

"Tarka," Grayson's voice came again, "Bastendorff's got reinforcements on the way. If you want to live, get in now!"

Her arm throbbed, and so did her head. She glanced quickly at Rochelle and the wall of foliage beyond her, still unsure.

Grayson jumped out of the chopper. "Tarka, if we weren't trying to save you, you'd already be dead." He pointed back to the missiles mounted on the attack helicopter. She easily recognized them as AGM-114 Hellfire air-to-surface missiles, or "ASMs." Tarka knew it would take less than a second for those weapons to wipe her and Rochelle off the face of the earth.

"Okay. We're coming out!" Tarka yelled.

"You sure about this?" Rochelle asked.

"Yeah," Tarka lied.

As Grayson helped them aboard, she wasn't sure if they were going to take Rochelle back to Booker, or if they would let her go with the original plan, which meant a trip to see Vonner. There was also the possibility that Tarka, or both of them, would be dumped into the Pacific.

# CHAPTER FORTY-ONE

P aul Grayson turned out to be the angel he claimed to be. After receiving medical treatment for their injuries, and a brief stay on one of Booker Lipton's remote islands, Tarka and Rochelle were released. Hudson immediately messaged the Wizard.

"She's free!"

The Wizard, in turn, let Gouge know. The three members of the Tire Shop Gang all felt a little freer themselves, and more relieved than they ever could have imagined.

Vonner set Rochelle up with a new identity, complete with social security number, driver's license, passport, and even a bank account containing $25,000. For now, he wanted her to stay in a small rental property he owned in a secluded area on the Hawaiian island of Oahu. He promised that once it was safe, she could resettle near her family in Ohio.

Hudson, pleased with the news, instructed Fitz to find a reason for him to visit Hawaii. Vonner gave his approval, as long as it remained secret, but it would still take at least a month before Hudson could get there. Presidential schedules and logistics were immensely difficult to arrange.

He'd waited decades to see Rochelle again, and was anxious to talk to her. In the meantime, both he and Vonner braced for Bastendorff to use whatever he had learned from Rochelle against them.

During the next few weeks, NorthBridge launched more attacks, specifically targeting the 3D system, NSA, and even one directly at Covington's office. Covington declared that the attack on his office proved NorthBridge was lying.

"These animals know we're getting close to their leadership. The hundreds of arrests that *AKA-whomever* pretends weren't real terrorists, have given us innumerable leads to the heart of NorthBridge," Covington said on a news show. "Their faux outrage and the attacks on me personally verify that the vermin we've detained were members of NorthBridge."

The female host fawned over Covington, who was used to the attention. He was a handsome man with thick black hair, and at six-foot-four, he could have been a star athlete. Instead, he'd pursued connections and money. Covington had cultivated his aura of power for decades, and had reached the zenith of his success. But the frustration caused by Pound's insubordinate actions left him constantly furious.

He pulled out a roll of Necco wafers, carefully peeled back the wax paper, and offered the pretty host a pink one, the only flavor of the classic sweets he didn't like. Covington actually loathed the pink flavor, and normally took great pleasure in crushing them under his shoe, reveling in the crunching sound as the intruder of his otherwise candy utopia was destroyed.

That day, on his show, Thorne said: "The United States is

becoming Nazi Germany. FaST is the SS, and Covington, while maybe not Hitler yet, is certainly Joseph McCarthy, the 1950s senator who made false claims about many Americans during the 'red scare,' when fear of communism overtook the nation. 'McCarthyism,' which destroyed many innocent lives, became synonymous with the term 'witch hunt.' One day, I predict the name Covington will be equated with these dark days when anyone who disagrees with the mission of the state, dictated by the elites who hold the leash of politicians, will be unjustly imprisoned, tortured, and destroyed. A time when Three-D cameras invade our every moment, and the most private conversations are monitored and recorded. Even Orwell and Kafka could not have imagined the extent of the power wielded by American intelligence agencies. The media calls him a hero, a savior. To me, David Covington is the Antichrist!"

An assistant ushered Linh and another man onto the expansive back porch of the Florida beach house. After the president hugged Linh, she introduced him to the man she had brought along.

"Mr. President," she said formally, "this is the person I told you about. The one who, like you . . . died."

Hudson looked into the man's eyes as he shook his hand. He could tell immediately that the man had also seen something that few others had, might even know what Hudson saw, what he felt like. "How long?" the president asked. Anyone who'd had a near-death experience knew what the question meant. *How long were you dead?*

"Seven minutes, seventeen seconds."

Hudson nodded. "How?"

"Same as you," the man said, his gentle eyes squinting, as if in pain. "Took a few bullets."

Hudson glanced at Linh. She hadn't told him the man had also been shot. Hudson had only agreed to meet him because Linh asked for the favor, said it would help the man. Hudson knew she'd probably thought it would help him as much as the man himself.

Maybe she was right, he'd thought. Although he'd received thousands of letters from NDE survivors around the world, he'd never actually talked to one. He really hadn't wanted to, because even though he relived those nine minutes every day, Hudson would have been happy to never think about them again.

Still, here he was, face-to-face with another person who'd "slipped the surly bonds of earth."

The two men strolled up the beach, side by side, talking quietly while Linh trailed behind, the ever-present Secret Service agents a bit farther back, a few more walking ahead of them. Half an hour later, an assistant jogged up and told the president his next appointment was waiting.

"Thank you, Linh," Hudson said as they bid each other farewell. "And I look forward to seeing you again," he added, gripping the hand of Paul Grayson.

## CHAPTER FORTY-TWO

The president's next guest might have been more surprising than a man who had also been shot to death. Even several aides, who hadn't been briefed, were stunned to see the president greet one of his most vehement political opponents.

"I'm amused that you actually went through with this meeting," Thorne said as Hudson ushered the shock-jock out to the beach.

"I did it for two reasons," the president began. "First, I wanted to know if your obnoxious and arrogant personality was real, or just a front that you put on for your show."

"There is only one Thorne, and I'm as sharp as they come," he said, smiling proudly, as if he'd said something profound. "We both know I should have your job, and you should be mixing colorants into gallons of paint, maybe duplicating car keys. But, like always, the voters were tricked."

The president stopped and studied Thorne's face, trying to decide if the radio commentator was being serious.

"So, now that you've got that answer," Thorne said with a straight face, "let's hear your second reason."

Hudson still couldn't tell for sure if it was an act. He hoped so. Hudson narrowed his eyes, and in a tone sharper than Thorne's attitude, said, "We may have a lot more in common than it seemed during the campaign."

"I doubt that," Thorne replied, caught by the president's tenacity.

"Hear me out. Specifically, we might have a mutual enemy.

"Who might that be?"

"Assuming you *aren't* actually a member of NorthBridge," Hudson said, giving Thorne another long, probing stare.

"I can tell you this," Thorne said. "I sure as hell don't consider NorthBridge to be my enemy, if that's who you think we share a dislike for."

"You'd be surprised to know that I'm interested in true, perhaps even radical change, as you are."

"I must be on candid camera," Thorne said, looking around as if he were part of an elaborate practical joke.

"Seriously," Hudson said firmly. "I'm hoping to break the grip of those wealthy elites who seem to think the world's governments and their populations are pieces on a chessboard, pawns to be played with."

Thorne returned the president's stare with an incredulous look. "You work for one of those wealthy chess players you just described."

"So do you," Hudson said, raising a brow.

"No," Thorne argued. "That's the difference between you and me. Vonner may own the company I work for, but that doesn't mean I work for him. Your situation is different, he actually *owns* you." Thorne had the smug smile of a man who had just landed a blow and knew he could handle whatever was coming back his way.

"You've never understood my relationship with Vonner."

Thorne laughed. "No, *you've* never understood your relationship with Vonner."

"This will be a lot easier if we just stop arguing about the past and who we both are, and instead talk about our goals for the future. I really think you'll see we have common ground."

"I assumed you brought me here because you're worried about NorthBridge. You think I have influence. Maybe you're starting to believe the talk that there really could be a revolution, or civil war, in America. Perhaps you think I have the power to sway that course."

"You're correct that you're here because I believe you can help, but not because I think you can stop NorthBridge. I want you to assist us when we go after the REMies."

Thorne looked startled, clearly surprised by the word "REMies", enough so that Hudson knew Thorne had most certainly heard it before, and therefore understood the seriousness of the situation. This wasn't just talk about the Illuminati, wealthy families, or global elites, whom Thorne had railed against numerous times on his radio shows.

Hudson could see Thorne trying to figure it out, wondering if this was a REMie effort to lure Thorne in so he could be neutralized, or if Hudson might be the first president who really planned to do something about it. The fact that Thorne knew the word, yet had never used it publicly, meant even the brazen shock-jock feared the cartel of billionaires who ran the world. That sobering thought prevented Hudson from smiling at Thorne's plight, a man who had never been at a loss for words trying to figure out what to say.

"Are you for real?" Thorne finally asked.

Hudson nodded.

"What about Vonner?" Thorne pressed, looking over his shoulder as if waiting for the assassin. "You do know he's a REMie?"

"I told you, he doesn't own me. I don't work for him," Hudson said firmly. "I work for the American people."

Thorne nodded slowly, a slight smile creasing his face. "When? How long has this been going on? Maybe it wasn't NorthBridge taking shots at you all those times. Maybe it was the REMies."

"Tell me what you know about the REMies," Hudson said.

"Why don't you go first, Mr. President."

They talked for another half an hour. Thorne, reluctant to trust the president at first, finally agreed to help after Hudson told him about Cherry Tree.

# CHAPTER FORTY-THREE

Melissa smiled as she entered the Oval Office, happy Hudson had returned from Florida earlier than expected. "How'd it go with our friend?"

"Good. Let's go for a walk."

The first couple wandered the White House grounds in what had become a nearly daily ritual. Hudson filled her in on Thorne, gave her the latest update from Crane's efforts at building a case against the REMies, and was most excited to tell her about Rochelle's new home in Hawaii.

"Yeah, but have you heard Schueller's latest song?" she asked after listening to his ramblings.

"No, is it good?"

Melissa squinted as if maybe she suddenly didn't recognize him. "Aren't all of his songs good?"

He laughed. "You know what I mean."

"You should hear it. Spend some time with him. You, more than any of us, know how short life is. Don't forget to smell the flowers." She winked. "And listen to the music."

Hudson checked in with the Wizard on his way to a recording session where Schueller would be laying down his new song. It was only the third time he'd left the White House since the Air Force One attack to go anywhere other than the Florida beach house or Camp David. But even Fitz agreed that the president of the United States could not be seen as a prisoner in the White House, or, worse yet, a coward.

"Dawg, don't you feel it? Since Rochelle's been free, it's like the internal energy flow is more powerful. Wild how no matter how much the force increases, it's still interdependent on everything else," the Wizard said. "When are you going to see her?"

"In two weeks."

"Does she know you're coming?"

"No, I'm afraid she'll refuse to see me."

"Even after you had her rescued?"

"Thirty years too late," Hudson said as the motorcade rolled down 16<sup>th</sup> Street, closed off for his protection.

"I guess so," the Wizard replied. "Gouge would like to see her, too, but he's afraid."

"Of Rochelle?"

"Of whoever's killing the people who were there that night."

"It's been a while since they struck."

"Well, yeah, they can't get you, and they can't find Gouge, his dad, or me."

"His dad's still in hiding?"

"Yeah, wouldn't you be? I still can't believe how shaky his voice got when I told him that someone knew what had happened."

"He must have been thinking there was a connection between the deaths and Rochelle."

"He'd lost track of a few of the guys, and didn't know."

"Any idea where he went?" Hudson asked as the limousine turned onto Georgia Avenue.

"No, and I don't want to know."

"Then how do you know he's still alive?"

"He checks in with Gouge every few days," the Wizard said. "Dawg, you gotta talk to Gouge. He really wants to see you. You haven't seen him since everything went down— Zackers' drive, all the killings, Rochelle going free . . . "

"Man, I can't," Hudson said. "It's way too risky, for both of us."

"I'll tell him you're gonna try."

"I have to go," Hudson said as The Beast pulled up to the recording studio.

Hudson expected another one of Schueller's "protest songs." His son had become quite popular among college students. His debut album, filled with anti-global elite anthems and cloaked references of their domination, without using the term "REMie", had actually been receiving considerable radio play. He wanted to go on tour, but the security concerns and risks made it impossible.

A minute into the song, Hudson became emotional, as he realized this was no political song. Schueller had composed a beautiful tribute to his late mother.

Hudson nodded to his son as he sung the last words and opened his eyes. Afterwards, he hugged his son. "Will you sing it again?"

Schueller did. When he finished for the second time, he noticed his father was unusually sad. Schueller sang the chorus again, and then again, while looking into his father's eyes, coaxing him to sing along. He repeated the words, again and again. Father and son sang together, softly at first, and then louder, egging each other on. They sang loudly, over each other, reaching a ridiculous high, causing the other band members to laugh out loud. The engineer actually recorded them together! Hudson and Schueller ended up laughing uncontrollably, harder than they had since Schueller's mother died. With tears streaming down their faces, they hugged long and hard.

When Hudson finally pulled away, he wiped his eyes and said, "She would have loved it. Mom would have been so proud of you, and so am I." He paused, and whispered almost inaudibly, "She can hear your songs."

Tarka, her left arm still in a cast, lingered on a rooftop near the recording studio. Now that the president was back in circulation, she had resumed her primary mission of protecting him from all kinds of threats. She sat quietly, monitoring the area, alert to anything remotely out of the ordinary. She observed several Secret Service CAT members, but they didn't see her. A two-person VS backup team was stationed at a nearby restaurant; its Art Deco motif and colored lights illuminating the front entrance were visible from Tarka's vantage point. She could even smell the cooking grease. If all went well, her team would get her takeout, and she'd eat it en route back to the White House, and then, eventually, get back to the hotel and sleep.

Crane, because part of his cover was being a member of

Schueller's band, was also at the studio. He looked the part of a garage band rocker—long frizzy hair, scraggly beard and mustache. He might pass for a twenty-year old drug dealer, but he was twenty-eight, and could code and dance across the DarkNet unimpeded. Instead of playing an instrument, he was working in the corner on a secure laptop. Schueller and Hudson huddled with him as the other musicians cracked some beers in the breakroom.

The Secret Service agents were all outside, every entrance covered. Only two agents covered the inner studio—007, and another whom the president trusted.

"Are we getting closer?" Hudson asked in a hushed tone, even though no one could hear them.

"We're so close. Like train-on-the-tracks close," Crane said. "I've totally got them on the nineteen twenty-nine stock market crash. They planned the whole dammed Great Depression. Check this out."

Crane pulled up several screens in succession showing various graphs, financial data, and other facts which purported to prove the links between REMie activity, the media, and the end result of what they created into historical reality. It was hard to follow, but Crane was working to make it simpler and more digestible, at least for the initial announcements. The Cherry Tree plan called for all the supporting work to be released, documenting the entire REMie history of what was, in fact, an endless series of MADE events and conspiracies.

"And see this?" Crane asked as he pulled up another screen. "You may have heard of what was called 'The Business Plot' or 'The White House Coup,' which took place back in 1933 when a group of 'wealthy businessmen,' which included J.P. Morgan, the DuPonts, the Remington Arms family, and even Prescott Bush— whose son and grandson became president—tried to recruit

Marine Corps Major General Smedley Butler to oust President Franklin Roosevelt in a coup d'état."

"Yes, I always thought of it as just an odd and obscure foot-note in history," Hudson said. "But now, thinking of it in context of all we've learned, it's another piece of the puzzle fit into place."

"Yeah, they weren't just 'wealthy businessmen,' they were REMies, and it was a CapWar," Crane said. "Can you imagine if it had been successful?"

"If I recall correctly, the House of Representatives investigated," Hudson said. "The McCormack-Dickstein Committee on Un-American Activities. But much of it was done in secret, and then the transcripts were heavily edited and redacted. I think the full transcripts of the hearings actually disappeared."

"You really were a history teacher, weren't you?" Crane said. "I think records of the hearing might exist. During the past twenty years, the National Archives has done an amazing job at organizing and digitizing their massive trove of documents."

"I still don't get how incriminating documents would just be left around," Schueller said.

"Remember the first lesson," Hudson replied. "Those who believe the Illuminati exist have always assumed they were one group. That was never true. We now know that it was the REMies, and they do not act as one. Rather, they've been at war with each other for well over a century."

"I know, but—"

"They keep dirt on each other," Crane interrupted. "So somewhere there are documents showing what that coup was all about, and who was involved. And it doesn't stop there. The same bad actors helped fund the Nazis and coerced the US into World War II."

Crane brought up a screen filled with financial transactions between German and American companies and banks during the 1930s, and continuing into the war years. Next, he showed them an overlay of each major war. Hudson had seen the list before, but now Crane was actually documenting how the REMies CapWars had transpired, resulting in a dramatic increase in REMie MADE events.

"Look back at the first world war," Crane began. "Prescott Bush's father, Samuel P. Bush, a close buddy of the Rockefellers, was appointed to the War Industries Board as chief of the Ordnance, Small Arms, and Ammunition Section, meaning he was basically in charge of government dealings with munitions companies. He was also on the board of the Remington Arms Company!"

"REMies sure know how to profit from war," Schueller muttered.

"Remington sold weapons to both sides," Crane said. He switched the screen to the list of major CapWars. Hudson had also seen the list before, but now there was also a color-coded section showing false media stories at the time that helped shape public opinion.

- *1913 – US Federal Income Tax begins and Federal Reserve Bank System established, creating the authority of the private bankers to issue Federal Reserve notes (known as US Dollars today).*
- *1929-1935 – US Stock market crash and worldwide depression. After which the pyramid with the all-seeing eye in the capstone first appeared on the back of the US dollar bill.*
- *1939 – World War II begins.*
- *1963 – US president John F. Kennedy assassinated for refusing to cooperate with the REMies.*
- *1976 – US president Jimmy Carter elected – REMies involvement unclear.*
- *1987 – US and world stock markets crash.*

- *2001 – Terrorist attacks of September 11th.*
- *2008 – Financial crisis and great recession which followed.*

Schueller asked Crane to enlarge another interactive table illustrating how major media companies had aided in selling every US war for the last hundred and twenty-five years.

"It's incredible how many people have died for no reason other than greed and a lust for power," Schueller said.

Through the glass separating the studio from the sound engineer's room, 007 caught Hudson's attention and pointed to his watch. Time to go. They'd been in one place too long. Hudson nodded to agent Bond.

"Much of the media in this country has long been nothing more than an extremely efficient propaganda machine for the REMies," Crane said. "And I have proof. Gypsy is linking it all together."

"How soon until it's ready for prime time?" Hudson asked.

"A few more weeks."

"Make it sooner."

Just before the president headed back to the White House, he told Schueller that Thorne had already begun to implement the early stages of Cherry Tree.

"He's laying the groundwork," Hudson said. "Crane's work will be stage two."

"Do you really think we can trust Thorne?"

"He hates the REMies as much as we do. That's enough."

"I hope you're right," Schueller said. "It's almost like we're putting the REMies on notice. I'm not sure they need any more advantages."

"All we have is the truth," Hudson said quietly. "We have to start telling it."

# CHAPTER FORTY-FOUR

Fitz interrupted the president during a meeting with his secretary of state and other senior advisors about the diplomatic efforts to avoid war with China.

"Mr. President, there's been another NorthBridge attack," Fitz said. "They hit one of our bases in Texas, wiped out seventeen long-range UAVs."

The President and Secretary of State exchanged a worried glance. UAVs, or Unmanned Aerial Vehicles, commonly known as drones, had become the backbone of the US Military's ability to project power around the world. For years, they had been used to bomb targets in more than a half a dozen countries, and they provided a major advantage against China, should war come.

"Predators? Reapers?" the president asked, naming two of the most advanced drones.

Fitz nodded.

"How do we know it was NorthBridge?"

Everyone in the room knew where the question was coming from. NorthBridge had never claimed responsibility for the Air Force One attack, although most people assumed they had done it. The experts knew that NorthBridge had never been linked to an attack that they had not claimed.

"It's on their website," Fitz said. "Along with a statement from AKA Washington about drones not being a fair military tactic. He called UAVs a cowardice tool meant only to advance the corrupt empire of the elites."

Another man entered the room, the administration's expert on NorthBridge. "Sir, we have more on the situation in Texas," he said, addressing the president. "No injuries. Apparently, they timed the strike so it would result in no casualties of any kind except for the UAVs."

"How could they know that?" the president asked.

"They're making a point that they can get anywhere, anytime," the man replied.

"And something else," Fitz added, bristling. "Thorne has already cheered the attack on his radio show, calling for Americans to realize that drones make war too cheap and too easy."

"Covington's going to have a field day with this latest garbage from Thorne," the Secretary of State said. "I can't believe there hasn't already been a FaST raid on Thorne. The guy is a North-Bridge sympathizer at the very least, aiding and abetting after-the-fact, and, for all we know, he might actually be one of their leaders."

The Secretary of Defense walked in with two uniformed aides. "Sorry, Mr. President, I was delayed in overseeing the locking down of all our bases worldwide. We've raised the alert status and already launched an investigation in Texas."

"Any guesses how they could have breached security and timed it to avoid human casualties?" the president asked.

"The Chinese," the Defense Secretary said. "We have indications that the MSS is backing NorthBridge."

Hudson wasn't surprised to hear his own Defense Secretary blaming the Ministry of State Security of the People's Republic of China. It had become fashionable to blame China for every-thing. The media was full of anti-China stories every day.

"What indications?" the president asked.

The Secretary of Defense produced satellite images which purported to show Chinese-made weapons being transferred to NorthBridge in remote areas of Canada, as well as CIA photos of known MSS agents meeting with alleged NorthBridge members.

None of it impressed Hudson. He knew the REMies could easily make anything look the way they wanted.

"All right, keep me posted," the president said. "I've got another meeting."

Fitz gave him a puzzled look. The chief of staff wasn't aware of anything on the schedule until two o'clock, at which time they would be meeting with the Russian ambassador to discuss the Chinese situation, and it certainly seemed they still had more to discuss concerning the NorthBridge attack and the link to China.

Hudson had intentionally allowed longer for the meeting with the secretary of state than he knew it would require, knowing he could carve out some free time from the official calendar to have a quick chat with Fonda Raton on the White House grounds. The unexpected NorthBridge attack made his exit a bit more awkward, but he had his own shadow timetable to consider. Cherry Tree was underway. The REMies were finally going to be challenged.

---

# CHAPTER FORTY-FIVE

F onda smiled as Hudson approached. "You should've seen the look on the man's face when he saw I was whom he had to escort out here."

"Nobody in his right mind can imagine why I would ever meet Fonda Raton, especially these days."

"These days?"

"There's been so many leaks from the administration, and you're the queen of capitalizing on leaks."

"Am I?" Fonda asked, exaggeratingly batting her eyelashes. "You flatter me so."

"Come on, you've got more inside sources than the CIA," Hudson said, smiling.

"But I don't have *all* the sources," Fonda said, turning serious. "There are people inside your administration, very close to you no doubt, who are leaking things—embarrassing things, *important* things—to undermine your popularity and your credibility."

"I've got enemies everywhere, but if you know people inside the White House who are leaking, then name names!"

"Oh, if it were that simple." Fonda turned and walked to admire a rosebush, then faced him again. "But I can tell you why they're doing it. They're preparing for your opposition to the war, and for your attack on the REMies. They're using the leaks to control you and make you seem ineffective, possibly even diminished from your near-death experience. What *did* happen in those nine minutes, Hudson?"

He stared at her for a moment, but said nothing.

"Anyway," Fonda said, smiling awkwardly. "It's working. Your rock-solid approval ratings are beginning to falter."

"I don't care," Hudson said. "As you may already know, I'm planning to give a speech this week in which I will take the military option off the table."

"No." Fonda shook her head. "I don't like the timing."

Hudson scoffed. "I wasn't asking your permission. I really don't care if you like the timing, but I expected your support."

"Oh, Hudson." Fonda started to reach for his shoulder as if she was going to brush imaginary dust off, but she stopped, catching a glance from the Secret Service agents. They always seemed too close. "Sometimes you just have to trust others who have been at this a lot longer than you."

"Trust?" He wanted to trust her, but knew better. "You can't be trusted."

"Of course I can't be trusted, Mr. President. Do you mind if I call you Mr. President?" Fonda winked. "In any case, you're going to oppose the war. What do you think that's going to get you?"

"Hopefully it will get me peace. Hopefully it'll stop this damn war before it gets started. You know there's no real issue for the war; this is all the REMies. It's another REMie MADE event, and the media, as always, is going along for the ride. We have no more business fighting China than we did fighting Russia all those years. This is nonsense."

In his peripheral vision, Hudson noticed a Secret Service agent behind a machine gun emplacement on the White House roof and imagined the man receiving an order to shoot him. Would he follow it? Was he a good one, or one of the agents Bond had described as trained in the 'Critical Move' to kill, or let a president die, for the good of the country? Hudson stared at the agent on the roof for another moment, and then jumped back into his rant.

"Do you know that Frederic Remington, of the REMie Remingtons, was sent to Cuba by newspaper magnate William Randolph Hearst to cover the war? But when he got to the island, nothing was happening, and no trouble was expected, so he sent a cable to Hearst that 'There will be no war,' and Hearst cabled back, 'You furnish the pictures, and I'll furnish the war.' The REMies have been doing this forever, and the media has been *helping!*"

"Of course they have, and of course I agree with you," Fonda said. "And obviously it's the REMies using the media to create the war with China, but if you come out against the war now, they'll just ridicule you, destroy your reputation, and make you into an unpatriotic communist sympathizer bought off by the Chinese. They'll even turn on you and say that the big corporations—ironically, the very ones that the REMies control—have convinced you not to go to war because it will hurt their sales. After all, we import half a trillion dollars of goods a year from China."

"Yeah, before Bill Clinton handed the keys to China, we purchased almost nothing from them. People forget that now . . . now that China is the enemy," Hudson said. "I wish I could take your advice, do everything at the perfect time, but we're a little short on time."

"That we are," Fonda said. "But that doesn't mean doing things in a rush is going to save time."

"Funny, you're in agreement with Vonner, a man you profess to hate and disagree with entirely. He also doesn't think the time is right to oppose the war—or anything, for that matter."

"Of course he doesn't. You keep forgetting he's a REMie. He's the one who's controlling you. Vonner doesn't want you to oppose the war the REMies want. He doesn't want you going after the REMies."

"And he doesn't want me going after NorthBridge either."

"NorthBridge? Then I agree with him again," Fonda said. "What you need to do is start reforms slowly. Don't declare your opposition to the war yet, don't be some big crusader, and don't make yourself a target for all the extreme groups. The right and the left will both hate you. The REMies will take you out. If they don't, then NorthBridge will. *Everybody* will come for you."

"What else is new?"

She frowned. "Come on, Hudson. We need you alive. It's not about opposing this or that, changing who or what. The only hope is to first take the fangs out of the intelligence agencies. That's what keeps the REMies in power. You've got to do this smart."

"*Is* there a smart way?"

"Look, since 1900, only three presidents have defied the REMies," Fonda said. "McKinley—assassinated, Kennedy—assassinated, Carter—"

"*Jimmy* Carter?"

"He refused to play along, but the REMies decided the country was too fragile following Vietnam and Watergate for another dead president, so they made sure he had an ineffective, do-nothing, one-term presidency."

"What about the Camp David accords? Peace between Israel and Egypt?"

"Come on, you know your history," Fonda said with an

incredulous look. "It meant nothing, and led to the assassination of Egypt's leader, Anwar Sadat."

"They haven't tried to assassinate me."

"Haven't they? Who tried to kill you on Air Force One? Everyone thinks it was NorthBridge, but why didn't they take credit for it? They always have in the past."

"If the REMies wanted me dead, then I'd already be dead."

"There are lots of ways to kill a man, and they don't all involve death," Fonda said, picking up some flower petals that had fallen from a rosebush. "People have been so polarized, but there's no difference between what Democrat and Republican presidents do. It's only the media, the propaganda of the elites, that makes it seem so. Just look at Bill Clinton, a darling of the liberals, and yet, as we noted a moment ago, he gave away the economy to Walmart, China, and NAFTA. Clinton made a further gift to Wall Street by repealing Glass-Steagall, and deregulated the risky derivatives market. The guy was a Republican. He expanded the war on drugs more than any other president, made sixty more crimes eligible for the death penalty, and was responsible for massively swelling the prison population with his crime bill that included the brutal 'three strikes' law. I won't even mention Monica. She was just to keep the public distracted—works every time."

"I thought you were a liberal," Hudson said, amused. "What about Bush's taking us to war with Iraq for the invisible weapons of mass destruction?"

"That's my point. They're all the same, and I am a liberal, but Clinton wasn't, and Obama wasn't, at least once they got into office," she said. "They all change because the REMies let them know who's really in charge. But you haven't changed. Well, you have, but in the right way." Fonda gave him a look like a woman about to kiss her lover. "That's why I don't want them to kill you."

"I cannot be the man that ushers in World War III," Hudson said. "I have to stop them from tricking the American people into yet another war . . . the *last* war." He took a deep breath and put his hands in his pockets.

"The public isn't as dumb as you think," Fonda said. "A lot of them have already realized that all the presidents are the same people, just wearing different masks. They know the two-party system—us-versus-them—is bogus. Why are there parties at all? Why can't anyone run for president and get on the ballot? Let them all debate."

"You know why. They control both sides of the table."

"But you, Hudson, you were a mistake. Somehow, they let you slip in. Don't blow our only chance. Don't do it the wrong way." She inhaled the scent of the rose petals, then blew them off her hand, smiled at him, turned, and walked away.

Back in the Oval Office, in advance of the meeting with the Russian ambassador regarding the Chinese situation, Fitz and an aide resumed briefing the president about the NorthBridge strike on the drone base. They read him a new statement from AKA Jefferson saying that NorthBridge was going to continue to destroy the war-making abilities of the United States.

"It is the official position of NorthBridge that a war with China would be catastrophic. Not only for the two countries involved, but for the entire world."

Hudson couldn't believe the timing. Now, if he opposed the war, in addition to siding with Thorne and Fonda Raton, he'd appear to be giving in to NorthBridge's demands.

He sat there a moment, waiting for the Russian ambassador, and replayed Fonda's advice.

*Take the fangs out of the intelligence agencies.*

He shook his head and let out a small, frustrated laugh. "Why not try something easier, like, control government spending?" he said to himself, then pressed a button on his desk and asked for a cup of tea.

# CHAPTER FORTY-SIX

B astendorff placed the final few Legos on the four thousand piece Death Star replica as an assistant waited.

"Okay, what is it?" the billionaire asked with a tone of annoyance very familiar to all who worked for him.

"News broke that a new kind of listening device has been found in millions of Chinese-made products, and millions more computers have preinstalled malware which collects data and sends it to server farms located in China."

Bastendorff smiled. "Let's see how our young American president handles this situation. How is he going to oppose the war now?"

"And have you seen what Brown said?" the assistant asked, handing him a copy of the interview that Vice President Brown gave to a prominent internet news site.

Bastendorff started reading, occasionally mumbling quotes out loud in a sarcastic tone. "Such guff! 'War is always wrong, but I'm not saying I wouldn't do something 'wrong' to defend our country. If I were president, and we were threatened, I would act.' Isn't it nice that Vice President 'Pacifist' Brown would resort to violence under the right conditions? Maybe I should arrange for a group of armed Chinese mercenaries to start shooting up San Francisco. I wonder if that would qualify." Bastendorff pushed a cream-filled pastry into his mouth. "Damn Vonner for giving us this mess to deal with. That loser couldn't choose a decent president even if he was at the signing of the Declaration!" he said through his food, several crumbs hitting his assistant in the face.

Bastendorff stormed into the elevator, leaving his beloved Lego collection behind. As they arrived on a floor of the building that resembled NASA's mission control, only a few technicians looked up from their monitors.

Bastendorff went on reading and ranting as they walked. "The vice president suggests that nations focus their armies solely on the defense of their own established borders. 'That way,' she says, 'the world can know real peace. But in the meantime, if someone tries to invade America, we'll blow the expletive out of them.'"

"Maybe it's a message," the assistant speculated.

"An *irresponsible* message," Bastendorff snapped. "Make sure we bury her with coverage."

The assistant understood the order, and immediately left the billionaire, who continued on alone to a viewing room. The assistant quickly approached a woman seated at a large console surrounded by computer screens and phones.

"US Vice President Brown just gave an anti-war interview," he began. "We need US and European media to ridicule her 'irresponsible and unrealistic statements.' Question her ability to lead, should the need ever arise. Questions should be asked about her ties to China. Dig up some campaign contributions, inappropriate meetings with Chinese officials. You know the drill. Oh, and make sure there are stories in Japan and South Korea media as well. She is to be bombarded with negatives."

"Starting when?"

"Now."

The woman began clicking keys. "How long?

"Until she resigns, or you hear differently."

With the aid of the 3D system, and NSA communications monitoring, the pace of FaST arrests increased daily. The public
applauded as more "NorthBridgers" were put behind bars.
Meanwhile, Crane and the Wizard had turned Gypsy onto
Covington's tactics and "storm troopers." By analyzing those
who'd been arrested, Gypsy showed that those detained had no
links to NorthBridge. Instead, they were mostly people who had
views deemed "inappropriate" by Covington. Most had only
expressed a dislike of 3D, fear of going to war with China, and a
general distrust for government or the media.

Hudson reviewed the findings and called Vonner. "I'm going
to fire Covington."

"You can't do that," Vonner said. "They won't let you."

"You mean *you* won't let me."

"I mean that Covington is the REMies' man."

"He serves at the pleasure of the president," Hudson said.
"That's me, and this thug gives me no pleasure."

"Be that as it may," Vonner said, glancing over at Rex, who
was rolling a handful of multi-colored dice as he watched a bank
of monitors. "You're stuck with him."

"Why?" Hudson pressed. "What happens if I fire him?"

"One, you'll wind up with someone worse—"

"Not if I make Colonel Dranick DNI."

Vonner scoffed, but made no comment. "Two, I think it
would be your last official act as president."

"Is that a threat?" Hudson asked angrily.

"Not from me," Vonner said in his friendliest tone. "It's a warning, though."

"We'll see," Hudson said, ending the call.

Vonner turned to Rex. "Make sure he doesn't do anything stupid. I'll call Fitz, but get some of our other assets mobilized to talk some sense into Hudson."

"Speak of the devil," Rex said. "David Covington, line eight."

Vonner gave him a surprised look. "Can that be a coincidence?"

"Get your boy under control," Covington said as Vonner opened the line.

"He's concerned about FaST."

"I know what troubles the president, but FaST is what's keeping order in this country. Without us, NorthBridge would have the country sliding into a state of anarchy by now."

"Some people see it differently," Vonner said, pouring a scotch and mounting his exercise bike. "There are those who think FaST is a vehicle to remove those who don't want war."

"War *is* coming," Covington said. "The president does *not* get to decide."

"It should at least appear—"

"You want to talk about appearances?" Covington whined. "He runs the country *barefoot* from some Florida beach!"

"We're working on it," Vonner said breathlessly as the digital speedometer passed ten miles per hour. "Just keep cool. These are tricky times. You may think you have a handle on what's going to happen next, but the funny thing about surprises is that they tend to surprise you."

# CHAPTER FORTY-SEVEN

With the stunning success of the FaST raids, people began to support the government's case for war with China. Thorne asserted it was because those opposed to the war had been simply disappearing, but he couldn't prove it. The day that polls first showed a majority of Americans believed war against the communist nation was both necessary and winnable, President Pound did the unthinkable: he gave a speech declaring his opposition.

*"How can we willingly commit to a war that could easily lead to the end of civilization, even our species?"* Hudson began. *"For nearly half a century following World War II, we avoided war for that very reason. Mutually Assured Destruction, or 'MAD,' made it clear that the Soviet Union and the United States would be insane to allow the cold war to heat up into a nuclear confrontation. And yet, for reasons not entirely clear, we are now on the brink of just such a nightmare. The United States and China, both economic and military superpowers, must not allow our differ-*

*ences, suspicions, and competition to escalate. For if they do, we may find events quickly spiraling out of control. That is why, as Commander in Chief, I am taking the unprecedented step of pledging not to order the use of force to resolve this dispute.*

*"Let us not pretend that war is anything other than monstrous, horrific violence on a massive scale. Violence against humans. Militaries and weapons exist for one reason—to kill humans. This is not what we should be doing; we, the only known intelligent life in the universe, at least looking out eighty trillion miles in any direction. Please stop and think about that for a moment . . . We humans are huddled together on this beautiful blue planet, a fiery rock covered with water, flying through the dark, cold, vastness of space at sixty-seven thousand miles per hour, able to survive only because we are exactly the perfect distance from a spectacular little yellow dwarf star. We are truly clinging to life. Do we want to risk all those miracles for a few dollars? Because that's what these disagreements boil down to at the end of the day; a few dollars. Perhaps we are worth more than that."*

The media immediately condemned the speech. Most members of congress were highly critical of the president's "reckless" action. Various pundits speculated that the president's near-death experience had made him "too soft." Sources within the White House leaked that Hudson had met several times with the leader of the controversial Inner Movement. Once again, the 25th Amendment was debated across the Internet. *"Could the president be removed?"*

Many in the media reminded viewers that Vice President Brown, although a longtime anti-war stalwart, had recently signaled she would not back down and would use force if the US were attacked, something the president, apparently, was now unwilling to do.

The White House quickly attempted to clarify the president's remarks, saying that of course he would order the military to defend the nation if China, or any other nation, violated US borders or airspace. However, the damage had been done. Hudson's approval ratings plummeted from the mid-seventies, where they'd been since he survived the Air Force One attack, to below fifty percent.

Even Ace, the president's brother, thought the speech was a bad idea. "You've taken away our leverage with the Chinese," he told Hudson. "Never telegraph our intentions."

Still, there were those that supported him. Scattered peace demonstrations sprang up as a minority of Americans resisted the call for war. The largest event, in Washington DC, saw tens of thousands march for peace. It ended with a sea of people on the National Mall chanting and listening to a series of anti-war speeches, including one by Thorne. The rally brought a swift show of force from FaST. Two-hundred and sixty-eight demonstrators were arrested. A FaST spokeswoman told reporters that the agency had reason to believe that most of those taken into custody were NorthBridgers who'd been seeking to use "the disturbance" as a recruiting tool.

Hudson, with firing Covington still under strong consideration, and in spite of Vonner's warnings, told Fitz he wanted a list of potential replacements for the director's job. Hudson expected Fitz to tell him that Covington worked for Vonner and not the president, but the chief of staff said nothing.

The president's decision to come out against the war reignited the controversy over the nine minutes, as both sides debated the significance of his near-death experience on the decision. During an interview with a well-known cable news anchor, Hudson further flamed the divisive fires when he said, "It makes a lot more sense to me that instead of war, I should declare peace."

"Is that what you're doing?" the anchor asked.

"Yes," Hudson said thoughtfully. "If I have the power to declare war, I should also be able to do the more noble thing."

"Congress might object to that premise," the anchor said. "In fact, leaders from both parties have already said they'll go around you if necessary."

Hudson gave his best politician laugh. "Last time I checked, I was still Commander in Chief."

"What do you say to your critics who wonder if those nine minutes, when you were clinically dead, changed you, and, uh—"

"Let me tell you something that all those veterans watching us today can identify with. Being shot changes you. Being close to death, however it comes, changes you. I've been shot at a lot in my life, going back to my days in the army. Then again once I decided to run for president, and NorthBridge seemingly painted a target on my back. But all Americans have experienced death in one form or another; the loss of a loved one, a serious illness, disease, accident. Every moment, each of us is only a single breath away from death."

# CHAPTER FORTY-EIGHT

C rane issued another report to Hudson and the Wizard detailing more links and proof of REMie Manipulate and Distract Everyone, or "MADE" events, between 1913 and the present day. He was focusing increasingly on the 2008 financial crisis and the Great Recession that followed. At the same time, the Wizard was tracking digiGOLD, and Hudson began to see that the two researchers were on a collision course, not just with each other, but with the REMies.

"You realize it's still possible that the REMies are either behind NorthBridge, or, at the very least, effectively using the terror attacks to further their own agenda," Hudson said to the Wizard during a SonicBlock-protected video call.

"That's where the REMies have proven so brilliant," the Wizard said from his elaborate storage shed. "We're living in the new paradigm! As Crane has shown, and the Gypsy program has laid out, REMie-initiated MADE events are only a small part of the equation. Most of the time, stuff just happens naturally, be it a major hurricane, earthquake, some popular movement, or even a war, and the REMies then use it. They're incredible at reacting."

"Not hard to do when you control all the money, the media, and almost every politician." Hudson, sitting on a small sofa in the President's Study, marveled at all the Wizard's computer equipment visible through his monitor.

"We're going to nail them," the Wizard said, his face lit by the glow of at least seven different monitors. "Did you see the other part of Crane's report? That it's a REMie going after all of us who were there that night, thirty years ago?"

Crane had used Gypsy to track all the events surrounding the deaths of each of the people who'd assaulted Rochelle and murdered her brother, plus he'd fed in the attempts on Hudson, Gouge, and Gouge's father. The conclusion pointed to one of two people ordering the hits, and neither was a surprise.

"Yeah, I saw," Hudson said. "Bastendorff and Vonner. I didn't need a fancy computer program to tell me that one of them was behind the killings. They're the only two men who have held Rochelle captive since her 'release' from prison."

"Would Vonner do it?"

"I asked him, and of course he denies it," Hudson said.

"As he always does."

"Yeah. He's certainly had plenty of opportunities to have me killed."

"But what about the other guy?" the Wizard asked. "He has a good motive."

"What? To stop the men from talking who didn't even know we were there? The people who have as much a reason to keep the truth hidden as I do?"

"Vonner is a cautious man."

"True, but Bastendorff is the obvious one to have gone after me, if it really wasn't NorthBridge."

"But why would he kill all the other guys when their story would hurt you?"

"Because they were never going to talk, and they didn't know we were there. But if it's only Rochelle who's left, *he* controls the story. Hell, maybe he made a deal with her. I don't know." Hudson took off his shoes and stretched out on the sofa, exhausted. An email came in from Crane. Hudson sat back up thinking it might be important. Instead, Hudson laughed to himself as he read it.

*Washington, D.C., is twelve square miles bordered by reality.*

The quote was attributed to President Andrew Johnson. Crane had taken to sending Hudson smart and pithy political humor every few days. His timing was often good, or better.

"No doubt Bastendorff is evil," the Wizard said, too busy with his own distractions pouring in from the DarkNet to notice Hudson's smile. "But I've never trusted Vonner. Anyway, there's no such thing as a *good* REMie."

"What about Booker Lipton? You seem to like him," Hudson said.

"I like his Universal Quantum Physics. I mean, the stars, planets, galaxies, everything we can see up there, makes up less than four percent of the universe. The remaining ninety-six percent is dark energy, or dark matter. No one really knows what it is, what it does, they can't even truly *find* it. Don't you find that awesome? Doesn't it blow your mind? Don't you want to know?"

"Not right now," Hudson said, trying not to look annoyed.

"Oh well. Anyway, lots of REMies fund lots of positive things."

"And that doesn't make them good?"

"No," the Wizard admitted. "Booker could be as bad as the rest of them, or he could be different, just like Vonner might have wanted you to help him stop Bastendorff, or he's using you so *he* can get the CapStone."

"It won't matter in the end, if we do our job," Hudson said, slumping back down on the sofa. "It's another reason I have to stop the war . . . to show they can be beat."

"Big job, Dawg."

"Yeah," Hudson said. "Meantime, you and Gouge need to stay alive."

"You, too." The Wizard pointed into the screen as they signed off.

A few minutes later, Hudson was drifting to sleep on the sofa, still worrying about his two oldest friends and wondering if Bastendorff was going to have them killed.

Or would Vonner do it?

Congressional leaders met with Hudson at the White House to demand he reconsider his stance. Afterwards, he met with Fitz in the Oval Office.

"They're going to pass a resolution," Fitz said.

"I won't sign it," Hudson said, leaning against the Resolute Desk.

"They have the votes to override a veto."

"Damn it, I'm the Commander in Chief. They can't make me order military action."

"They'll use the courts," Fitz said, sipping his favorite drink, Coke Rocks, a Coca-Cola over Coke-ice cubes.

"The Supreme Court will never usurp the executive branch authority in matters of national security."

"They might because of the nine minutes."

"What does my dying have to do with anything?" Hudson said, pacing over to the window. But he knew the answer even before Fitz replied.

"There's a lot of buzz about the Twenty-Fifth Amendment."

"You know it'll go nowhere. And Brown will never sign on."

"I agree, the vice president won't be a party to your removal," Fitz said. "However, there are other ways. It is still unlikely your opponents will succeed, it's just that we don't need any of this right now. NorthBridge is ripping the country apart from the inside. We're on the brink of the biggest war since World War II, and every aspect of it is a hell of a lot more frightening."

"Not to mention the country is still bitterly divided between liberals and conservatives, half a dozen international terrorist organizations are dangerous enough to threaten us, the prospect of war with China has begun to fracture the global economy . . . "

"It's ugly," Fitz said. "Remind me why you wanted this job?"

Hudson thought of Rochelle and the REMies. Nearly sixteen months in office, and he hadn't accomplished anything. North-Bridge, other than Covington's false arrests, seemed as invincible as ever, the REMies were still running the world, and Rochelle wasn't quite free enough to return to her family. He hadn't even been able to introduce his simple education reforms.

"We are the change," Hudson said softly.

Fitz heard him, but didn't comment.

"I don't understand why congress won't give sanctions time to work," Hudson said, walking back to his desk and sitting down.

"When have sanctions ever worked, in the history of sanctions?" Fitz said. "Sanctions are only used so it can *look* like politicians are doing something. In fact, you want to avoid war. There are many experts who believe it was President Clinton who set the stage for Bush's invasion of Iraq. People forget that in 1998, Clinton began the most sustained bombing campaign since Vietnam, with daily attacks on Iraq in the no-fly zones. And it was Clinton's administration that made regime change in Iraq an official US policy."

"We were talking about sanctions."

"Exactly. Clinton   implemented   the   most   devastating

economic sanctions in history. Your friends at the United Nations have estimated those sanctions cost a million Iraqi deaths, most of them children."

Hudson nodded, taking the point. "I recall a *60 Minutes* interview with Madeleine Albright, Clinton's UN Ambassador. Leslie Stahl said to Albright, 'We have heard that a half-million children have died. I mean, that's more children than died in Hiroshima. And—and, you know, is the price worth it?' Albright replied, 'I think this is a very hard choice, but the price—we think the price is worth it.'"

"I remember, too. Shocking," Fitz said. "There have been a lot of studies that dispute the UNICEF numbers."

"I'll bet there have been, but we know for a fact that there was not enough food or medicine getting in, that a large percentage of the population was malnourished, and the Iraqi healthcare system all but collapsed during sanctions. The REMies were trying to starve the country and bring what had been a thriving wealthy country into economic ruin so they could regain control of the oil and financial system. The per capita income in Iraq dropped from $3,510 in 1989 to $450 in 1996."

Hudson agreed that in the majority of situations, sanctions just hurt companies or industries instead of the government they were targeting.

"Diplomacy then," the president said as he put his feet up on the Resolute Desk.

Fitz raised his glass of Coke. "To diplomacy." Then he rolled his eyes.

"I'll see the bastards in court, then."

# CHAPTER FORTY-NINE

Melissa tried to reason with Hudson as he arrived in the family quarters. "You're going to be the first president in history to be bypassed by Congress," she said, handing him a glass of wine.

"So?"

They're calling you a coward."

"So?" Hudson repeated. "Do *you* think I'm a coward?"

"Of course not."

"Do you think I should start World War III?"

"You don't have to start it, I think you just need to keep the option on the table."

"Damn it, Melissa, I am an honorable man. I cannot in good conscious say that I am willing to risk the extinction of our species."

Melissa admired his conviction, his calm determination, his knowing for certain that what he believed was right. Yet it frustrated her. "How is everyone so sure they're right?" she asked. "Not just you. Half the country believes with all passion that they're right about what they believe, but the other half is just as sure that *they're* right. Two polar opposites. Both can't be right. I have no idea if *I'm* right most of the time."

"Nor do I, but of one thing I am sure. War is *not* right."

In the wake of a series of ninety-two coordinated attacks on 3D surveillance hubs and 3D monitoring stations, Covington ordered an aggressive increase in FaST raids and arrests. AKA John Hancock issued a statement claiming responsibility for the sabotage and noted that no humans were injured.

*Only the artificial intelligence bots that invade the privacy and daily lives of every citizen were harmed. These Orwellian creatures and the MONSTERS who run them must be shut down. Those who believe they have nothing to hide because they have done nothing wrong should be especially careful since the rules can be changed at any time without notice. Something that is allowed and innocuous today could be classified a grievous offence tomorrow. A citizen is only a single decree away from becoming a criminal.*

Hudson read the statement several times and noted that the word "monsters" was all in capital letters. He didn't think that was an accident. He had only recently learned that most federal agencies contained a select individual known as a MONSTER, "Mission of National Security Transfer Every Resource." This key person, appointed to this secret post by some covert committee with unknown origins, even within the realm of top-secret clearances, had enormous power. The

MONSTER could access all the resources of an agency, a department, or any military branch instantly, and often invisibly, for a special Veiled Ops unit, known to the MONSTERs simply as "the Unit."

The MONSTER structure was put into place as part of the Patriot Act following the September 11, 2001 terrorist attacks. MONSTER, like so many other provisions, was hidden from public knowledge and withheld from Congress. Even those few inside the government who knew about the program believed it to be a resource-sharing plan which could be used to cut through red tape in times of national emergencies and threats to national security. But MONSTER was so much more than that.

The MONSTERs were pulled from the upper ranks of the NSA without input or oversight. None of the presidents in powers since the MONSTERs' inceptions had been briefed on the program. Fonda had told Hudson about them during their last meeting, and he'd been trying to dig up more about the MONSTERs and the Veiled Ops Unit they facilitated. Fonda had said, "MONSTER really only exists for a single reason: to make the Unit the most powerful force in the world. I believe Covington is using MONSTERs to expand the Unit, may have, in fact, folded the Unit into FaST. If my sources are right, and this is true, imagine what he can do with that kind of power."

Enjoying the quiet of the Oval Office before the day began, Hudson sat at the Resolute Desk, thinking about the MONSTERs. He checked his watch: 6:10 a.m. He knew Fonda put up her daily post every morning at six. Hudson walked over to his study and navigated his web browser to the *Raton Report* to check her coverage of the latest from NorthBridge.

He'd found that Fonda often had better intelligence than he

got in the President's Daily Briefing, which was no surprise, since the PDB was prepared by Covington's office. The *Raton Report* had wide coverage of the NorthBridge attacks against the 3D system, including a post by Fonda herself citing several sources with knowledge that the 3D system had recently expanded to include the use of drones.

*"Thousands of small, unmanned aerial vehicles, as well as dozens of full-sized UAVs, are being utilized,"* the report said. She questioned whether the original Deter and Detect Domestic Terrorism Act allowed for drones to be used in that way.

Even before AKA Hancock claimed responsibility for the strikes against the 3D surveillance system, privacy rights groups had been clamoring for the network of cameras to be dismantled, but now, with Fonda's reporting, even those who hadn't been bothered by the loss of privacy might take issue with drones constantly monitoring their lives.

*"It's a slippery slope,"* AKA Hancock had warned in his statement. *"They keep taking more and more, until they have it all."*

Yet many in the media, as well as the majority of public officials, believed that the need for 3D was mostly due to North-Bridge and other criminal threats. "We're only trading a little privacy for security," the Senate Majority Leader had said. "What good is privacy if you're not alive to enjoy it?"

Fonda's story went on to reveal that the 3D system now included advanced recognition technology that could put names to faces even when they were obscured. But even more frightening was the system's ability to identify people by their clothing and posture. 3D could also determine a potential threat based on facial expressions, and in certain situations, 3D cameras, when placed near video or poster displays, were able to "read" a person's thoughts by analyzing his or her expressions after viewing certain content.

*"An image of President Pound might illicit a negative emotion*

*from a Democrat, and 3D would pick that up and feed the data
base. It's not about security, it's about feeding the data base. He
who controls the data controls us all,"* the report concluded.

Hudson's thoughts were interrupted by an urgent message
from the Wizard. He shoved the SonicBlock drive into his laptop,
and twenty seconds later was looking at the tense face of his
oldest friend.

"Crane just called. Gypsy picked up that FaST is going after
Fonda and Thorne," the Wizard blurted. "The squads are out
now. Both are to be arrested and detained."

"Damn Covington," Hudson said. "It must be her story about
Three-D."

"I haven't seen the story," the Wizard said, "but, Dawg, I'm
betting it's Cherry Tree. Thorne's only connection to Fonda is
that they both speak out against Covington and FaST. I think this
is Covington making a preemptive strike for his REMie masters
to shut down Cherry Tree before you launch."

"Two can play at this game," Hudson said. "It's time to get rid
of Covington."

"Just make sure you announce it publicly first," the Wizard
said. "I've been applying fractal mathematics to the stuff from
Crane, the patterns Gypsy has found, and it seems to indicate a
fluctuation in the electromagnetic field. I think we're about to get
buried in trouble. The negatives are . . . are you following me?"

"No, I never do."

"How could our universe be random? It could not."

"Can you get messages to Fonda and Thorne anonymously?"
Hudson asked, ignoring the Wizard's ramblings. "To tip
them off?"

The Wizard's face fell. "I think we can manage that. I'll do
it now."

"Maybe they can hide out until I can get rid of Covington
and terminate the FaST squads."

"And, Dawg, while you're at it, I talked to Gouge last night. He and his dad are still holed up in some old trailer, a shack really, out in the sticks, and he's scared."

"Okay, I'll think of something," Hudson said, realizing that he knew too many people—the Wizard, Gouge, and now Thorne and Fonda—who were in hiding. Maybe he was next. "Send those warnings out right now!"

## CHAPTER FIFTY

Covington walked into the Oval Office and exaggeratedly checked his watch. "National security?" he asked sarcastically after seeing no one else in the room. The president had had an aide summon the DNI to the White House immediately, citing a national security emergency. "What's the crisis?"

"*You're* the crisis," the president said. "FaST is out of control."

Covington smiled smugly, as if he'd already guessed the true reason for the "urgent" meeting.

"Mr. President, you are the one confused." Covington walked over to a chair opposite the Resolute Desk, sat down, and pulled a green Necco wafer from his jacket pocket. "You mean *North-Bridge* is out of control. The nation is under attack from within, and FaST is the only thing standing in the way of total anarchy." He held the candy in his hand.

"You've gone way beyond the original scope of FaST," the president said, trying to control his anger. "This isn't about NorthBridge anymore, this is about your personal political enemies."

Covington squinted at the president, trying to ascertain if Hudson could somehow know about the pending arrests of Fonda Raton and Thorne. "I'm in charge of FaST," Covington said. "I'll decide what's enough."

"No, you won't. That's not how it works."

"Oh really?" Covington smirked. "Why don't you tell me how it works, then."

"I guess I'll have to, since you don't seem to understand that the President of the United States is in charge. *I'm* your boss, David, at least for a few more minutes."

"You?" Covington scoffed, disgusted. "You're just a figure-head, a paid actor . . . *I* control the government, you idiot!"

Hudson stared disbelievingly at Covington. He'd suspected it, deep down probably actually knew it, but to hear Covington so blatantly claim a greater authority than the president's was still shocking and disarming. Yet it only took Hudson a second to gather himself and his seething anger and respond. "Then tell me, David, which REMie do you answer to?"

It was Covington's turn to be surprised. "So, you've figured that much out, have you? Maybe a bit smarter than I thought, but not smart enough to know how to do your job. Does Vonner know you know?"

Hudson could see the DNI tactics—answer a question with a question—but he had to push. This would be his last chance to get a clue as to which REMie controlled Covington. It could have been dozens of people, but Hudson was betting it was either Bastendorff, Booker, or Vonner. Obviously if it was Vonner, then Hudson had bigger problems than just challenging the DNI.

"Do you think Vonner can save your job?" the president asked. "Or will you call Bastendorff?"

Covington shook his head, clearly startled to hear Basten-dorff's name. "Busy boy, aren't you, Hudson?" It was the first time the DNI hadn't addressed him as "Mr. President." Hudson noticed.

"I might not have you charged with treason if you tell me which one gives you your orders."

"Why do you want to change things, you fool?" Covington growled. "You see this piece of candy?" He held up the green Necco wafer. "This company has been making these wonderful little sweets since 1847. Union soldiers carried them during the Civil war. And then, in 2009, some knucklehead decided to change the formula and replace the artificial sweeteners and colors with natural equivalents to appeal to the health-conscious consumer. Only they weren't exact equivalents, so they tasted different. In fact, they dropped the green color all together."

"Your point?" Hudson asked, annoyed and a bit baffled at the odd timing of the irrelevant story.

"My point is that the company received thousands of complaints, and sales of Necco Wafers plummeted thirty-five percent. Two years later, they reverted to the original formula, flavors, and ingredients." He popped the green candy into his mouth. "You see what I'm saying, Hudson? Don't change something that's working."

The president stared incredulously at Covington, and then walked over to him. "Either way, David, you are no longer the Director of National Intelligence. In fact," Hudson checked the time, "the news of your dismissal has just been released to all the major news organizations, including the *Raton Report*. Thank you for your service."

The president held out his hand to shake his adversary's. Covington, ignoring the gesture, gave Hudson a contemptuous look, shaking his head slowly, as if disgusted.

"My service has only just begun," Covington said before turning and walking out of the Oval Office, as if leaving a party that had run out of alcohol.

# CHAPTER FIFTY-ONE

From his car, Covington called the one man in the world who could solve this problem; his true superior, not some silly shopkeeper who thought the presidency still meant anything.

"Pound has to go," Covington said as soon as the man answered. "He thinks he's just fired me."

"Surely you can handle him. He's just a schoolteacher, after all. A couple of years ago the man was selling screws for a living."

"I agree the president is an idiot, but he's a smart idiot," Covington said. "He's figured things out."

"So what? Presidents have put the pieces together before," the man replied, sounding almost amused. "And if they're clever enough to get that far, they're also bright enough to know they have to cooperate with us. They always have. Well, aside from a few glitches . . . but we dealt with those." The man grunted, as if the thought of those situations was uncomfortable.

"I'm telling you, Pound is different. He hasn't accidentally stumbled into the reality—he's gone looking for it." Covington paused, before raising his voice. "The guy is hunting REMies."

"Hunting us? What does that even mean?"

"He's trying to bring down the whole system," Covington said. "Pound aims to stop the REMies."

The man laughed.

"Seriously, he seems to think the people can do a better job running the world than we can."

"Don't be ridiculous, he knows better than that."

"*I'm* the one charged with managing the US government. Listen to me, he's a real threat."

"It's tricky," the man said. "Apparently the president announced publicly that you were 'dismissed.' Interesting choice of words. In either case, you're on all the news channels right now. We can hardly get you back into your old job, but we'll get someone. Don't worry."

"I want to take this to the council."

"No, no, no," the man said irritably. "You know with this CapWar raging, the council is no longer relevant."

"They can still be called together."

"No, I think not."

"I'm calling them. Everyone needs to know the threat."

"Bad timing, David. Lay low for a while. Write a book. We'll get you something."

"I'm *not* laying low. I'm going to bring the president down."

"Pound is nothing," the man said as ice clinked in his glass.

"You're wrong. He's taking advantage of the CapWar. He knows the REMies are divided right now, more than ever before, and that the system is strained."

The man on the other end of the phone whistled. "Strained? That's a nice way to put it, but we've got contingency plans—six different ones. If the economy collapses, there are even those who think it would be the best thing. I can think of one individual that believes a complete economic implosion would give him the CapStone."

"I can guess who that is, but it may happen," Covington said as his driver turned onto Constitution Avenue. "Then tell me this: what is a victory in the CapWar if the world is reduced to chaos?"

"REMies thrive on chaos," the man said. "There is no real advantage to Pound, whatever he may be doing. However, if you're so certain he's a threat, send me a report. If I agree, I'll see to it that the president is brought down."

"You don't need a report," Covington said, breaking a stack of pink Necco wafers into tiny pieces.

"I'll have to think of something interesting," the man mused. "The people are pretty bored with sex scandals and the like, unless maybe we did something with him and young boys?"

"I'm not talking about removing him through some scandal," Covington said tersely. "Pound has to be killed, and soon."

"I'm not sure that is the wisest course, and anyway, Pound has proven himself almost invincible."

"But he's not," Covington said, wishing he was a billionaire so he could compete with the man to win the CapWar. He knew he was smarter than most of the super-rich "frat boys." He unwrapped a new package of Necco wafers and began extracting the pink intruders. "You know we could have Pound dead tonight if you authorized it. It can look like anything we want. He could choke on something, have a heart attack, a brain aneurysm, maybe even kill himself. How about that?" Covington asked. "We've never had a president commit suicide. Everyone knows he's been unstable since the Air Force One attack, those nine minutes weighing on him. He could leave a note. The public would eat it up. Everything he saw during the near-death experience made him want to go back."

"I must admit, I do kind of like it," the man said.

"The president is under a lot of pressure, the poor man wanted to die again, that could be really entertaining for the public, something new and different." Covington gave up on the pink candies and pushed a handful of his favorite orange ones into his mouth. "It could be fun. How about the president offs himself in some spectacular way? Give me a few minutes, I'll come up with a list of exciting ways. Hey, what if he jumps off the White House roof? We could even have some grainy footage of it released. Maybe he—"

"You might be getting a little too theatrical—"

"Theatrics are what sell," Covington said, as his car passed the Washington Monument. "Or didn't you pay attention to Trump's election and presidency? Ratings were through the roof."

"Let's just bring him down in a quick scandal," the man said again, losing interest in the flashy suicide.

"A quick scandal was the plan to finish Bill Clinton. That guy was an easy set up, but there was nothing quick about the scandal, and it never brought him down."

"Okay, David. Put together a proposal, something solid, and nothing *too* flamboyant. I'll take a look at it and make a final decision, but tell me this; are you really ready to deal with a President Brown?"

"Absolutely. That woman will make *any* deal to avoid war."

# CHAPTER FIFTY-TWO

The next day, Thorne did his radio show from an undisclosed location. Although Covington was officially out as DNI, FaST remained operational, and still had active warrants for the shock-jock, as well as Fonda Raton. The latter was also "at large," but that was nothing new for the reclusive journalist who never seemed to be home. This had long frustrated Vonner, who had ordered Rex, on numerous occasions, to find out who was protecting her. Rex had also picked up the advance plan by FaST, and Vonner had been hoping she might finally be removed from his "most wanted" list.

Schueller stopped by the Oval Office, where Secret Service Agent Bond was standing guard at the door.

"Hey, 007," Schueller said, not surprised to see him there. Schueller knew his dad was being extra careful after firing Covington. It was very possible that the REMies would retaliate. NorthBridge, through AKA Franklin, had issued a statement applauding the action as the second decent thing President Pound had done. The first had been announcing his opposition to the war in China. Hudson did not welcome the endorsements from the hated terror group. "They said I could go in," Schueller said.

Bond nodded.

Hudson barely looked up as his son entered the room. "Come look at this," he said, staring at his computer screen. "We're *so close* to being able to go forward with Cherry Tree."

Schueller looked at the latest data from Crane and started to laugh. "We're going to get them!"

"I think so."

"What's going to happen when their system all comes crashing down?" Schueller asked. "Couldn't it be an epic disaster?"

"I've got a small team of economists working on just that," Hudson said, "but there's no question that it may not be pretty. The 2008 financial crisis gives us a clue, or the 1930's worldwide depression, but those were actually carefully controlled chaos."

"Right, the REMies were locked in CapWars, but they were still pulling the strings."

"The trick to all of this will be taking the REMies out of the equation. We need to be sure they cannot impact the economy."

"How?"

"I'm hoping the economists can do that."

"Can you trust them?"

Hudson raised an eyebrow. "Hard question these days, but I went to school with one of them, and he brought in two others that he trusts."

"What's that?" Schueller asked, pointing to a small icon on the screen.

"Crane sent a little video of Oliver Stone at an awards show some years back." He clicked on it, and the famous movie director spoke.

*"It's fashionable now to take shots at Republicans and Trump and avoid the Obamas and Clintons. But remember this: In the thirteen wars we've started over the last thirty years and the $14 trillion we've spent, and the hundreds of thousands of lives that have perished from this earth, remember that it wasn't one leader, but a system, both Republican and Democrat. Call it what you will: the military industrial money media security complex. It's a system that has been perpetuated under the guise that these are just wars justifiable in the name of our flag that flies so proudly."*

"Wow, maybe Oliver Stone should make a movie about your presidency and bringing down the REMies. He sure seems to understand what's going on with his 'it's a system.'"

Hudson smiled. "Wouldn't that be great? Hope I live to see it."

He and Schueller stared at each other for a moment, then continued listening to Stone's speech.

*"But we continue to create such chaos and wars. No need to go through the victims, but we know we've intervened in more than one hundred countries with invasion, regime change, economic chaos. Or hired war. It's war of some kind. In the end, it's become a system leading to the death of this planet and the extinction of us all."*

"Smart man," Hudson said.

"So are you," Schueller said.

"We'll see." Hudson looked back at Crane's data. "If I can stop the REMies without spiraling the world economy into rubble while avoiding World War III at the same time, and not get myself killed."

# CHAPTER FIFTY-THREE

G ouge looked at the lines crisscrossing his father's face. His old man had lived a hard life. Born in poverty, he became a father at seventeen. Four kids later, Gouge came along, then two more after him. A lot of drinking, tough physical work, bar fights, and scrapes with the law were all etched into his tan, rugged face. Gouge studied the man he'd detested and idolized. He looked older than seventy, a *lot* older.

"What the hell you lookin' at, boy?" his father barked. The old man now knew his son had been there that night when Rochelle and her brother . . . That's why they were "livin' like trash," hiding out in the woods in a broken-down trailer. But he hadn't known all those years. If he had, there would probably have been even more wrinkles.

They still hadn't spoken about it, but sitting there in that dilapidated trailer, with not much to keep them company other than a radio and some old magazines, Gouge couldn't hold his tongue any longer.

"Dad, I want to know about that night."

His father looked at him with an angry, bitter expression. "We ain't goin' to talk about that."

"Yes, we are," Gouge said, his voice rising. "We have to. I've been paying for your crime every day of my life for the last three decades."

"Don't you blame *me* for your screwups, boy. I gave you a good life. I did right by you." He spat some tobacco into a can.

"Some of that's true, but all of it was erased that night when those terrible things happened. Why'd you do it, Dad? Why'd you kill that man and rape Rochelle? She was just a girl."

"I said we're not talkin' about this, now shut your damned mouth!"

"And I say we're going to talk," Gouge said, standing up, towering over his father. His arm hit a box of cornflakes, sending it spilling off the table. "You're going to tell me how you could do such a thing, and how you could stay silent about it all those years."

"Like hell I am."

"You start talking, Dad, or I swear, so help me, I'll tell Sissy and June everything."

His father looked as if he'd been smacked. The thought of Gouge telling his precious daughters about the horrors of that night were unbearable to him.

"Damn you, boy! I should have whupped your ass more, didn't teach you no respect. Damn you!"

"What happened?"

"It was Corbett," his father said, resignation in his words. He stared at his son, eyes burdened with a hated look back into the greasy, grit days of Southeastern Ohio three decades earlier. "Those Corbett's ran that town, they ran everything. The whole bad lot of them, used to doin' whatever they wanted. Oh, that night Tanny Corbett looked at that poor girl, figured she was just another thing he could have, do what he wanted with her. That's what he was like. He didn't care, just was gonna use her, then crumple her up and throw her away. Didn't care . . . Corbett's didn't care," he kept mumbling.

"Why didn't you say no?" Gouge asked.

"Ain't no one said no to the Corbett's. I know you may think I was a rich king with my own tire shop, but most of my business came from the Corbett's. They could've shut me down anytime."

Gouge had never known his father's business was that fragile. "Back to Rochelle."

"See, Corbett and his buddies, they couldn't stand to be questioned by that black boy. He come in there all high-and-mighty-like. Damn, he was askin' for trouble."

"He was looking for his sister. He knew y'all had her."

"Yeah, well, he should've had more respect. They weren't gonna take guff from that boy. He just made it all worse." His father shook his head over and over.

"But you raped her, too, Dad. You raped Rochelle before her brother got there. Did Corbett *make* you rape her?"

"Careful of your tone, boy. You remember who you's talkin' to." He looked at Gouge as if he was considering taking a shot at him. "See, that was in those days. You may not recall, but I did some drinkin' then."

"I remember all right," Gouge said. "I remember the beatings."

"Good, see?" His dad pointed a gnarled finger at him. "Just didn't teach you enough, though, did I?"

"You taught me plenty," Gouge said, looking down at the tattoo across his knuckles."

"Poor baby," his father sneered. "Well, I was drunk that night, you can't doubt that. I don't even remember the girl much, but I didn't know from which was right. I just went along with everybody."

"That's too easy, Dad," Gouge said, appalled that after all

these years, that was all he was going to get. "Did you sober up when you killed her brother?"

"Now, wait a minute," his father said, standing up, his bloodshot eyes fiery with rage. "I'm not the one who killed that damned boy."

Gouge stared down into his father's face, only inches away. "You killed him, same as everyone who—"

The door of the trailer suddenly smashed into the tight space, and before Gouge or his father could react, four men dressed in black and armed with FN F2000 Assault Rifles and stun guns filled the dank room. Gouge and his father never saw the fifth man.

Gouge woke up coughing. Everything was burning; black smoke and heat, so incredibly hot. He tried to stand, but there was already too much smoke in his lungs. He began to crawl, but didn't know where to go. He didn't know anything. He kept crawling anyway, trying to get away from the flames that surrounded him. At the same time, he saw a rack of tires burning, and heard his father scream.

Before it fully registered that he was in the old tire shop, he saw his father, on fire, stumbling through the inferno. Gouge tried again to get up, but there wasn't enough strength in his body. He struggled to pull himself in the direction of his father, but the heat was too much; his skin was already blistering.

Gouge watched helplessly as his father collapsed, melting into part of the hellish blaze. He coughed violently, dizzy with pain. Blindly trying to see a way out of the toxic furnace, he took one last look at where his father was, but nothing was left. He'd vanished into the raging flames. A thought flickered into his brain, his last before losing consciousness.

*This is the perfect place, and a fitting way for us both to die. A fine welcome to Hell.*

# CHAPTER FIFTY-FOUR

Hudson reset the SonicBlock and took the call near the fountain on the South Lawn. The Washington summer made it easy to understand why the city was called "the swamp". It was more than the humid weather, the tangle of bureaucrats, "leaches," "snakes," other "reptiles," and mud . . .

Hudson stopped his spiraling thoughts. Even at seven-thirty a.m., the sun glared, and the humidity, at ninety-one percent, was winning its daily race with the temperature. Later in the day, it would be a meteorological draw, as both would be in the upper nineties. Still, it was already hot and sticky enough that he congratulated himself once again for giving up neckties.

"How are you? *Where* are you?" the president asked Fonda as soon as he was out of earshot of the closest Secret Service agent.

"The first answer is too long to bore you with," Fonda said, "and the second is better if you don't know."

"But Covington is gone."

"There are plenty more where he came from. He has a lot of friends, and not just REMies. I bet two-thirds of the Congress has criticized you for firing him."

"Congress acts as if they're so important, but they're just REMie employees. 'Keep Covington! Declare war!' It's so frustrating. Even the so-called liberals join in."

"We've had this talk about Republicrats and Democans."

"I don't understand how I, the president, have term limits, and yet we've got congressmen and senators who serve for *decades*. These 'professional politicians' are not what was envisioned by the Founding Fathers. They've proven to be ineffective. Most are only interested in seeking their own fame, power, and riches on the backs of working Americans. I think we'd get a lot more done and see far less partisan bickering if senators and congressmen were limited to two terms, just as the president is. I wouldn't be opposed to a single term limit for *all* of us."

"It'll never fly," Fonda said.

"Why can't I just go on TV and tell the American people the truth?"

"They aren't ready for the truth."

"You sound like Vonner or Bastendorff, deciding what's best for the people, what they need or don't need."

"You have to remember," Fonda explained, "the population has been lied to, manipulated, and brainwashed for more than a hundred years. They don't even know how to believe the truth anymore."

"That doesn't mean I can't try."

"Do you really think you're the first president to attempt that. Let me read you something that I keep with me so that I don't forget: *We are opposed around the world by a monolithic and ruthless conspiracy that relies primarily on covert means for expanding its sphere of influence—on infiltration instead of invasion, on subversion instead of elections, on intimidation instead of free choice, on guerrillas by night instead of armies by day. It is a system which has conscripted vast human and material resources into the building of a tightly knit, highly efficient machine that combines military, diplomatic, intelligence, economic, scientific and political operations."*

"John Kennedy," Hudson said, recognizing the speech.

"That's right. Some say he was talking about the communists, but he was warning us about the REMies."

"Knowing what I know now, it sure seems that way."

"And what about President Eisenhower?" Fonda added. "I'm sure you recall his farewell address. His deep concern was quite apparent when he warned us: *We must guard against the acquisition of unwarranted influence . . . by the military-industrial complex. The potential for the disastrous rise of misplaced power exists and will persist. We must never let the weight of this combination endanger our liberties or democratic processes. We should take nothing for granted. Only an alert and knowledgeable citizenry can compel the proper meshing of the huge industrial and military machinery of defense with our peaceful methods and goals, so that security and liberty may prosper together . . . We must also be alert to the equal and opposite danger that public policy could itself become the captive of a scientific-technological elite."*

"I know those words, too," Hudson said. "So, I'm in good company."

"Maybe, but before you go out there calling for term limits, remember one of those presidents only uttered that warning on his way out of office, and the other didn't live to see the end of his term."

Hudson returned to the Oval Office and asked Fitz to come in. Fonda may have been trying to discourage him, but instead she made him more determined to speak to the American people about government corruption and to build support for term limits.

"With all due respect, Mr. President, I think that's a bit ambitious," Fitz said after the president told him about his term limits proposal. "You're not popular enough to drum up support for anything more than a tax cut."

"I was going to do that, too," Hudson said. "It's time. I'm planning to officially propose term limits, campaign finance reform, new banking regulations, military cutbacks, tax reform—"

"May I speak frankly?" Fitz interrupted, taking a sip of his Coke. "I may need a little rum for this. I mean, Mr. President, that's crazy talk. Do you really need more enemies? That many?"

"Between Congress trying to usurp me, and all the leaks trying to undermine me, it's incredible the American people haven't noticed there's a slow coup going on."

"Mr. President, did you ever wonder if maybe *you're* on the wrong side of these issues, especially war?" Fitz asked. "It's worth considering that if *everyone* else is 'wrong,' then maybe it's flipped around. Perhaps you are the one who is wrong, and everyone else is actually right."

"Fitz, I appreciate that you're always willing to confront me on my ideas, but it's interesting that we rarely seem to agree these days. In fact, I'm not sure there were many days we ever *did* agree. I wonder if some of those leaks aren't coming from you, or at least have been sanctioned by you—"

"Wait a minute, Mr. President." He set his drink down on an end table. "I serve you and your agenda with full loyalty."

"Loyalty to whom? Vonner?"

"Vonner is not your enemy, Mr. President." He stared Hudson in the eye. "If you want my resignation, just say the word. However, think carefully about the timing with Congress debating the Twenty-Fifth Amendment, and about to vote on declaring war without you. The country never more divided,

NorthBridge running unabated, Covington just fired . . . is now really when you want more disruption?"

Hudson couldn't afford to let Fitz go yet. He didn't trust him, but he didn't trust anyone outside his family, so that didn't count against his chief of staff. Fitz was right, though. Congress *was* about to declare war; not just against China, but against his presidency. He needed Fitz to help him navigate that unprecedented storm.

The main thing was stopping the war with the Chinese. He believed Linh, the mysterious leader of the Inner Movement, when she said that: *"If we don't stop this war, it will end civilization."*

That evening, Hudson was trying to get to bed early. He'd issued a statement calling for term limits, and would have to spend the following day on the phone with dozens of senators and members of congress. In the morning, he also planned on calling for other governmental reforms. The media was already whipping up a firestorm, with most commentators saying that the ballot box was the only term limit needed. However, there were early indications that a majority of the public supported his call for mandatory limits. This was stage one of Cherry Tree. His idea was to keep the momentum going for a few more days until Crane had enough so they could go to stage two and publicly release the REMie data.

Melissa, surprised to see him before midnight, smiled when

he came in, but before he could join her in bed, an urgent signal sounded on his laptop. The Wizard needed a call.

He looked back at his wife. It wasn't the CIA or Pentagon, so it wasn't a matter of national security. Maybe he could ignore it.

Then Hudson recalled the two other times the Wizard had contacted him in the past two years, and knew it must be a real crisis.

After the SonicBlock flash matrix ended, the Wizard came through, already in mid-sentence.

"There were two victims, and I haven't been able to reach Gouge!" the Wizard said breathlessly.

"Victims of what?"

"The fire! The whole tire shop was leveled!"

"How? Gouge wouldn't be there," Hudson said. Melissa sat up in bed and looked over at him when she heard his upset tone.

"I checked with the hospital, but since I'm not a relative, they wouldn't confirm anything except that two victims of the fire had been brought in. One was a fatality, and the other is critical."

"But they wouldn't have been there," Hudson repeated.

"I hacked into the hospital's computer network. The deceased is still unidentified—they've got him listed as a John Doe—but the one in the ICU, with burns on over eighty-five percent of his body, is listed as Thomas Gouge."

"Oh, no."

"But as you know Tommy's dad is also Thomas, so I don't know which one it is. But even if it is Gouge, I'm not sure I want it to be. He might be better off dead."

Hudson put his hand to his mouth. "What were they doing at the tire shop?"

"I keep asking myself that same thing."

"I'm a relative. I can call the hospital and find out if it's Gouge or his dad in the ICU. They'll tell me how he is."

"You may be related, but you're also POTUS. I don't think you should call."

"I'm going to call."

"Have Ace or Jenna call," Melissa suggested. Hudson agreed it would be the wiser course to let his brother or sister call. After all, they were just as related to Gouge. Melissa texted Ace.

The Wizard and Hudson continued to speculate on why Gouge and his dad would have come out of hiding to go to the tire shop. A few minutes later, Melissa interrupted to say that the hospital had confirmed the man in the ICU was Tommy Gouge.

"The nurse told Ace that the burns are so severe and that, combined with the smoke inhalation, his chances of survival are minimal," Melissa said loud enough that both Hudson and the Wizard could hear. "They're hoping to stabilize Gouge enough to airlift him to Cleveland sometime tomorrow. Ace promised to go to the hospital first thing in the morning."

Hudson took a deep breath.

The Wizard's eyes filled. "It's down to just you and me, Dawg. Everyone else is dead." Then he looked down and muttered almost silently, "Matter cannot be created or destroyed . . . that's a law of the universe . . . it just is."

"Gouge may pull through," Hudson said.

"No, I saw his chart." The Wizard shook his head slowly. "We're his best and oldest friends. We owe it to him to pray . . . pray that he dies tonight."

# CHAPTER FIFTY-FIVE

Crane pecked away at his keyboard, spurred on by his astonishing discovery. The hacker rubbed his thin, stubbly beard, impressed with himself. He couldn't stop smiling. "I got you, NorthBridge!" he said to himself.

Although he didn't yet have the true identities of all the AKAs, Crane had IDed the big shots and secured conclusive evidence of the driving force behind the most secret and successful terror network the world had ever known. As he sat flying through the DarkNet, cross-corroborating details and data, Crane was in awe and edged with fear. NorthBridge had the ability to bring the United States to its knees, and it was going to happen soon. The terror organization was closer than anyone realized to igniting a second American Civil War. He could see it all there on the screen, no longer a prophetic theory. There would be battles in the streets.

Crane hadn't even been looking at NorthBridge, but came across them while scouring the complex world of international crime, conspiracy, and corruption that lay in a labyrinth of arms deals, money laundering, payoffs, murder, and betrayal. Viewed from the DarkNet, that shadowy world showed the REMies connected to everything. They used the population's naïve belief in the illusions of "free markets," "democracy," and "fair, objective media" to steal more wealth and take more control. The strings of power were pulled, cut, and tied into knots.

While scouring REMie transactions, Crane found that the trail led through the central banks, corporate tax havens, and eventually into cryptocurrencies, and, of course, digiGOLD. That's where the paths crossed. Once he stumbled upon NorthBridge, he took all he could find on their digiGOLD transactions and fed it into Gypsy. The computer program automatically overlaid and churned through a hundred years of data, looking for patterns, anything with similar markers.

Suddenly, the shocking answer to a question he had never asked, appeared. An untrained eye might have missed it, particularly if they weren't looking for it, but Crane caught the anomalies and followed the sequence, still expecting something different. Now that he had the explosive information, he didn't know exactly what to do with it. Publicly releasing the names of the founders and force behind NorthBridge could create as many problems as it solved.

"That's above my pay grade," the hacker said to himself as he continued to plow through the endless code in front of him, unconsciously sucking down Red Bulls. "The president will have to figure that out."

But even as he muttered the words, he wondered if it was wise to give the source to Hudson.

There would be time to think about that later. Right now, he still needed to focus on confirming two more things, and everything had to be preserved with at least triple redundancy. Crane had learned one thing during his thousands of hours of wandering the DarkNet: information, particularly in the digital realm, could change or vanish instantly. He looked up to a pegboard above his workplace and fished out a flash drive from a bin. A poster caught his eye, a photo of a lone backpacker at the base of Denali, something he'd always longed to do. He wished he were there now.

Back to the screen, navigating the most treacherous place on earth—the canyons of code on the DarkNet. Just as he found the final confirmation, he heard the noise. It wasn't very loud, but when someone lived alone and worked in the dark, he heard every sound; a filter in the subconscious deciding if it could be ignored, or warranted a nervous system alert, maybe even the more critical fight or flight reflex. Crane, used to traveling through billions and billions of bits of information every waking hour, searching for anything incriminating on the world's most powerful people, constantly lived in a paranoid state, on edge so that even a trip to the grocery store had him looking over his shoulder. His best friend Zackers had died on the same quest—to bring back proof of the REMies' crimes.

The sound, like cloth rubbing against drywall, magnified, and alarmed him more than it normally would because of the North-Bridge find. Crane, not a big, tough, physical man, fancied himself a secret agent type, but in truth, he was a coward. So after the second sound—a slight creak—his mouth went dry. It still might be nothing, but it could also be a killer.

*Preserve the data,* he thought. *It might be all that saves you.*

Crane had two choices and almost no time to make them. First, he could grab something and fight. The only thing close was a putter. He kept the slender golf club around as a reminder of his father, who had putted golf balls into fancy crystal glasses on his office floor. Crane had done the same into a red plastic cup, but not nearly as often. He stole a quick glance at the club and the balls. Maybe he could throw the balls at an intruder, then swing the club, but a swift look back at the screen told him those weren't good options with the type of information he'd been delving into. NorthBridge or the REMies wouldn't send some-body who could be defeated by a computer geek with a putter and a couple of cheap golf balls.

That meant the only other option was to run. The small room where he worked was windowless, but the adjoining bathroom had a window. He didn't think the drop to the ground was too far, but he'd never really thought about having to drop from there. His caffeine-infused mind came up with another thought.

*Maybe I'm imagining the danger. Those sounds, even if they'd been real, might've been nothing more than one hears occasionally in apartments and houses when alone—settling, plumbing, furnaces, whatever.*

That made him feel better, but just to be sure, he hit a series of keystrokes to preserve and protect the data.

Crane stood quickly, looked at the golf club, then at the bathroom door. He peered down the dark hall toward where he had heard the sounds. It only took an instant for him to make the decision.

*It must have been nothing.*

Just in case, he picked up the golf club and the balls and headed down the hall. He'd make sure, and then grab another Mountain Dew from the fridge.

The computer blinked and continued working as he headed down the hall. In six or seven steps, he reached the light switch. Just as he flicked it, an amber glow lit the hall, and he saw a shadow move at the other end. Crane dropped the balls, turned, and ran back toward the bathroom.

He never made it.

# CHAPTER FIFTY-SIX

As usual, the Wizard had eight monitors full of data open in front of him as his servers filtered and saved endless streams of data. He was deep into looking for clues as to who was behind the tire shop fire, and pushing to obtain information Hudson could use to pressure members of congress to vote against war.

Just before nine p.m. Pacific time, hundreds of encrypted files came in from Crane. However, the stream had been interrupted before all the transfers had been completed. Crane regularly sent data backups, and sometimes there were glitches. The Wizard gave them only a fleeting glance, figuring it was a routine upload.

After a couple of hours, when Crane still hadn't resumed the transmission, the Wizard figured he might have gone to bed since it was around two a.m. Eastern time—a little early for Crane, but not a red flag. He kept working on digging for dirt on the congressmen and senators on his list. Finally, at two-twenty on the West Coast, the Wizard checked the files Crane had sent.

Seeing the magnitude of the contents, he immediately tried to contact Crane, first via computer, and then by phone. Getting no response, he called Schueller just before six a.m. Eastern time. The Wizard told him enough to scare him. As the president's son, getting out of the White House for an unscheduled outing was neither quick nor easy, but Schueller moved with urgency, fearing for his friend.

Schueller checked his phone again as he pulled up to the apartment. He'd left several messages for Crane. Nothing. The two Secret Service agents accompanying him followed as he entered the building. After getting no answer from quickly repeated knocks on the apartment door, he used his key and entered. One agent remained in the hall while the other went in with Schueller.

They found Crane hanging by an extension cord from a ceiling beam in the windowless room where he worked. His feet dangled five inches above the floor. A typed suicide note on the floor next to a knocked over chair claimed:

*Life is too dark and lonely. I cannot go on now that Schueller has ended our relationship. I'll love him forever, but he cares more about our band than me. Good luck finding another bass player.*

The Secret Service agent was already on the phone with the police. Schueller, too furious to mourn the loss of his friend at the moment, called the Wizard.

"They killed him! It's Zackers all over again!" He told him about the fake note. Crane wasn't really in the band, couldn't even play an instrument, and certainly was not romantically involved with Schueller. "They made it look like a suicide, but—"

"It's not," the Wizard said, swallowing his emotions. "This is no time to get upset. We can mourn later. Right now, we've got to get through this. It may not have been the REMies. Crane discovered enough on NorthBridge . . . check his computer, see if they wiped it."

"Okay," Schueller said, wiping his eyes and inhaling. "Hold on."

"Schueller, what are you doing?" the Secret Service agent asked. "You can't touch that, this is a crime scene. The police are on the way."

Schueller ignored him. "Nothing," he said, talking to the Wizard again. "The only thing on here is the bogus note. No one's going to believe this set-up."

"You'd be surprised by what Washington will accept as truth."

The president was up early working the phones, trying everything he could to convince senators and members of congress to vote against the war resolution. A congressman from New Mexico who was waffling told Hudson that all but one paper in his state were running favorable stories in support of the war.

"How can I go against that?" the congressman asked.

"There were hundreds of editorials supporting George W. Bush's disastrous plan to invade Iraq," Hudson responded. "In the months before the Iraq war, even the incredibly liberal *Washington Post* ran one hundred and forty-one stories on its front pages promoting the war, while the editors buried any dissenting articles. And *The New York Times* ran even more than that. Even liberal darling Michael Moore said, 'I blame *The New York Times* more for the Iraq war than Bush.' The media's been selling the wars of the elites for more than a century. 'Remember the Maine!'"

"Maybe," the congressman said, "but the polls."

"The polls are not real." The president laughed. "There's

nothing easier to fake. At best, the polls simply measure the effectiveness of the media's spin. At worst, they just spit out bogus results, and somewhere in the middle answers can be manufactured by phrasing the question in the right way and selecting a favorable sampling area or demographic. You simply cannot believe them." He stood up, walked over to the portrait of George Washington, and thought, *When all seemed lost, how did you know to follow your instinct?*

"But the media cites them," the congressman said.

"It's a vicious circle of lies!"

"Maybe. I wish I could go with you on this, but your approval ratings are just too low right now."

"My point exactly," the president said. He knew he wasn't going to convince this politician of anything. *How do these people get elected?* he wondered. He knew, of course, and the answer made him sick to his stomach. On to the next call.

Hudson got the news about Crane in the middle of a call with a senator from Texas. Already weary from a morning spent trying to convince politicians, all of whom were owned by REMies and defense contractors, that war was a bad idea, Hudson abruptly ended the conversation with the senator. Yet another victim of his war with the REMies, Hudson paced the Oval Office, eyeing different items he could smash—a historic vase, an antique lamp, the damned Remington sculpture.

Crane had had a lot in common with Schueller, in spite of not really being a musician. Hudson had known him better than Zackers, and Crane had always felt like another son to him. He grimaced briefly, remembering the funny email Crane had sent him two days earlier: *What's the difference between a politician and a flying pig? The letter F.*

Hudson shook his head and made a silent vow to find who was responsible for Crane's murder. Whoever it was had made sure that Schueller would be embroiled in a scandal. Not today, but it was brewing. The contents of the note would not be released immediately, but at the most inopportune time, it would leak. Then the whole Zackers mess would be rehashed and the media would smell blood—in this case, actual blood—but they would pursue the wrong man, the wrong angle, sent off in entirely the wrong direction as happened again and again and yet again.

The president, still reeling from the fire at the tire shop, his uncle's death, with Gouge clinging to life, tried not to give way to his emotions. Even if Gouge managed to hang on, his life would be excruciating and distorted, lived in a completely disfigured form. Hudson clawed at the Resolute Desk. He didn't even know whom to blame. Had Bastendorff ordered the Gouges killed? Or could Rochelle have somehow orchestrated the vigilante hits on everyone who had been there? In the many years since that night, nothing had happened to any of them until she got out of prison. And what about Crane—the REMies or NorthBridge? All he knew was that the "accidental" fire at the tire shop and Crane's "suicide" had been deliberate attacks on him, and he couldn't help but think how different things would have been if he hadn't come back after those nine minutes.

*Maybe I should have stayed dead.*

# CHAPTER FIFTY-SEVEN

B y the end of the day, the president had failed. The House and the Senate had both passed a Joint Resolution approving war on China. The REMies had won. Incredibly, the vote had been bipartisan, with only sixty-four nays in the House and eighteen against in the Senate. The REMie influence was easy to see. The war made no sense, and yet the peoples' representatives had chosen to start it.

Hudson immediately issued a statement: "This is an unjust and perilous decision which jeopardizes our national security, and, more importantly, risks our very existence as a species. In spite of the decision by our legislative branch this evening, I, as your Commander in Chief, refuse to act upon its call to arms."

Fitz entered the Oval Office carrying a six pack of Cokes, the classic, tall, thick green glass bottles imported from Mexico, where they still made the beverage he called "the nectar of the gods" with real sugar. He waited until Hudson completed a call with the president of Taiwan. "I just spoke with the Speaker of the House," the chief of staff said, downing a swig of his own Coke and handing the president one of the icy-chilled colas. He'd just pried the top off with an old Sharon Steel opener Hudson always kept in the table between the two sofas. "He isn't happy with your defiant statement, says they're going to censure you."

"Let them."

"And then they will impeach."

"Clinton survived impeachment."

"You won't," Fitz said. "As you know, Clinton was impeached by the House, but the Senate didn't follow through. I've also had a call from the Senate majority leader. The Senate will also vote for impeachment if you don't carry out the war resolution. Then, you'll be removed from office."

"That'll take a while."

"Maybe, but in the meantime, they'll sue you in the Supreme Court."

"I've got the US Constitution to defend me. Separation of power."

Fitz shook his head. "What are you trying to prove? This is a necessary war. Otherwise, the Chinese will be running the world for the next hundred years. Do you really want to be the president who let that happen? The fall of the American empire will be on your hands."

"Why do you think the REMies can do a better job than average people at deciding their own fate?"

"REMies?" Fitz asked as if it were a foreign word.

"We've never had this conversation about the REMies, and don't insult me by pretending you don't know what I'm talking about."

Fitz opened another Coke, then stared at the president for a few moments. "You can't take them on," he finally said.

"I *am* taking them on already."

"Mr. President, don't."

"I have to, Fitz, I just have to . . . " he said, sounding regretful.

"They won't let you," Fitz said. Silence hung as the two men held each other's eyes. "And I'll tell you why you shouldn't. First, you can't possibly win. Your power, as president, is mostly for show. *Their* power is virtually infinite. The second reason is that they're better at deciding than the average person. Look at the amazing world we live in. The REMies created it!"

"It has lots of amazing aspects, that much is true," the president said. "But there's plenty that could be better."

"Sure, and they're working on it. Vonner's one of the ones leading the way at improving the world."

"You could have fooled me."

"Seriously. Do you know that the Illuminati was originally founded as a group meant to liberate the world from oppression? They were known as 'the enlightened ones,' the few who understood the truth. This was back when religion and government were ruling and controlling people's lives."

"They still are."

Fitz smiled. "Not like they once did. You should know, history teacher, the Illuminati tried to spread what they knew to the masses."

"I know the history of the Illuminati," Hudson said, sipping tea and ignoring the soda. "It didn't take long for some of those 'enlightened' few to use their knowledge and position to accumulate wealth and power for themselves, to start manipulating the masses as their own pawns. Power corrupts, and the REMies have carried on that tradition quite impressively."

"Many of them, yes," the chief of staff said. "But Vonner wants to bring democracy and peace to the world, no matter what cost. He thinks it can happen."

"Even if it means using the military?"

"Short term pain, long term gains," Fitz replied. "He's fighting the others. You know about the CapWars?"

"I do."

Fitz nodded, as if sizing up Hudson anew, maybe even

impressed with how far the hardware store owner had come. "The war with China is going to happen. You can't stop it, but it won't be World War III. The REMies don't want to destroy the planet. Not only will it ensure America as the center of power for another century, but it'll give Vonner and his allies the advantage in this final CapWar."

"Vonner is just another snake in the swamp," Hudson snapped.

"If that's true," Fitz said in a severe tone, "then you've got bigger problems than you think."

# CHAPTER FIFTY-EIGHT

The Wizard had been trying to reach Hudson all day, but it was after midnight before the two men finally connected. The president made the call from his private study, the small room that adjoined the Oval Office. The matrix took longer than usual to clear. His old friend appeared, and Hudson was struck by his drawn and weary face. It was the first time he could remember the Wizard without his long black hair pulled back in a ponytail. His splayed hair made him look even more disheveled.

"Dawg, Crane made a big breakthrough. I mean, I don't have it all yet, because it looks like he was sending it to me when whoever killed him . . . they may not know I have it. I mean, that he got *any* of it out . . . " The Wizard was rambling, his eyes darting around. "But he did. He hid it on the DarkNet."

"Can't they get it?"

"No, Crane was too smart. He used a freeze grid and sent me the key encrypted with just a few other details, but it's big stuff. It's hard to explain how to use it, but it's not like a key where I can just punch in a series of numbers and unlock all his data. It's more like scanning trillions of bits out there until we get a match and then we rebuild it one step at a time. Slow, but reliable. It'll probably take a week. But he got me enough to know—" The Wizard looked over his shoulder. "He gave me three NorthBridge names. Crane identified AKA Washington, AKA Jefferson, and AKA Hancock, with more to follow."

"Tell me," Hudson said, knowing the information could potentially save thousands of lives, and his presidency.

"AKA Washington is Booker Lipton."

Hudson let out an audible gasp. "You're telling me that Booker Lipton tried to have me killed? *Multiple* times? Back in Colorado, on the campaign trail, that was NorthBridge. They took responsibility for that and the stadium attack! And who knows what else. That bastard burned my house down!" Hudson realized his fists were clenched. He went on a rapid power-trip, imagining sending the FBI, the marines, a CIA assassin to kill Booker. "I told you, Wizard, there's no such thing as a good REMie!"

"I just can't believe it. I know the man. It doesn't fit, but Crane was sure."

"I believe it!" Hudson said. "And Booker probably had Crane killed to stop us from finding out. Maybe even had the tire shop torched. If Gouge dies—"

"Now wait, we don't know that Booker had anything to do with the tire shop, that could—"

"Are you defending . . . " Hudson stood up and yelled into the monitor. "Don't you dare defend Booker to me!"

"I'm just saying we don't know everything. NorthBridge may not have been behind those attacks."

"You're defending terrorists now? They claimed responsibility!"

"Maybe they didn't. You know how things can be faked. We should give Booker a chance to explain—"

"Oh, I will," Hudson said. "I'll track him down and see what he has to say for himself. But one thing you always seem to forget about Booker is he's a *REMie*."

"So is Vonner."

"Thank you, you've just won my argument," Hudson said, but he was already thinking about Linh. She was never far from his mind, ever since he'd first met her at an early fundraiser during the election. She possessed both youth and wisdom, power and charity, amazing insight and a contemplative pres- ence that Hudson found addictive. Booker was the chief backer for the Inner Movement she led. Could she be involved in NorthBridge? Was the Inner Movement just another front? He'd heard that the IM had had a radical side known as Inner Force during its early years—perhaps that was another arm of NorthBridge.

The questions battered him. It was impossible to believe such a woman could be a terrorist.

The two men debated Booker and discussed Linh for a few more minutes, neither able to reconcile the facts with their own experiences. But when the Wizard finally told him who the other two AKAs Crane had uncovered were, Hudson lost all his remaining fight.

After little more than four hours sleep, the President was back at his desk. His secretary handed him a cup of hot tea. "Your favorite," she said with a smile, and told him she'd managed to reach Booker Lipton.

Hudson picked up the phone. "Good morning, Booker. Or do you prefer AKA Washington?"

"Hudson, I always knew you were worth the trouble. Congratulations."

"You aren't even going to *try* to deny it?" Hudson said,

wondering if he should disable the SonicBlock so the call could be recorded. "What arrogance."

Booker had his own scrambler making it safe for him to speak. "This is a complicated time."

"I've noticed," Hudson said. "I'm deep in it. But is that the best you've got? Why don't you tell me about Colorado, or the stadium?"

"Colorado was a surgical strike to take out Fitz and rogue Secret Service agents, but it went wrong and got out of hand. Revolutions are a risky business."

"Fitz?"

"He's a Vonner plant, as you must have known. Tells everything to the codger." Hudson had assumed, but it went back to the old question—was Vonner good, or bad?

"And the stadium?"

"NorthBridge," Booker said, "but there were circumstances which must be taken—"

"Liar." Hudson couldn't believe this conversation. "Are you trying to rationalize attempting to assassinate a presidential candidate?"

"Careful, Hudson. Don't let your emotions get in the way of your intellect," Booker said very calmly, yet emphatically. "You're smarter than this. Get the facts."

"You expect me to trust you to give me the truth?"

"Yes."

"You were trying to kill me?"

"No."

"But you just said those attacks, on *my* life, were from North-Bridge. And you're part of NorthBridge."

"Yes."

"It can't be both ways. Knowing this, do you *really* expect me to believe anything you say?"

"Yes."

Hudson was silent.

"I understand that since the Air Force One attack, you meditate," Booker said. "You really should meditate on this, Hudson."

A sick feeling suddenly hit the president. "Was Air Force One you, too?'

"No, that was David Covington."

Hudson sucked in a breath. The shocking accusation made perfect sense, but he didn't believe it because everyone knew Covington couldn't stand him. "You're trying to deflect."

"Covington has a covert military unit at his disposal—"

"Covington is gone."

"Not really," Booker said.

"Do you have proof it was him?"

"I have satellite photos showing the unit's movements. If you'd like, I can even provide audio transcripts of Covington discussing it, but they're not for public consumption. Just between you and me."

"Why not give it to the FBI?" Hudson asked, imagining Covington being arrested, the trial, prison forever.

"My companies are the largest suppliers of surveillance equipment to the federal government, from satellites to servers."

"You can't be trusted."

"You're wrong."

"Wait, did you know about the Air Force One attack before it happened?"

"Yes."

"Incredible! And you . . . Why did you *let* it happen?"

"I had reasons which I'd be happy to share with you, but this is not the time," Booker said. "*That* is a conversation we must have in person."

"You think there's a reason good enough to risk my life?" the president asked incredulously. "Go to hell, Booker!"

# CHAPTER FIFTY-NINE

Covington worked the room, knowing just whom to speak to and whom to ignore. The upper echelons of Washington power and New York business elites were in attendance at the party, hosted by the Swiss ambassador. He saw several REMies, but didn't think he should speak with them in public. There were plenty of people to schmooze, and Covington thrived at such events. He could talk art as easily as stocks, geopolitical issues as comfortably as wine, sports, technology, even philosophy if need be. He had years of experience navigating between politicians and REMies. He knew influential people. He traded in their wares.

However, this time the situation was a bit different. He'd made an enemy of the president, and although the president was subservient to the REMies, he was still a celebrity—the *only* president of the United States. With that position came prestige, and as a result, Hudson Pound wielded a little more power than one might think, even more than the president himself probably thought he had, because although the REMies had chosen him, owned him, and ran him, as long as he acted within their agenda,

Hudson could use that presidential cachet to interesting effect. The REMies gave him a long leash, the bureaucrats were usually star struck, and this made Hudson Pound potentially dangerous.

Covington was there seeking allies. Over the years, he'd done many things to make sure the right people owed him favors, and now it was time to collect. Hudson Pound had to die, and Covington wanted it to be tomorrow. He'd already sent his superior a proposal to have the old hit squad ready, but he doubted it would be acted upon. And if that arrogant REMie decided to remove Pound, it wouldn't happen as soon as Covington wanted.

He'd put an interesting twist in his proposal: that Covington should be the next president. It made sense that at a time of great unrest and turmoil, both domestically and internationally, when the country had never been more threatened in its entire history, to elect a president with extensive experience in the military and intelligence. The Director of National Intelligence had gained popularity and distinction by being the first one to push back on NorthBridge, and several editorials had already criticized President Pound for firing him.

The REMies liked to give the public new and different conversation topics to keep them distracted and amused. How often through the years had Covington heard REMies quote Juvenal, the Roman poet: *"Just give them bread and circuses."* The line referred to the practice of Roman leaders during the declining years of the empire, giving the citizens free grain and putting on elaborate circus games to keep the populace fat, happy, and distracted. The REMies had long ago adopted the process with the modern equivalents being fast food, TV shows, sporting events, and Walmart.

Covington had just spoken to the ambassador from Russia. Before that, it had been a British Parliamentary official. *The public has no idea the amount of international affairs and domestic policy that are determined and decided on the Wash-*

*ington social circuit,* Covington thought, smiling broadly as he moved on to a familiar congressman. Minutes later, he spotted the CIA director, a man who had answered to him up until the moment that Pound had fired him. He could count on his support, and wanted a quick face-to-face. However, before he could reach the director, he was intercepted by a lovely woman he did not know.

As he talked to the woman, who had introduced herself as an aide to the president of Greece, he continued to scope the room. Twenty feet away, the FBI director was in a hushed conversation with Colonel Dranick, both Pound loyalists. He'd be sure to avoid them. A contingent from the French government, two of whom owed him favors, was near the CIA director. He needed to excuse himself and keep moving. Yet, as the woman continued to speak, he could not help but be enchanted.

The attractive woman stole his attention, so that for a few moments he actually stopped scanning the room and listened as she spoke, even while thinking about sleeping with her, even though Greece couldn't offer him much of anything in his current situation. The REMies had all but financially taken over the country a number of years earlier, so there was no real leverage there . . . unless . . .

*Perhaps she might want to start a revolution in Greece, a coup. Hmmm . . .*

"I wonder," he began, using his most charming voice, which was quite convincing, "do you have any close connections in the military?" Covington thought of his backup plan: if he couldn't get the REMies to agree to take out Pound immediately, and establish Covington as the leading candidate to be the next president, then Plan B was to stir up trouble by destabilizing multiple countries around the world simultaneously. But he'd much rather be president.

Momentarily, he became lost in his own thoughts again.

The election was only two years away. That would give him a year to declare his candidacy. He was the perfect choice—all his success with NorthBridge, and tough talk about the Chinese, ISIS, Al Qaeda would make him popular. Of course the election would be very close, but he'd win. The REMies liked to keep them close, more drama for the public. *Bread and circuses.*

"Yes, as a matter of fact." Her voice brought him back. "My brother is an advisor to the Hellenic National Defense General Staff."

"Really?" Covington smiled. "What a coincidence, I have influence with most major governments, but Greece is so insigni . . . er, small. Meeting you is very convenient." He looked at her figure. "A pleasure, truly." He put his arm gently around her, and led them to get drinks.

Hopefully he wouldn't need Plan B. Still, she might be a helpful ally. *I really should sleep with her.* Covington looked down at her and playfully whispered the only phrase in Greek he knew, "*S'agapó.*" Her eyes widened and she smiled at hearing "I love you" in her native tongue.

He had the connections and strategic mind to make Plan B happen. He didn't really need Greece, but it would be an easy target. If this woman had the clout, and he didn't doubt that she did—someone so beautiful, intelligent, and obviously ambitious, in a little country like Greece—she'd probably slept with every-body important. Greece could be fun. *She* could be fun.

Plan B wouldn't be that hard to initiate. Of course, it would be done covertly, so that even the REMies wouldn't know where it was coming from, and they would need him to help restore order.

He raised his eyes to the server, then looked deeply into his prey's eyes. "What would you like?"

His multi-tasking mind never stopped. Or, if the REMies

didn't want order, he could assist in manipulating each crisis to their liking. Covington was a master at that.

But this woman definitely required more attention, preferably in a bed. He had other people to see. He'd arrange to meet her later. Covington handed her a drink. "I need to see someone over there, but I'll give you my number." While reaching for a pen, he found a roll of Necco wafers. "Care for one?" he asked.

"Oh my, I haven't seen these for years," the woman said. "They were my favorite as a girl."

"You could get them in Greece?"

"Oh, yes, we had a wonderful international candy shop in Athens."

Covington smiled. "Which flavor?" She deserved a choice. He wasn't going to force a pink one on her.

"I can't choose between orange and chocolate," she said, moving her fingers as if playing the piano.

"I often have the same problem." Covington knew it was going to be good sex. "Here," he said, peeling back the wax paper, "have one of each."

She took them and smiled as if he'd just given her diamonds, then seductively put the orange one on her tongue and savored it as if it were a sexual experience. "I'll save the chocolate for later."

There was so much electricity between the two of them that, as he handed her the card with his personal number, he found himself breathing slightly heavily.

"I must go, but I hope we can continue our discussion later."

"I'd like that."

He slowly put a chocolate wafer into his mouth, winked at her, and then made his way across the room.

A Japanese banker caught Covington before he made it to the CIA director. He was still thinking about the woman, but when the banker mentioned the pending war with China, Covington managed to put her out of his mind. Ten minutes later, he made it to the French contingency and, after a quick conversation, set up a meeting for the next day. A few eastern European countries later, and a lobbyist from a big defense contractor, he finally reached the CIA director. But Covington suddenly didn't feel well. He started to perspire, and wasn't sure his lungs were getting enough air. Each breath grew more labored. He thought he might be slurring his words.

"Are you okay, David?" the CIA director asked.

"What's happening?" he said, but no one could understand him. "Damn it, drugged." He collapsed. Several people pulled out phones and called 9-1-1. Someone yelled for a doctor. The CIA director tried to revive him.

David Covington, former Director of National Intelligence, lay dead, surrounded by the upper echelons of Washington power, New York business elites, and several REMies.

The fact that he died so suddenly and publicly meant there would be an autopsy, but as Tarka quietly left the building, she knew the findings would confirm that Covington had died of natural causes. She got into a waiting car driven by another VS agent, carefully took the chocolate wafer out of her pocket, and slipped it into an envelope. "Too many sweets can be a dangerous thing."

## CHAPTER SIXTY

The president was on Air Force One over the Pacific Ocean en route to Hawaii when he got the word about Covington's death. They told him preliminary indications pointed to a heart attack, but Hudson knew better. Someone had killed him. Most likely Booker ordered it so Covington couldn't deny his involvement in the Air Force One attack. Easier to blame a dead man. He wouldn't miss Covington, but Booker's words, *"There is always another rodent waiting,"* kept repeating in his mind.

He tried to focus on the chores ahead of him: a long-awaited meeting in Hawaii, and then, after that, he would take the gamble of his life. If he survived that much and returned to the White House, he'd still have to deal with the other two NorthBridgers—that is if they hadn't fled the country. Surely, Booker had tipped them off.

It was a nice house, ocean view, easily $3.5 million, maybe more. The land surrounding it was an artful combination of manicured and natural, giving the house a welcoming appearance. After the Secret Service checked the house, he insisted they break protocol and all of them remain outside. They were reluctant, but these agents had been handpicked by Hudson.

Tarka was nearby. She couldn't get too close because of the nature of the location. However, she sat with a listening device and a high-powered scope about two hundred yards away, shielded by a line of palm trees and flowering shrubs.

Finally, Hudson found Rochelle standing in a sunroom with a ceramic tiled floor that looked like sand, surrounded and almost enveloped by lush tropical plants.

Hudson stood staring at the ghost of his lost innocence, a ghost who knew the truth of his failings and lies. In the lines of her face, he saw decades of his own guilt and shame. Mirrored in her eyes was his past; a young man, scared and stupid with inexperience. She was not like him. Rochelle had never been afraid, even when surrounded by the thugs who would rape her, kill her brother, and leave her with a twisted, empty wreckage of existence.

He wondered in that moment, as he had so many times over the years, what he would have done if he had been her. Would he have killed the man who killed his brother? Would he have gone after all of them? But those questions had always been burned out by a question so big it terrified him.

What if he had told? What if he had reported what really had happened that night? Would she have gone on to kill the governor? Or would she have simply been content that justice had been done?

But would justice have actually prevailed in that corrupt place, that corrupt time? These things had eaten away at him, robbed him of so much sleep and stolen his peace.

Now, all these years later, as he stood staring at Rochelle Rogers, he could still see the girl of that night, the horrors of that scene, the awful men . . . The same images had exhaustedly tormented him. Could it finally end? Those thoughts pummeled him, ricocheting in his mind, threatening to engulf him yet again.

He summoned all the strength he could muster, reached into the depths of his being, and drew upon everything that had happened since, and with a hoarse voice, pushed out the words, "I'm sorry," unsure if his apology had even been audible enough for her to hear.

"I'm sure you are," she said, holding his stare. "But now look at this. You've done become the president of the United States of America, and what have I become? I spent my life in prison."

He started to say that he hadn't been the one who did that to her, that he hadn't been one of those men, but they both knew that wasn't true. He could see it in her accusing stare. If he had acted differently that night, everything would've been different. And that's when those deeper questions surfaced, the worst ones that had almost killed him, the same ones that had ruined Gouge and the Wizard.

What if he had tried to stop the rape? What if he had tried to stop the killing of her brother? By doing nothing, he was, in fact, an accessory to those heinous crimes. Because he'd never reported them, he was also an accessory after the fact. He should have gone to jail.

Standing before that strong, brave woman, he wanted to hide. She'd known all along what a coward he'd been, yet she had never come forward. Had she told Bastendorff? Did he have some sort of confession or story of that night recorded, ready to air? Because if he did, Hudson knew he could never deny it. He would be ruined. He didn't think anyone could understand who wasn't *there* that night, who hadn't grown up in *that* little town, back in *those* days. He didn't. Not even with the excuses he'd so often repeated to himself when he dwelled within that nightmare. Hudson Pound knew he was as guilty as those other men for letting the rape and murder happen, and he was as guilty as Rochelle for the governor's death.

"I wish I'd acted differently that night. It's haunted me every second since," Hudson said, his voice still raspy. "The thing is, when we make a mistake, especially when we're young, that's so big and causes so much damage, it kind of buries us in quicksand." He paused, but she gave no reaction. "We're forever trying to get free from that sinking, the mistakes of our youth, as we grow older and try to figure out how to make it right, but we're still in that damned quicksand." His voice cracked. "You see, it won't ever set us free. It's not the same as a normal person trying to figure out what to do, trying to make it right, because we're trapped in that dark, cold, wet, quicksand. We're trying to figure it out, but at the same time we're struggling for our own life, our own sanity, trying to—"

"Just save yourself," Rochelle finished.

Hudson looked at her, his eyes brimming with tears, hers still stoic and wise. He nodded. "I just wish I could go back . . . "

"You were trying to save yourself that night," she said. "You were barely older than me. I know how scared you were . . . " Her eyes widened. "But they weren't doing it to *you*."

Hudson's lips tightened. Her stare was unblinking.

"And when they did that, you just stood there, silent," she said bitterly. "And when they were killing my brother, you still stood there, Hudson Pound . . . while they were *killing* him! You watched. *WATCHED!*" She let out a cry, gnarled and deep, years of repressed emotion erupting, then stopping as suddenly as it had appeared.

Hudson shook his head in shame. He wished she had a gun, and could finish it.

"And then, after, you didn't never say a damn thing." Her tone had shifted from bitter to disgusted.

Hudson opened his mouth, searched for words. Nothing.

"I kept waiting for you," Rochelle went on. "I kept thinking, 'That boy is gonna do the right thing, that boy is gonna tell the truth of what happened that night. He'll make sure my brother's killers pay for what they did.' I thought there were witnesses that saw, I counted on that, knew you'd do the right thing." She let tears well in her eyes. "But you didn't do it," she growled. "You never said nothing!"

Hudson still couldn't get anything out, as if someone held an old dirty rag over his nose and mouth and he had to keep reminding himself to breathe.

"And you think that by pardoning me, or rescuing me from some kind of captivity, that makes it right? It don't! It don't even *begin* to make it right!"

Hudson shook his head. That wasn't what he thought at all.

"What you think you're doing? Giving me back my life? Is that what you think? 'I'm saving her now.' Well you ain't! You can't save me. I died that night with my brother!"

"I know," he whispered.

"You *don't* know!" The intensity of her rage seemed to stop time itself.

*Please*, he thought.

"Don't you get it? That's why it didn't matter what I did afterwards. The governor, whoever, because I had to go out there myself and do what you were afraid to do. I had to make it right, to get justice!" She wiped her nose. "People might think it was revenge but it ain't revenge. You can't revenge something like that ... that *massacre*."

He nodded.

"But it would be justice!" she said, shouting now. "It was the only way to get justice when you were too scared, scared like a little boy, to do the right thing. Now you're the president. God help us, what are you going to do with that?"

The lump in Hudson's throat was too big to let him speak. He swallowed hard a couple of times, couldn't breathe for several seconds. Not many people ever get to confront the demons of their past in such a way, and he was ill-prepared. He realized just then that somewhere in the back of his mind, he'd thought when they finally met that she might hug him, tell him it was all right, that she forgave him and would thank him for rescuing her.

"For a politician, you don't got much to say." She moved closer and lowered her voice. "Or are you still afraid?"

"Why didn't you ever tell anybody that I was there? That I saw?" He regretted the question as soon as it slipped out.

"Because who the hell was going to believe me?" She clenched her fist, took a step toward him, just another half-step, not in any way threatening, but incredibly intimidating. She looked up into his eyes, their faces only inches apart. "You think that I spared you because I had some noble thought about your intentions? Or, not wanting to drag you into it? No! I spared you because no one would believe a little Negro girl against all those high-positioned white men. That's the only reason you didn't get dragged into it, 'cause I know how it would've gone down, and you know it, too."

"Yeah."

"And you think anybody'd believe me? Because if you do, I'll happily go out and tell my story right now. See, Hudson Pound, I'm still looking for every scrap of justice I can find. I'll take it from you, I'll take it from your friends, I'll take it from those beasts that did it . . . " And then the tears finally came. "Why? Why didn't you stop them? Why didn't you tell?"

"I'm sorry," Hudson repeated. "I was too afraid."

Her appalled expression gave him no relief, no forgiveness, but he had no other answer.

While she dried her tears, Hudson informed her that all the perpetrators were dead. He told her the details of each death, finishing with Gouge's father in the tire shop fire.

"So it's burnt to the ground?"

"Yes."

She nodded, her lips quivered, but she didn't break again. "Good."

"Is there anything I can do?" he asked.

She shot a look as if to say, *too late*. Then she turned away. "I'd like you to leave. And, Hudson Pound . . . "

"Yes?"

"Please don't ever come see me again."

# CHAPTER SIXTY-ONE

Hudson, dejected and feeling worse than when he'd arrived, had no time for self-pity or regret. The world stood on the brink of nuclear war. The media thought he was in Hawaii for a long weekend, and he'd been widely criticized for taking time off with so much turmoil swirling around his administration.

But he wasn't there for a break, and hours after his ill-fated meeting with Rochelle, he was back on Air Force One, this time joined by the First Lady, Schueller, the Wizard, Colonel Dranick, and several other of his closest aides. The president and his small entourage were headed to Beijing on a secret peace mission.

Hudson's phone began playing the familiar tune, "Bang on the Drum All Day." He ignored it, but five minutes later, when the ringtone played again, Hudson answered.

"What do you think you're doing, going to China?" the chief of staff asked, obviously furious.

"Damn it! How'd *you* find out?" the president asked, worried the media had already discovered his stealthy mission.

"I'm you're chief of staff, or had you forgotten? I find out everything. It's my *job*."

"I don't want this in the media."

"Really? They're going to find out, and when they do, they'll crucify you!" Fitz ranted. "Pandering to the Chinese is going to make you look even weaker. Come on, you're smarter than this. Tell the pilot to turn the plane around before you give your enemies in Congress more fuel for impeachment."

"Do me a favor, Fitz. Keep the media away from this, and let me worry about doing my job. I'm the president . . . or had *you* forgotten?" Hudson said, ending the call.

"That wasn't nice," Melissa said.

"I know. Can you believe—"

"I meant *you* weren't nice. Fitz is just trying to keep you out of trouble."

Hudson looked at her and laughed. "Oh, you're on *his* side? Do you really think he's got even half a chance of keeping me out of trouble?"

She smiled. "Lord knows I can't. But Fitz is right, this is a huge risk. And not bringing the Secretary of State or Defense, or anyone with negotiating experience . . . "

"This isn't about diplomacy or negotiation tactics," Hudson said. "This is about the truth. That's why I convinced the Wizard to come. With Crane dead, it's the Wizard, Dranick, and Schueller who know the most about what the REMies have been doing. The reasons for this war aren't real."

"The REMies are real."

"Don't worry," Hudson said, taking her hand. "I have to try this. There's nothing left to lose."

Hudson knew this would work only if the Chinese president weren't controlled by the REMies. It was a gamble, but they had good evidence that he wasn't.

"Fitz said Congress is going to impeach me," Hudson said to the Wizard.

"Funny you should mention that," the Wizard said. "I've been wanting to show you this. Remember after the Air Force One attack, you had that huge bounce in the polls, but then the media and members of Congress kept questioning your competence?"

"Sure, they used my opposition to a war with China to make me seem 'confused' and weak."

"Yeah, they made you into a MADE event," the Wizard said. "Anyway, I found a way to get into Three-D and uncovered private conversations of people in Congress."

"Really?"

The Wizard smiled triumphantly. "Dawg, every tool of the Empire can be flipped on them."

Hudson allowed himself a small smile.

"Anyway," the Wizard continued, "they won't impeach you because many of them are afraid the REMies have gone too far, and that with NorthBridge and everything else going on, the country is in grave danger. They're scared to risk a leadership crisis."

"Wow," the President said. "If they're scared, I guess we should be terrified."

"People in Congress are extremely concerned that the CapWars have gotten out of hand and too dangerous."

"But the REMies put them in power."

"Sure, but they're still human. They don't want the country to go down the tubes," the Wizard said. "They're also petrified that NorthBridge is going to cause an all-out revolution, and for the first time since the Civil War, they're wondering if the Union can survive."

"REMies don't care about a country or a people, only about consolidating power. They'll continue on, all wealthy and fat, even if America doesn't."

"It might serve the REMies better to have America split into five or six separate nations, some parts crippled, and some at war with each other for years. Dawg, even if you stop the war with China, there could be regional wars in North America and other countries on and off for decades."

# CHAPTER SIXTY-TWO

When they arrived, without fanfare or publicity, the presidential motorcade went directly to the central headquarters for the Communist Party of China. Hudson and his group were ushered into an opulent private room deep within the Zhongnanhai complex, adjacent to the Forbidden City. They were met by the Chinese President and eight of his closest aides and government officials.

Initially, those gathered did an awkward diplomatic dance, as none of the normal protocols existed in this unprecedented furtive summit. Hudson noticed that none of the high ranking Chinese officials, including their leader, were wearing neckties. He found out later that this was out of respect for him, since the whole world knew he'd given up neckties after his nine-minute death.

As the two leaders, arguably the most powerful men in the world, shook hands, their warm politician smiles belied the fact that the two largest militaries on the planet were faced off in what could easily escalate into an extinction event.

In Hudson's desperate attempt to avoid the potential war,

he'd worked through every back channel between the two nations to arrange and keep this moment secret. The Chinese leader had agreed to the eleventh-hour meeting because of Hudson's public stance against war, a conflict they also wished to avoid. China's President had also been impressed by Hudson's willingness to come to them.

Still, other than the two leaders, there were no other happy expressions in the room. Even Melissa wore a scowl. The two superpowers were less than weeks away from armed conflict, perhaps only days if a mishap in the South China Sea mushroomed. Amongst the tension, the US President began his plea openly and honestly.

"There need not be war between us," he said. "We are old friends who have fallen victim to schemes and manipulations by a global cartel of billionaires with no allegiance to any nation. These people, known as REMies, play the planet like a chess board, and they've made us their current pawns."

The Chinese leader, who spoke perfect English, looked startled for a moment. Hudson held his breath, terrified he'd guessed wrong, that the REMies owned the Chinese government, too. A scurry of activity among the top Chinese officials added to the muted chaos of the anomalous scene. The head of MSS, their intelligence agency, whispered into the Chinese leader's ear. Hudson looked over to Melissa and Dranick. Both shrugged with their eyes.

A group of soldiers suddenly entered the room and stationed themselves at each window and door. The president's Secret Service detail tensed. Someone handed the Chinese leader a digital tablet, which he studied for several moments before finally turning back to Hudson.

"Forgive me," he began, his expression still anxious. "These 'REMies' have attempted to infiltrate our country for many years. We consider them deadly dangerous."

"How have you kept them out?" the president asked, relaxing a bit.

"Execution," he replied, his face angry and bitter.

"Well, you've missed a few," the president said carefully, motioning to the Wizard, who presented the proof Crane had secured of REMie infiltration into most aspects of Chinese society, including their government.

The MSS minister looked on nervously as the Chinese leader tried to hide his embarrassment over their failure, but Hudson explained the history and intent of the REMies, and told them that based on everything they'd learned about the elites, China was the country with the least amount of REMie control.

While that news didn't quite allow the MSS minister to relax, Hudson did notice the man seemed to stand a little easier. Then the Wizard and Schueller gave a detailed report filled with evidence of the REMies' MADE events around the world. Again, China ranked among the countries with the fewest major events. However, the entire run-up to war had been created by several top REMies, including Bastendorff. The Wizard provided them with the actual links of how the REMies had created the crisis between the two superpowers, and why.

"We are long past the days when the media could be trusted, when we could believe what we see on television, even in intelligence reports," Hudson said. "There have been too many wars fought, too many lives lost, for no reason other than to advance the greedy agendas of the global elites."

The two leaders spoke for hours, and forged an agreement to avoid armed conflict. China's president also pledged to help Hudson take on the elites, a pledge which could prove to be as important as stopping World War III if the leaders of the two largest economies on the planet could ally in the secret fight against the REMies, and perhaps return the CapStone to the people.

The president would face a firestorm at home for negotiating with the enemy, defying Congress, and making a deal with the Communists, who, according to the media, were bent on dominating the Pacific rim and beyond. *"China is the threat"* had been hammered into the headlines for years, but the president had chosen to no longer serve the lie.

Hudson had averted war. They were safe. The REMies had lost this one.

# CHAPTER SIXTY-THREE

"Nice work, cowboy," Melissa said as they rode in The Beast back to Air Force One. "But you do realize that one day you'll have to deal with China? They aren't really on our side, even though right now we share a common enemy."

"I know. They're a dictatorship, but hopefully when we expose the REMies to the world, people everywhere will demand more freedom, more say, more openness."

"You're a dreamer."

"Maybe, but we can't take on the REMies if we're in the middle of a nuclear war, and we have a *much* better chance at beating them with the Chinese on our side."

"I hope you're right," she said, giving him a quick peck on the lips. "You usually are."

He put his arm around her.

"It's not going to be easy to go after REMies if NorthBridge keeps attacking," she added. "Now that you know who they are, what are you going to do about it?"

"I have a few ideas," he said as he held her tightly, humming their song in her ear. Melissa hardly dared to breathe, because for this beautiful moment, he was exactly the man she had fallen in love with. She knew it couldn't last, but she would enjoy each precious second.

As they flew back to the United States, Hudson reflected on his accomplishments. On Inauguration Day, he'd pledged to himself to free Rochelle, stop NorthBridge, and destroy the REMie hold on the world. Mixed results, but progress across the board. Rochelle was out, but that was as much as he could think about that one. NorthBridge had finally been cracked. He would soon face the task of bringing them down. And the REMies, although still as powerful as ever, had suffered their first major defeat— there would be no war with China.

Schueller came over and sat next to him. "I'm proud of you, Dad. Look at what you've done. You've stopped the war with China and turned an enemy into an ally in the fight against the REMies—a big and powerful ally."

"It was a good day."

"Day?" Schuller echoed. "It's been a good month! We know who's behind NorthBridge. Now we'll be able to stop them."

"I plan on making Dranick DNI, and he can use FaST to go after the real NorthBridge terrorists," Hudson said.

"What about Booker and the others?"

Hudson still had to face the two other NorthBridgers Crane had fingered. He didn't look forward to it, but it was his first priority once they landed in DC. "Dranick will get their side of the story, but there's no justification. They'll all end up indicted and jailed."

"Cherry Tree has a better chance now that Covington is no longer interfering and the Chinese are helping."

"I hope so, but the government's still filled with people who don't want us to succeed in cleaning up the corruption. Loyalists to the REMies, although most don't even know it's the REMies, cling to the system that feeds them. Which means that, ultimately, the REMies are no less powerful than before," Hudson said.

"That's not true. Your being president makes them less powerful. If we can stop Bastendorff . . . "

Hudson nodded slowly, but he knew the odds were overwhelmingly against him. The REMies were gunning for him.

*How many attacks can I survive?*

Later in the flight, the president went and found the Wizard, who'd spent most of the trip reviewing and decoding more of Crane's work.

"I wanted to thank you again for coming," Hudson said. "It's good seeing you in the flesh after two years of seeing only the digital version of you."

The Wizard smiled. "You too, Dawg."

"I know you prefer staying in the shadows, especially with someone out there killing all of us who were at the tire shop that night . . . "

"I've been thinking a lot about Gouge," the Wizard said.

"It's hard for me to breathe when I think about his pain," Hudson admitted.

"Who would have done it?" the Wizard asked. "Bastendorff wouldn't want to kill all the witnesses. He'd want to be able to parade all the rednecks out, show how brutal it was, and then say how *you* let it happen. Killing everyone doesn't help him."

"Who *does* it help?"

"You. And since you're not doing it, then it has to be one of your supporters," the Wizard said, stroking his beard.

"But no one knows about it."

"One person does; a person with the means to get it done . . . Vonner."

Hudson had thought the same thing himself, but hadn't wanted to deal with that possibility. Yet with the Wizard making it sound so obvious, he could no longer deny the fact that Vonner was responsible for all those killings, for Gouge's tortured state, and, presumably, for more things yet to surface.

# CHAPTER SIXTY-FOUR

Hours later, when they were only a few miles from entering US airspace and the plane was dark and quiet, with most of the passengers sleeping, Schueller found his father awake, working in his office.

"Can I interrupt?" Schueller asked.

"Sure, I've just been finishing my speech," Hudson said. "It might be my most important one yet. The media and Congress are going to roast me on this peace mission, but if I can convince the American people that we can trust China, and that war must be avoided . . ."

"How are you going to do that without telling them about the REMies?"

"I'm working on it," Hudson said. "I wish we were ready to unleash Cherry Tree, but Crane's death has slowed us down a little."

"That's exactly what they wanted it to do."

Hudson nodded sadly.

"Dad, can I ask you something?"

"Of course."

"About the nine minutes?"

Hudson tensed, but nodded.

"Crane and I had become good friends, and I'm having a tough time . . . I mean, Zackers and Crane were both killed trying to help us."

"I know, and one day the world will recognize what they did, and know their sacrifice," Hudson said. "We couldn't have gotten this far without them."

"That's true, but what I'm getting at . . . what I'm trying to ask is more about Mom, I guess." Schueller was looking away, avoiding his father's eyes.

Hudson made a point of finding his son's stare. "Hey, Schueller, what is it?"

"You *know*," Schueller said. "You know what happened to Mom, I mean, when she died. What she saw, where she went."

"Oh, Schueller." Hudson hugged him. "It's not . . . I wish it were that simple."

"Those nine minutes, *what* did you see?" Schueller asked. "Whatever it was changed your whole world view. You're infinitely more patient. Believe me, I grew up in your home, I know."

Hudson flashed a brief smile.

"You went against everyone to stop the war," Schueller continued. "You quit eating meat, dropped so many of your old conservative ideas, you don't seem to care about material possessions, and it's not just all that. I *see* the change in you."

Hudson's face was full of tenderness as he looked at Schueller. He shook his head slowly, not sure he could finish this conversation, but knowing he must.

"Dad, so many people have died for your crusade. And you *know* . . . " Schueller repeated.

Hudson thought back on Zackers and Crane, all the Secret Service agents and other law enforcement members who had died, all the people who'd been lost rescuing Rochelle, and all the others. Rage surged through him. Each life seemed too high a price, and yet whenever he considered the millions lost in all the REMie wars over the last hundred years, the countless lives destroyed by poverty, hunger, poor health, because of REMie corruption, he realized the cost was tiny compared to allowing things to continue under REMie rule.

Hudson looked out the window. The lights of the West Coast had just come into view, as if looking into an inverted universe, each city a solar system scattered across a vast black sea; a Hubble deep field stretched and bright. He took a long breath, and turned back to his son. "I saw nothing," Hudson said slowly.

Schueller, mouth slightly agape, stared back at his father, confused. "Nothing? How can that be?"

Hudson shook his head, anger welling. "NOTHING!" he said, too loudly for the quiet cabin. "Nuuuuuthing." He looked down at his hands, and then back into Schueller's eyes. "But I *felt* myself go," Hudson said, suddenly whispering. "I was *aware* of passing."

Schueller strained to hear every word.

Hudson continued, his tone that of awed reverence. "It wasn't like dying with finality, more like going into another place, different. The change was subtle, yet marked. Kind of like going outside on a hot day when you've been hours in air conditioning." He checked Schueller for recognition, then leaned closer and lowered his voice even more. "I also became aware of my consciousness, and that it survived. Those nine minutes were an eternity."

"No tunnel of light?" Schueller asked. "No angels?"

Hudson shook his head. "No visuals, just feelings." He stared past his son with a faraway look. "Oh, but the truth, the knowing, the peace."

Schueller searched his father's eyes for more.

"Mom isn't gone," Hudson said. "I know people say stuff like that, and we believe it's just to comfort those left behind, but I'm here to tell you that death is not what we think. The physical loss is what confuses us, but our essence goes on."

"You mean the soul?"

"I don't like that term. People have attached so much meaning—spiritual or religious—to it. But my physical body had died. Think of it this way—if you and I went into an underground cave, completely devoid of light, and we had a whispered conversation, you would still know me."

Schueller nodded.

"Without my physical body, I was still me. My energy went on, but with so much more force. I could see everything without seeing it—the information, the knowledge, the . . . everything, just flowed into me."

"Did you sense Mom?"

Hudson nodded. "It's like being filled with the love of everyone you've ever cared about, not just from this lifetime, but across all existence."

Schueller smiled at the passion in his father's voice.

"Then it's suddenly a pull—do I want to go back, or stay in this glorious realm? And that's when I knew there would be more."

"More?"

"Lifetimes, but different." Hudson stood up and looked as if he were searching for something. "I don't know how to describe it, how to relate much of the experience, but I can tell you this for sure: We. Go. On."

Schueller nodded, and was silent for a few moments. "So you didn't *have* to come back?"

Hudson gazed faraway and shook his head slowly. "No, I didn't, but even with all that enormity and mysterious awe ahead, it actually makes this life seem even more precious. The best I can do is to describe our life on earth as us being kids, and you wouldn't want to miss your childhood, would you?"

# CHAPTER SIXTY-FIVE

Hudson waited in The Beast until 007 and the rest of his elite Secret Service detail cleared the building one last time. He had not told them he would be meeting one of the leaders of NorthBridge, just that this was a meeting of the highest sensitivity. The location had been suggested by Schueller. One of his band mates had spotted it when scouting locations for a new studio. Located only a few miles from the White House, the abandoned delivery depot had been outdated by its small size. The same problem made developing it into something else a challenge, so the landlord was looking for unusual uses.

The president walked across the dusty concrete floor, his footsteps echoing off the white painted brick walls. The space, about the size of three or four basketball courts, was mostly empty, save for a few large tables, some scattered chairs, and a pair of large aluminum ladders. Light filtered in from high windows that looked as if they hadn't been cleaned in his lifetime. Hudson could taste the dust, a musty scent mixed with used motor oil that made him cough.

In the next room, the NorthBridge leader had been searched, and stood waiting for him next to a pair of battered folding chairs.

"AKA Jefferson," the president said. "Thank you for coming. You'll excuse me if I don't shake your hand."

"But we're old friends," Fonda Raton responded with her usual coy smile.

"No," Hudson said. "Friends don't lie to each other, don't conceal the fact that they're part of the leadership of a ruthless and brutal terror organization that has tried to kill me more than once, and has murdered people who were trying to protect me."

"Now, hold on!" Fonda fired back. "Those people trying to 'protect' you were bad agents who would have killed you or let you die."

"Save it, Fonda! NorthBridge wanted me dead, and you knew they were trying to assassinate me, didn't you?"

"No. Yes," Fonda said. "You don't understand NorthBridge."

"You're right, I don't understand anything about them except that they kill people. They tried to kill *me!*" he repeated.

"There are different factions—AKA Adams, AKA Franklin, Washington, Hancock . . . "

"You say factions, I say criminals."

Fonda shook her head dismissively. "Some want more action, some less, some of them trusted you, some did not. Vonner is an enemy, a REMie, and you belonged to him."

"It seems NorthBridge is full of REMies."

"No, Booker is the only one, and he's not anything like the rest."

"He's worse. Booker's working both sides. He's nothing better than a war profiteer. He sells the government most of the equipment for Three-D, most of the tech the NSA uses to spy, satellites, drones—it's a long list—and then he uses NorthBridge to destroy the very materials he sold, and to attack his biggest customer."

"You don't get it!" Fonda snapped, trying to keep her voice under control. "We're in the middle of the final CapWar. There are at least ten REMies going for the CapStone."

"Including Booker."

"Sure, Booker, but there are dangerous REMie-backed groups—Omnia, Aylantik, Mirage, Techtrains, others. *They* must be stopped if we're ever to regain control from the elites."

"You've told me all this before, but back then I thought you were a journalist." He glared at her. "We can't kill our way to freedom."

"It worked in 1776."

"That was a war, a revolution."

"So is this."

"No," Hudson said, shaking his finger. "This is *terrorism*. There's a difference."

"I don't think so."

"Of course you don't. At least Thorne—AKA Hancock—is honest about his views, but you're like two different people."

"Booker said I shouldn't have come, that you aren't strong enough—"

"Strong? Booker and I have different methods. Take DNI David Covington. He was a problem, a REMie tool, so I fired him. But I guess that wasn't good enough for AKA Washington. So Booker had Covington killed?"

"He did not." Fonda looked shocked at the accusation. "Booker had nothing to do with his death. Anyway, Covington died of a heart attack." She winked.

"Then who did?"

"Most likely Vonner."

"What are you talking about? Why would Vonner have Covington killed?"

"I'm not sure, but his top assassin was at the Swiss Embassy party."

"He has *assassins*, as in more than one?"

"Vonner Security? All those VS agents running around protecting you?" Fonda said. "A great many of them are assassins, mercenaries, or terrorists."

"Terrorists?"

"Ironic, isn't it?"

"I'll tell you what's ironic," the president said. "Covington was right about you and Thorne. The FaST squads should have arrested you."

"Are you going to send them for us?" Fonda asked, as if challenging him.

"Are you going to end NorthBridge's violence?" He stared at her pleadingly. "If NorthBridge stops, I'll forget what I know about you, Booker, and Thorne. I'd rather put the REMies in jail than you." He softened his tone. "We want the same thing—the REMie system ended—and it can happen. We can make more progress working together . . . peacefully."

"Is that why you wanted to see me?" Fonda asked. "Because I wish you were right, but the REMies have an iron grip. The only way is to go after their power. They will not give up their control, their money . . . it must be *taken* from them by force!"

"What if it comes down to having to kill them all?"

Fonda nodded slowly. "What *if* it comes to that?"

"I see," the president said. "I don't think we have anything more to say to each other."

"Careful, Hudson, remember what you just said. 'We want the same thing.'"

"No, we don't."

"Yes, we do." Fonda reached for his hand, but Hudson remained stoic. "Sometime, you're going to need our help, either to finish off the REMies, or to save you."

"I don't think so."

"You still have no idea of the power you're up against," Fonda said. "Don't you get it? It's such a long shot that we'll even succeed."

"Terror is the wrong road, Fonda. I can see someone like Thorne thinking armed rebellion was the only way, or Booker with his hundred-billion-dollar warped view of the world, but you? You're better than this. You know that truth can be told, that words have more power than bullets."

"I'm sorry, Hudson, I really am, but it can't be done in your fairytale, non-violence world. They are too strong, these modern-day emperors, lords, and we, the peasants, the indentured servants!" she said through gritted teeth. "The REMies have created this system where we spend our lives serving them. The greedy bastards harvest our output by disguised taxes and debt. You've seen it, you know! Their scams, phony monetary policy, fake news, manufactured economic booms and busts, lies for wars —they scare, agitate, divide us into blindness as we unwittingly remain slaves . . . they've stolen everything. REMies are evil!"

"I'm not denying that."

"But you think you can fight that kind of power using the very system they set up? They control it all. *Everything* has been infiltrated. You're smarter than that. Damn Covington for killing you that day," she said, her voice rising with emotion. "If you hadn't seen whatever the hell it was you saw during those nine minutes, you'd see that NorthBridge is the only hope. For God's sake, you were a soldier! We are at war!"

Hudson stepped close to Fonda, until their faces were only a few inches apart. "I'm offering you clemency, but the offer is only good for the next sixty seconds. If you refuse, you'll leave me no choice, and from now on, I won't just be going after the REMies. I'll be coming for you, too."

Fonda narrowed her eyes, slowly reached up and touched the president's lips with one finger. "Thank you anyway . . . shhh." She stepped away and began walking toward the exit. Then she stopped, turned, and flashed a Fonda smile, but it remained for only an instant before her expression turned deadly serious. "Mr. President, fasten your seatbelt and get ready for a bumpy ride, because you're about to find out that NorthBridge has *a lot* more friends than you do."

# CHAPTER SIXTY-SIX

"Did you have David Covington killed?" Hudson asked as he stood next to Vonner, overlooking the Potomac River at his estate just outside Washington, DC. Secret Service agents were stationed far enough away that they couldn't hear, unless one of them started yelling.

"Certainly not," Vonner replied.

"But he was working for you," Hudson said, still amazed at how easily Vonner could lie.

"Wait? Was he working for me, or did I have him killed?" Vonner asked with a comically confused expression. "Which is it? It can't be both."

"Yes, it can," Hudson said. "I believe he was working for you, and that's why you wouldn't let me fire him. Then you realized I was right. Covington had gotten out of control, so you had him killed."

"No."

"Well, there's an awful lot of people dying lately."

"Welcome to the CapWars."

"Do you realize I can have you arrested?"

Vonner looked at the president as if he'd said something funny, but the billionaire knew there was no humor in his statement. "Oh, Hudson, in some ways you've come so far, and yet you're still a child . . . "

"Do you know how many people have died because of me?"

Vonner didn't respond.

"Thirty-four!" Hudson's voice cracked. "Do you know how hard that is to endure?"

"Sorry to say, my boy, that I do." Vonner smiled like a grandfather. "And I don't mean to make you feel worse, but your estimate is considerably low. Many, *many* more people are dead because of you."

The Wizard retrieved the final Crane files on the REMies. There was still NorthBridge data out there, and he'd get it eventually. However, the REMie revelations were astonishing. As he sat there, staring at the material that got both Zackers and Crane killed, he couldn't help but think of the words he had once read on a poster about H.L. Mencken:

*"The most dangerous man to any government is the man who is able to think things out for himself, without regard to the prevailing superstitions and taboos. Almost inevitably he comes to the conclusion that the government he lives under is dishonest, insane and intolerable, and so, if he is romantic, he tries to change it. And if he is not romantic personally, he is apt to spread discontent among those who are."*

The Wizard made multiple copies of the newest information, then sent them to key people, including Schueller, Dranick, and the president. He had the proof that the REMies had looted the treasuries of the United States, and many other countries. They were operating a massive criminal enterprise disguised as the world economy. Through a nearly infinite series of manipulations, the rigged system was growing more unsustainable by the day. No one was safe. It could all come crashing down at any moment, and NorthBridge could make matters worse.

The Wizard had told Hudson repeatedly that they needed someone smarter than both of them to design a new structure that was actually fair, and that could be built out of the ashes of the REMies' empire. The most brilliant man the Wizard could think of was Granger Watson, a rogue futurist and technologist who might be able to figure out a way, but Watson might already be working for the REMies. So far, they'd had no luck in setting up a meeting.

*"They aren't just using digiGOLD to fund their operations. They have something far bigger in mind,"* the Wizard noted on the file before he sent it. *"NorthBridge appears to be planning to use the cryptocurrency to bring down the entire world's economic system."*

Hudson held an emergency meeting in the Situation Room with Dranick, Melissa, Vice President Brown, Schueller, and several other trusted aides to develop a plan for dealing with the looming crisis. They decided the time had come to enlist the help of other nations, starting with the top economic powers. The Gypsy program had shown that the leaders of Germany, the United Kingdom, France, Italy, and Brazil were under REMie control, so they would have to be excluded. However, the president would personally contact the leaders of China, Japan, India, and Canada, and inform them of the threats from both the REMies and NorthBridge.

It was a risky strategy, but coming off his major victory in stopping the war with China, and unmasking NorthBridge leadership, Hudson believed momentum was on his side. He would start with Canada. The prime minister was already scheduled for a state visit, and Hudson had developed a close relationship with his Canadian counterpart during their mutual time in office.

Dranick would send FaST squads to raid Booker Lipton's headquarters, Fonda Raton's offices, and Thorne's residence. The missions were to be done in absolute secrecy, as the president still did not want to publicly release the identities of the three top NorthBridge officials. The strategy was problematic, but as they lacked enough evidence to prosecute, there was little choice. The hope was that the raids would yield verification of their involvement, as well as additional data, and what Dranick called "the big prize," the names of the other AKAs—especially Adams and Franklin. However, raiding Booker's headquarters would prove no easy task, and Raton's offices and Thorne's residence were sterile. It was as if the AKAs only existed in the cyber realm, but the Wizard was having just as tough a time tracking them on the DarkNet.

Quickly, it all became part of what the Wizard termed "turbulent obscuring perplexities." Their best plans and efforts were thwarted by unanticipated difficulties, failures, and new information which buried what had seemed earlier to be a clear path in an avalanche of REMie schemes and obstructions. Even before they could contact the world leaders, their plan began to fall apart when the Wizard called with the news that Japan and Canada's governments were also compromised by the REMies.

"It's likely that India's leadership has also been corrupted," the Wizard said.

"Is there *anyone*?" the President asked, holding the phone, but staring at Melissa. She could tell by his face it was bad news.

"Maybe Iran, Jordan, Venezuela . . . "

"Anyone we can *trust*? Anyone with any power?"

"It doesn't appear so, at least not any governments."

"But the people," Hudson said, catching Schueller's glance. "If we get Cherry Tree right, then it's seven billion people against a few hundred . . . who do you think is going to win?"

"It'll be close," the Wizard said. "It's not just about people. They've got all the money. Imagine seven trillion dollars against a few hundred . . . "

"Then we'll just have to make the money worthless."

Without knocking, Fitz walked unexpectedly into the Oval Office, interrupting the meeting with the Canadian Prime Minister. The chief of staff looked pale, his expression reminding Hudson of how he looked at the height of the Colorado North-Bridge attack during the campaign when they all thought they might die.

"Fitz," Hudson said, raising his eyebrows and motioning to the Canadian Prime Minister and the others in the meeting, as if to ask *did you forget?* "What's wrong?"

Fitz seemed unable to speak at first, and then he suddenly blurted, "Arlin Vonner is dead."

---

# CHAPTER SIXTY-SEVEN

Several days after learning the news of Vonner's sudden death, Hudson still digesting the shock and its many ramifications, was readying for a busier day than usual. But it was still early, and he'd agreed to a quick meeting with a member of the household staff as a favor to the head usher. An African American man, who worked in the White House kitchen, had requested an audience with the president. Hudson, distracted and stressed, greeted the man in the Oval Office.

"Thank you for seeing me, Mr. President," the man said.

"Of course, of course, Elwood," the president said, looking down at his notes and seeing the name Elwood Allen, "but you know I only have a few minutes before my secretary comes in and starts telling me I'm running late." The president hoped he didn't sound too abrupt. "What can I do for you?"

"Actually, sir, I'm going to do something for you."

Hudson looked up and cocked his head. "Well, I can sure use all the help I can get these days."

The man nodded and smiled nervously. "See, Mr. President, my grandfather worked in the White House, too. He was here more than thirty years, and a ways back, after I got my position, he asked me to pass along a message to the president. But not just any POTUS. He said if I ever see a man inaugurated who seems *really* different, I should give him the message."

"Fascinating. And I'm different?"

"Yes, sir," Elwood said with a lingering gaze. "I believe you are."

"I appreciate that, Elwood, I really do. So, what's the message from your grandfather?"

"Actually, sir, it's from Jimmy Carter."

Hudson stood up and walked around his desk to stand face-to-face with Elwood. "You have my attention."

"President Carter was the first president since President Kennedy to use that," Elwood said, pointing to the Resolute Desk. "He found something hidden in there."

Hudson turned to the desk. "Really?"

"Yes, sir, something hidden by President Kennedy."

"What?"

"I don't know," Elwood admitted. "My grandfather passed in 2010, but he'd told me the story about the day they found it. President Carter was a bit of a carpenter, and when they brought the desk into the Oval Office, he and my grandfather spent a good bit of time inspecting it. That's when they discovered the hidden compartment."

"In the Resolute Desk?" Hudson asked, looking back at his desk suspiciously.

"Yes, sir," Elwood said. "May I?"

Hudson motioned him to go ahead.

Elwood walked around the desk, knelt down, and reached under near the floor. After a few seconds, a tiny, narrow slot suddenly opened. "There it is," Elwood said reverently. "Just like Grandpa said it was."

Hudson walked around and stood astonished as Elwood got to his feet.

"Mr. President, I believe your message is still in there."

Hudson knelt down and slid his finger into the small slot, retrieving a thick manila envelope, the kind sealed with strings. He quickly opened it and withdrew approximately twenty sheets of standard-size office paper folded in half. Momentarily forgetting Elwood was still there, he scanned the first few typewritten sheets and realized what they were.

Elwood cleared his throat.

The president, still kneeling, stood up. "Elwood, why didn't President Carter do anything about these?" He waved the papers.

"Sir, I don't know what those papers are, and I don't think my grandfather did either, but he did tell me that President Carter had been agitated when he read them, and said, 'Nothing good can come of this now.' He asked my grandfather to never speak of the discovery, and that was it until the day before President Carter left office. He called for my grandfather to come see him. By then they had a strong relationship. The President told him he had prayed on it, and had decided to leave those papers in the desk, that it was in God's hands."

"So why did your grandfather ask you to pass it on?"

"I don't know, but my grandfather was an honorable man, and he knew the importance of history. I'm guessing he just thought it was the right thing to do."

"Thank you, Elwood, it was. You and your grandfather did the right thing, a very important thing."

That afternoon, the president and Schueller, on their way to a cryptic meeting, talked quietly alone in the back of The Beast. Hudson explained the stunning find, and then showed him.

"These papers belonged to Kennedy?" Schueller asked.

"Yes. He must have hidden them maybe only weeks before his assassination."

Schueller's expression turned angry. "JFK was trying to bust the REMies, just like we are, and they killed him for it . . . and this proves it."

"I know," Hudson said. The papers detailed the REMies' corruption, and specifically their MADE events during the 1930s, 40s, and 50s, including the Great Depression, World War II, the Korean War, and even seeds of what would become the Vietnam War. There were other notes about the gold standard, and many more minor issues, but the proof was there—the REMies were creating trouble to enrich themselves, and Kennedy knew it.

"Why didn't Carter do anything with this?" Schueller asked.

"It was a different time. The country had just been torn apart by Vietnam and Watergate. He might not have thought it would have changed anything."

"He might have thought it would get him killed, too," Schueller said. "What are you going to do with it?"

"I'm going to let President Kennedy speak from the grave, and we're going to use this to help bring down the entire REMie empire."

# CHAPTER SIXTY-EIGHT

---

Hudson was unsure why the woman had insisted on meeting outside the White House. It seemed an odd request, which had been more like a demand, but given that she was Vonner's attorney, he figured it was one last favor for the man who'd made him president.

*Then I'm done with the devil,* he'd thought.

She'd seemed pleased when Hudson suggested they meet at the recording studio. He assumed the attorney was worried about their discussion being eavesdropped on. Of course, she didn't know about the Wizard's SonicBlock, which had proven itself reliable.

"Thank you for seeing me, Mr. President, Schueller," Kensington Blanchard said. "It's a pleasure to meet you both. As you know, I was Arlin Vonner's attorney. My firm, Blanchard and Weiss, has worked almost exclusively for Mr. Vonner for the last thirty-one years."

Hudson looked at the woman, wondering what she knew about his and Vonner's relationship. Based on her biography, she was in her mid-sixties, but she could have passed for a young fifty.

Her blonde hair had only a hint of barely noticeable gray. Hudson thought she was pretty, in a street-smart kind of way. *She's tough*, he thought, and yet the strong laugh lines around her hazel-gold eyes complicated that assessment. He could imagine her as a young attorney, decades ago, sparring with Vonner and his enemies. There was little doubt she could have handled them all, even then.

"As you may or may not also be aware," she continued, "Mr. Vonner was married twice. His first wife was *extremely* well-compensated at the time of their divorce, more than twenty-five years ago. His second wife, whom he loved very much, predeceased him four years ago. He had no children." The attorney's last sentence hung in the air a moment, as if it were her main point.

Hudson suddenly wondered if the old bastard had actually left him something, perhaps out of guilt for all the lies, manipulations, and killings. All Hudson wanted was Vonner's files on the REMies. That treasure trove of data could make all the difference in his war with the elites.

"I am here on behalf of Mr. Vonner's estate," she said, suddenly bringing Hudson's attention back.

The president nodded, gave her a serious expression, but the sudden hope continued that maybe Vonner had left him some of the files. All Hudson wanted was the truth.

The attorney looked from Hudson to Schueller, cleared her throat, and changed the world. "Mr. Vonner bequeathed a considerable portion of his estate to you, Schueller Pound."

"*Me?*" Schueller burst out. "Why me?"

"Yes, indeed," she said, shuffling some papers in a folder. "That's quite a question, and I'm not sure I can answer it fully today. You see, Mr. Vonner was an exceedingly complicated man, and—"

"Surely he had other heirs," Hudson said. "While I'm happy

to see Schueller getting an inheritance, it does beg the question . . . I mean, it's nothing I would've expected from Vonner."

"As I said, he was quite a complicated man. Most people had a certain idea about Mr. Vonner." Her eyes lingered on Hudson's for a long moment. "And most people were wrong."

"How much are we talking about?" Schueller asked hesitantly.

"Approximately fifty-two billion dollars." She paused, knowing the impact of her words.

Schueller gasped.

"That's crazy," Hudson said, jumping up and beginning to pace.

The attorney concealed a smile. "Mr. Vonner believed, Schueller, that you are best suited to carry out his work."

"His work? What do you mean?" Schueller asked.

"With respect, Ms. Blanchard," Hudson began.

"Please, call me Kensi."

"Fine, Kensi. Vonner was a . . . well, how should I say this? He wasn't exactly a *nice* man. We're talking about a manipulator . . . a murderer."

"Mr. President, I assure you that Arlin Vonner never killed anyone in his life. I'm willing to stipulate that my client operated outside generally accepted standards in pursuit—"

"Then maybe you didn't know him as well as you think," Hudson interrupted. "Maybe he didn't pull the trigger, but he did order killings."

For a moment, Kensi glared at the president, but then the expression softened to one a parent might have with a confused child. "Shall I continue?" she asked.

Fifty-two billion . . . the words kept thundering in Hudson's mind, giving him an instant headache. He glanced at his son, who looked as if he'd just won the lottery, wearing a grin and shocked expression that combined to make him look almost silly.

"Mr. Vonner had inherited and amassed great sums of money," Kensi went on. "He spent his time working to grow his fortune, but his main goal, what drove him, an obsession really, indeed what he believed was his sole purpose in life . . . " She paused once again to make eye contact with each of them. "Mr. Vonner wanted to win the CapWars."

Schueller and Hudson looked at each other, then back at her. It didn't surprise Hudson that Vonner wanted the ultimate prize. He'd known that for a long time, but whenever anyone mentioned either the words "CapWars" or "REMies," it always made him nervous. How did a person learn the truth about the conspiracy which had engulfed the world for more than a century? How much did they actually know? Which side was that person on? Could they be trusted?

Hudson stared even more suspiciously at Kensington Blanchard. Was this all true?

"Vonner wanted the CapStone?" Hudson asked.

"Yes, he did," Kensi replied. "However, you must understand, Mr. Vonner wasn't trying to win the CapWars so that he could be an emperor and rule the world." She smiled in an indescribable way.

"Vonner *wanted* to control the world, though. That's what he did," Hudson said, looking toward Schueller. He knew his son believed this about the man. Schueller had been the first one to point out that Vonner was evil and couldn't be trusted. But now, perhaps Schueller had been bought off by the dead man. Fifty-two billion dollars can change a lot of things, not the least of which is people.

"He wanted to win the CapWars," Kensi persisted, "so that none of the other SOB's—as he called them—would win and mess things up further. Believe it or not, Arlin Vonner was trying to fix things, Mr. President."

"Oh, he was good at that," Hudson said. "I'm living proof."

"I'm not certain what is causing you to be so hostile," Kensi said. "One might expect that when someone's son receives a life-altering windfall, there might be celebrations, at least some happiness."

Hudson just shook his head. "Incredible," he said, mostly to himself. "Fricking insanely incredible."

She considered Hudson carefully, then lowered her voice and said, "Mr. Vonner left you something else to help with the CapWars. Vonner Security."

"His security agency?" Schueller asked.

Hudson looked at his son as if surprised to hear him speak.

"Oh, you'll find it's a little more than a security agency," Kensi said. "But I'll be able to help you with that when the time comes."

"What is it then?" Schueller asked.

Hudson thought of Fonda's description of VS as "assassins, mercenaries, and terrorists."

"VS is more like an army. Think commandos," she said, turning from Schueller to Hudson. "There's one agent in particular, Mr. President, whom you should meet. Her name is Tarka. She's one of the top operatives in the organization, and she's saved your life more times than you can imagine."

Hudson nodded, but he was still barely able to express his thoughts. *Vonner, the CapWars, fifty-two billion dollars, Schueller, VS agents, Vonner as a "good guy"* . . . did he believe that? Did he finally have the answer he'd been asking since that day in the bank when Vonner asked him how he'd like to be president? Hudson knew that good guys were not always all good, and that bad guys weren't always all bad. He'd learned that in the world of politics, international intrigue, the REMies, and the CapWars.

He studied the attorney. Did she really know *all* about the REMies and the CapWars? What else did she know?

"Miss Blanchard, how much—"

"Please, it's Kensi." She smiled.

"Kensi, how much do you know about the REMies?"

"Enough to know not to answer that question," she said, suddenly looking hard and serious again. "I should tell you there's another reason that Mr. Vonner chose you to be president, and chose Schueller as a beneficiary."

Hudson sat back down, his palms clammy.

"Near the end of the nineteenth century," she began, "the early CapWars were waged. Two of the first conflicts among the titans of industry, who were vying for control of a young world economy, were the Panics of 1893 and 1896. Those CapWars were won by a man named John Collins."

"Yes," Hudson said, remembering. "Vonner told me about Collins the night I won the election. Collins was my great, great, great grandfather."

"That's right," she said. "John Collins was also Arlin Vonner's great-grandfather."

"What?" Hudson said, looking at her for confirmation of what he was trying to grasp.

"Yes," she whispered, as if revealing a great secret.

"Vonner and I are related?"

"Cousins. Distant cousins, but cousins."

"Dad, could that be true?"

"When I asked Vonner on election night why I grew up poor if I was related to Collins, a REMie," Hudson began, "he told me that the money had gone down a different branch of my family tree. I guess that branch ended up at him?"

"That's right. And now it's returned to your line," Kensi said.

Hudson and Schueller looked at each other again, stunned by the revelations, both imagining what they were going to do with fifty-two billion dollars, wondering if now maybe the CapWars were winnable, possibly even by them.

END OF BOOK TWO

CAPWAR **EMPIRE** (Book Three of the CapStone Conspiracy) is available now.

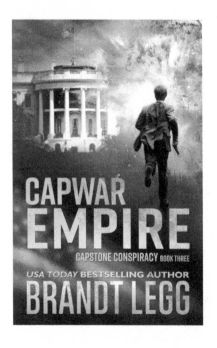

## A NOTE FROM THE AUTHOR

- ***Thank you*** so much for reading my book!
- **Please help -** If you enjoyed it, please consider posting a quick review (even a few words). Reviews are the greatest way to help an author. And, please tell your friends. Thanks!
- **I'd love to hear from you** – Questions, comments, whatever. Email me at my website, BrandtLegg.com. I'll definitely respond (within a few days).
- **Join my Inner Circle -** If you want to be the first to hear about my new releases, advance reads, occasional news and more, please join my Inner Circle at my website.

# ABOUT THE AUTHOR

USA TODAY Bestselling Author Brandt Legg uses his unusual real life experiences to create page-turning novels. He's traveled with CIA agents, dined with senators and congressmen, mingled with astronauts, chatted with governors and presidential candidates, had a private conversation with a Secretary of Defense he still doesn't like to talk about, hung out with Oscar and Grammy winners, had drinks at the State Department, been pursued by tabloid reporters, and spent a birthday at the White House by invitation from the President of the United States.

At age eight, Legg's father died suddenly, plunging his family into poverty. Two years later, while suffering from crippling migraines, he started in business, and turned a hobby into a multi-million-dollar empire. National media dubbed him the "Teen Tycoon," and by the mid-eighties, Legg was one of the top young entrepreneurs in America, appearing as high as number twenty-four on the list (when Steve Jobs was #1, Bill Gates #4, and Michael Dell #6). Legg still jokes that he should have gone into computers.

By his twenties, after years of buying and selling businesses, leveraging, and risk-taking, the high-flying Legg became ensnarled in the financial whirlwind of the junk bond eighties. The stock market crashed and a firestorm of trouble came down. The Teen Tycoon racked up more than a million dollars in legal fees, was betrayed by those closest to him, lost his entire fortune, and ended up serving time for financial improprieties.

After a year, Legg emerged from federal prison, chastened and wiser, and began anew. More than twenty-five years later, he's now using all that hard-earned firsthand knowledge of conspiracies, corruption and high finance to weave his tales. Legg's books pulse with authenticity.

His series have excited nearly a million readers around the world. Although he refused an offer to make a television movie about his life as a teenage millionaire, his autobiography is in the works. There has also been interest from Hollywood to turn his thrillers into films. With any luck, one day you'll see your favorite characters on screen.

He lives in the Pacific Northwest, with his wife and son, writing full time, in several genres, containing the common themes of adventure, conspiracy, and thrillers. Of all his pursuits, being an author and crafting plots for novels is his favorite. (see below for a list of titles available).

For more information, or to contact him, please visit his website. He loves to hear from readers and always responds!

BrandtLegg.com

# BOOKS BY BRANDT LEGG

CapWar ELECTION (CapStone Conspiracy #1)

CapWar EXPERIENCE (CapStone Conspiracy #2)

CapWar EMPIRE (CapStone Conspiracy #3)

The CapStone Conspiracy (books 1-3)

Cosega Search (Cosega Sequence #1)

Cosega Storm (Cosega Sequence #2)

Cosega Shift (Cosega Sequence #3)

Cosega Sphere (Cosega Sequence #4)

The Cosega Sequence (books 1-3)

The Last Librarian (Justar Journal #1)

The Lost TreeRunner (Justar Journal #2)

The List Keepers (Justar Journal #3)

The complete Justar Journal

Outview (Inner Movement #1)

Outin (Inner Movement #2)

Outmove (Inner Movement #3)

The complete Inner Movement trilogy

# ACKNOWLEDGMENTS

One of the things I like about writing series is being able to tell a bigger story. Another thing is getting to thank people multiple times for helping. Endless gratitude to my wife, Ro, who deals with all aspects of the story, including large parts that never make it into the books, and for the many interesting suggestions she offers which do get in. A million thanks to my mother, Barbara Blair, who reads and re-reads, proudly claiming to represent "the reader," and also amusing me by purporting to be "objective". Bonnie Brown Koeln, as always, pushes through the draft manuscript, looking for every typo and inconsistency as if she were on a grand expedition. Cathie Harrison, who, regrettably, I've never met in person, yet I fondly picture among blackberries, the green countryside of New Zealand, in a world of rabbits, alpaca, cats, dogs, other critters, and the occasional ice spirit. And for my late brother, Blair, who while I was writing this book discovered what happens in "the nine minutes" and beyond. I'm still hearing your echoes and feeling your presence. Certain scenes in this book were also aided by an old pilot friend, Glenn Turner, who made sure I had the information needed and arranged for me to speak with the right person to accurately handle Air Force One. Thanks, Glenn! Also, more appreciation to my copy editor, Jack Llartin, for taking care of the rough edges. And, finally, to Teakki, who patiently waited to build and play Legos until I finished writing each day.

Made in the USA
Monee, IL
26 January 2023

26357954R00215